MAGIC CLAIMS

Magic Claims
Copyright © 2023 by Ilona Andrews
Ebook ISBN: 9781641972567
KDP POD ISBN: 9798393691769
IS POD ISBN: 9781641972680

NYLA Publishing
121 W. 27th St, Suite 1201, NY 10001, New York.
http://www.nyliterary.com

MAGIC CLAIMS

KATE DANIELS: WILMINGTON YEARS
BOOK 2

ILONA ANDREWS

[1]

"Well, of course it blew up, Kate."

It was a beautiful September morning. I sat on a big log cut from a beached tree. A fire blazed in front of me, laid out in the firepit on the beach. Beyond it, the Atlantic Ocean lapped at the sandy shore. The water was an opaque aquamarine, the sky was a beautiful blue, and the flames in front of me were ruby red, fed by the mix of herbs and magic. About two feet off the ground, the fire faded into an image of my aunt.

The Rose of Tigris reclined on a carved wooden chaise decorated with lifelike Catalina mariposa lilies. Her white gown cascaded over her large body in artful drapes, setting off the warm golden tones of her bronze skin. I resembled her, but everything about her was...more. I was five foot seven, muscular, and strong, and she was over six feet, more muscular, and stronger. Our faces were very similar, but her eyes were darker, her lips were fuller, and her features were bolder. Her glossy brown hair spilled over one shoulder in a luxurious mane, clasped by a golden cord. She looked like a living painting that had blossomed from the ruby flames of the fire call, an ancient empress in repose.

We hadn't spoken for two months. She had been occupied

1

with something she couldn't or wouldn't share. It wasn't the first time she'd vanished from my radar. Once she was gone for nine months, while her subordinates made flimsy excuses, and when we finally reconnected, she told me that I was an excellent mother. Not that I didn't appreciate the compliment, but it came out of nowhere.

Since we finally got to talk, I decided it would be a great opportunity to clear up the exploding cephalopod issue. I had accidentally blown up a kraken. It had been... unexpected.

"*Karsaran* targets the highest concentration of magic within a living organism," Erra said.

"Yes, which for vertebrates would be bone. In the absence of bone, it will target blood, which has the next highest concentration of magic. I understand all that."

"Then what's your question?"

"Why did the kraken explode? I expected it to split, maybe to burst, but it detonated like it had swallowed a land mine, and then it rained kraken for about ten seconds."

She laughed softly.

In the distance, about five hundred yards out, a swimmer cut through the waves, moving fast, parallel to the shore.

"Oh great and powerful aunt, please enlighten this stupid one..."

"It exploded because you don't practice. You've been playing house for what, six years now? Seven?"

"I do practice. I practice every day." I had incorporated working on my bloodline powers into my exercise routine.

"Not in combat, you don't. You have no idea how much power you need to feed into a command to gracefully split a kraken along its blood vessels, and therefore it ends up exploding and landing on your face."

"So what do you suggest? Hunting down some krakens to calibrate?"

"Yes!"

"Seems cruel."

Erra gave me one of her patented ancient power stares, reached over, and slapped an invisible ball in front of her.

"Is that you smacking my head?"

"You are playing a very dangerous game. You've been trying to hide from who you are. First, you tried to do it in Atlanta, and now you're trying to do it here."

"You know why we left Atlanta," I said quietly. The city had slowly smothered me. I felt like I couldn't even breathe there, much less raise Conlan. "I wanted to give your grandson a chance at a normal life."

Erra waved her hand. "I do. I agreed with your decision then and I still agree with it now. Atlanta was too complicated. Too messy. Too many eyes and too many powers screaming bloody murder every time you sneezed. You needed to start fresh, away from all that. But you haven't exactly hit the ground running."

I counted off on my fingers. "Property cleared and warded, house repaired, Conlan enrolled in school…"

My aunt leaned closer. "You're puttering around on this beach, fixing this ruin, and trying to lull yourself into a false sense of security. Do you honestly think that you've solved your problems, child? That if you just stay in this little fortress on the edge of the continent, the world will forget about you, and you can have a quiet life? Even if you ran away to the most remote peak in the Himalayas, it wouldn't matter. Sooner or later, they will come for you, and you won't be ready."

A familiar discomfort rolled over me. "Why would anyone come for me?"

"For your power, for your blood, and for your son. If they take the boy, they can control both you and your husband. If they kill even one of you, they can make a name for themselves. And it won't be a run-of-the-mill enemy. It will be the kind of power who thinks they can take you."

For the past few years, a small voice in the back of my mind kept nagging at me. It started the day after I banished my father. I'd woken up to a sun-filled morning. Curran lay next to me, warm, sleeping peacefully, his muscular arm draped over me. Conlan was in his crib, making little growling noises in his sleep. I opened my eyes, looked up at the white ceiling, and thought, "Who will I have to fight next to keep us safe?"

I'd punched that voice back down, because I decided that I wasn't going to spend my life waiting for the other shoe to drop. Still, over the years, it kept piping up here and there. I thought it would go silent once we were out of Atlanta, but it only grew stronger.

"It's not just your enemies you have to worry about," Erra said.

I raised an eyebrow at her.

"One of the men I loved had a war dog," she said. "He was this huge drooling, farting, foul-smelling beast, bred for combat. Ugh, I hated that dog. I never hurt him, but I didn't want him near me, so I would stomp and shoo him when he got near. A surprisingly cowardly dog. He'd gone up against lions and men in battle, but he'd see me and run."

A six-foot-six woman built like an Olympic athlete wearing full armor and filled with roiling, terrifying magic. I'd run away too if she stomped at me.

"Is there a point to this story or did you just want to share your disturbing hobby of tormenting loyal dogs?"

Erra grimaced. "You take great advantage of my love for you. Anyway, the dog was only afraid of two things: me and thunder. Every time lightning split the sky, I would find him shivering by my bed and no matter how much I stomped and yelled, he wouldn't leave. He just sat there, shaking, until the storm passed and then he'd slink away."

"Aha."

"I finally asked Leo why the dog did that, and he told me that I was the most frightening creature the dog knew. When the

4

thunder came, he ran to me because I was so terrifying, I would scare away the thunder and keep him safe."

I laughed.

"Listen to me, you insolent brat! People are the same. Whether you like it or not, you married a First."

My laughter died.

"And yes, I know that your love is the greatest love there ever was under the sky and he left his Pack for you, but he took the reins of power when he was fifteen. He grew up being the Beast Lord. It wasn't just his identity; it has shaped his way of thinking. And I don't need to tell you that his successor isn't faring well."

No, she didn't need to tell me that. We've been hearing rumblings. Nothing concrete, just hints that things weren't going as well as they could be.

"Eventually things will fall apart in Atlanta. Perhaps this year, perhaps in five years, but in the end the Pack will destabilize. When that happens, the shapeshifters will panic. They will run from that thunder to the scariest person they know, expecting that he will make them safe. Do you think he'll be able to turn them away?"

The swimmer turned toward the beach and slid through the ocean, devouring the distance in fast, measured strokes.

"I don't know," I told her.

"Your face tells me that you do know." Erra fixed me with her stare again. "And even if he somehow decided to say no, you would say yes. All it would take is one vulnerable, helpless person with a sob story and you'll trip over your feet to take them under your wing."

"I have no idea what you're talking about. I'm retired."

"You need territory, a defensible base large enough to house many people, money, powerful allies, and connections to the local government to make it all work. Do you have any of those things?"

"No," I squeezed out.

"Then you should get busy, shouldn't you?"

"Thank you, dear aunt, for once again listing all of my failures."

"I'm trying to keep you alive. If you want someone to tell you how special and wonderful you are, go see your father. He wants you to fail so you'll be forced to run to him and beg for his wisdom."

"What happened to the dog?" I asked.

"He sired many puppies and lived to a ripe old age. I kept a pillow by my bed, and I would drape a special blanket over him when the storms came. I buried both the pillow and the blanket with him when he died, so he wouldn't be scared in the afterlife. Give your husband and your son my love and get to work."

The fire went out.

I didn't see Julie. Again. She used to fire call every couple of weeks, and then, about two years ago, the fire calls stopped. We still talked on the phone, but a long time had passed since I'd seen her. Too long.

Curran came out of the ocean, the hard muscles across his powerful frame slick with water. Oh wow.

My husband started across the sand toward me. At night he swam naked, but since it was morning, he wore blue swimming trunks and somehow that made him even hotter. But it wasn't his body that pulled me in, although it didn't hurt.

Looking into Curran's eyes was like coming face to face with an apex predator. There was steel will there, raw power, and confidence bordering on arrogance to back it up, but most of all there was love when he looked at me. Erra was right. He never stopped being the Beast Lord. He was the man who could dominate thousands of shapeshifters with a single look, and he was also the man who stayed up all night with a child who'd eaten some poisonous herbs in the forest and spent twenty-four hours throwing them up. One couldn't be separated from another. They were all aspects of Curran, and I loved all of him.

The Curran I knew was done with packs and shapeshifter hierarchy. A few years ago, Mahon came to him with this harebrained proposal of starting another Pack several states over, and Curran had shot him down flat. When Mahon demanded to know who would keep our family safe, Curran did his alpha stare and informed him that he was all the safety we needed. And yet if the Pack came to him now, desperate for his help, I wasn't sure what he would do.

Try as you might, you cannot change who you are. A son of Jushur, my father's former spymaster, told me this two months ago when I ran into him at the Farm. I didn't want to change who Curran was.

I didn't want to change who I was either. It would take a hell of a lot more than a sob story to force me out of my retirement. I'd earned my peace and quiet, and I would be keeping it.

Curran reached me.

"How was the water?"

"Invigorating. You should go for a swim."

"No thanks."

I loved swimming, but I liked my ocean to be right about the temperature of bath water. Our slice of the North Carolina coast was nicely swimmable in September, hovering around the upper seventies, but we'd had three days of storms and the water temperature dropped to the high sixties. I had no desire to get into it.

Curran leaned over and kissed me with cool lips. "What's the matter?"

Land, connections, money… "My aunt has given me a laundry list of things we don't have and need to get right away."

He laughed softly.

Connections would cost us our anonymity, and land would cost us money, which we didn't have. Curran and I owned a chunk of the Mercenary Guild. It paid quite well, but not well enough to finance us on the kind of scale Erra was envisioning.

7

"Do you think it was a mistake to move to Wilmington?" I asked.

"I have my smoking-hot wife, my troublemaker son, my fort, my beach... What else can a man want?"

"I'm serious."

"I can see that." He scooped me up off my log.

"What are you doing?"

Curran spun around and sprinted to the water with me in his arms. The beach flew by.

"Stop! Curran! Cu—"

He threw me. I hurtled through the air and splashed into the ocean. The water closed over my head.

Aaaa!

I flailed, broke the surface, and gasped. Curran locked me into his arms, his gray eyes laughing.

"You said invigorating, not fucking freezing. Let go of me!"

"Let me warm you up."

"I'll warm myself up!"

His smile gained a wicked edge. "Even more interesting."

I smacked him, kicked him in the chest, and launched into a frenzied freestyle, trying to warm up. I stopped about a minute later. In a calm lake, I would've ended up one hundred yards from where I started. In the ocean, against the current, I made it to about fifty.

Curran floated next to me, and he wasn't even breathing hard. It's good to be a werelion.

"Hey, baby."

"You are too much."

He pulled me closer, and I wrapped myself in his arms. We floated in the water.

"About what you said earlier," he said, his voice a deep rumble in my ear. "I enjoyed this summer. Conlan loved it."

They both loved it here in the fort. Erra was right—it really was on the edge of the continent, in a place where the land ended and the ocean began. We could get cornered here, squeezed between an angry sea and an enemy. If we were talking about safety only, I'd felt better when we were in Atlanta, hidden deep inside the subdivision where every neighbor was a friend. But Atlanta wasn't an option.

"Do you like it here?" Curran asked.

"Yes."

"Then it works for now. It's simple, baby. When we stop liking it, we'll do something else."

Maybe it was that simple.

Three weeks later

THE BEACH WAS AN EXCELLENT PLACE TO WORK OUT BECAUSE THE sand was soft and conveniently powdery.

Curran threw me over his hip. If I had let go, I would've landed on my back, but I had a death grip on his neck, and as he flipped me, I went with it and threw a handful of sand into his face. It bought me half a second, which I used to kick his feet from under him and get a triangle choke in place. Unfortunately, choking a werelion was a lot harder than subduing a regular opponent. A non-shapeshifter person would've tapped out. Curran got up, lifting me in the air while I hung off his neck.

I was about to punch him in the head when he tapped my thigh. His eyes were fixed on the fortress behind us.

I released him. He caught me, helping me to the ground, and I turned to look at the fort.

After the Red Horn gang attacked our home, Curran and Conlan decided to erect a flagpole. It jutted from our fort's tower, bearing a gray flag with stylized black stripes that looked either like tiger stripes or claw rips. When something happened, we raised a second flag below the first, an early warning system, green for shapeshifter, red for danger, and so on. When we left this morning, the gray flag flew alone. Now there was a blue flag under it.

Human visitors. Not from Conlan's school either. The lone time they came to visit after school started, he flew a ghastly orange to announce the occasion.

"Are you expecting visitors?" Curran asked.

The renovation crew had finished five weeks ago, and we were all paid up. The grocery delivery wasn't due for another two days.

"No." I scrambled to grab my shoes.

We found our visitors in the courtyard. A young Black woman with a wealth of hair piled on top of her head in a loose bun and a well-dressed older Black man. Our son had let them in, guided them to our outside lunch table, served them iced tea and cookies, and then parked himself on the side to keep them company. I could tell by Curran's face that a father-son conversation would be in Conlan's near future.

"Don't bristle," I murmured as we crossed the yard.

"I'm not bristling," he murmured back. "I'm perfectly welcoming."

The man was probably in his sixties, with dark brown skin warmed by a reddish undertone, and silver hair, cut short and half hidden by a light-colored fedora. His curly beard was silver as well, but his mustache was still salt and pepper. He was slightly shorter than average, with a trim build, shown off by a double-breasted gray suit, which he paired with a pomegranate-red shirt. He looked at the world through a pair of glasses with reddish-copper frames, and his eyes were narrow and shrewd.

The woman next to him wore a yellow tank top and a high-waisted black skirt. A large tote bag rested by her feet. She turned toward me and smiled. Solina.

"Is that one of the mermaids you rescued?" Curran asked.

"Mhm."

We reached the table, and both visitors stood up. Solina came around and hugged me. I gently hugged her back.

"You look well," I told her.

"Thank you. This is my grand-uncle, Edward Calloway. Grand-uncle, this is Kate and Curran."

Edward Calloway offered us his hand. "Please call me Ned."

Curran and I shook his hand in turn, and we all sat back down at the table.

Interesting. I didn't know Ned Calloway personally, but I knew of him. I first noticed the name because I kept seeing it on Paul's materials invoices during the renovations. I finally asked him about it. According to our general contractor, Ned Calloway was a "smart man who's done very well for himself." He owned many enterprises in everything from lumber and furniture to textiles and dual-engine car manufacturing. A lot of businesses in and around Wilmington carried the Calloway name.

"Your iced tea is delicious," Ned Calloway said. "What is it sweetened with?"

"Buckwheat honey," Conlan said. Thanks to his werebear grandparents, my son was a honey connoisseur.

"I'll have to remember that," Ned said. "My grand-niece told me a lot about you. Thank you for saving this child. Our family is grateful."

"It was a fortunate accident," I said. "I was looking for a different child."

"You found Solina anyway. I should've come to thank you sooner, but I was occupied by an emergency. I have a summer home in Carolina Beach. We're practically neighbors."

They didn't come here just to thank us, but rushing this conversation would only slow it down to the speed of cold molasses, so I settled in.

"That's good to hear," Curran said. "We've only recently moved in, so we don't know that many people. It's always good to meet a neighbor."

11

Ned smiled. "We are the welcoming sort. I'm sure you'll be a part of our community in no time."

Where was this going?

"Our family is from Penderton," Ned said. "That's not where we started, but where we ended up before Solina's parents and I moved on to Wilmington."

Penderton was a small town somewhere north of Wilmington.

"Where did you start?" I asked.

"My parents are from Wallace," Ned said. "They grew up with little means, married young, and my sister and I were born in Wallace, in an old farmhouse. My father had a head for business. He started in reclamations, then moved on to construction, and did well there. They bought a bigger home in town, but then the forest came."

"And ate the towns," Solina said.

Ned nodded. "Until about thirty years ago, that area was mostly fields, vineyards, and horse farms, with several small towns sprinkled in. Burgaw, St. Helena, Ivanhoe... Then woods started growing and there was no stopping them. The forest pushed people together. Smaller villages were abandoned, and Burgaw and St. Helena merged into Penderton."

A typical scenario that had played out all over the United States. Magic hated technology and high buildings, but it loved and nurtured plants. Trees grew like weeds, merging into massive forests that spawned things with scary teeth. People quickly realized that safety lay in numbers and sturdy town walls.

"Now, Momma didn't want to leave Wallace. Her family had been there for many generations. The family cemetery was there. The church where we were baptized was there. It didn't feel right to abandon that history," Ned said. "But they couldn't stay. To make the move easier, my father built their dream house in Penderton."

"It's a beautiful house," Solina said. "Memaw still lives there, and Grandma takes care of her."

"After my father passed, I tried to get them to move to Wilmington," Ned said. "But Momma wouldn't leave. Now they're trapped there. I love these cookies. I'm a sucker for sweets, and I have to say, these are special."

He dropped it very casually. *Yes, my mother and sister are trapped; wow, these are great cookies.*

"Good cookies are an essential food group," Curran said. "My wife is a great cook."

"I thought these were homemade. They just have that special touch of something."

"I'll pack you a batch for the road," I told him.

"Oh, I couldn't impose." Ned shook his head.

"I have made too many anyway. So why can't your mother and sister leave?"

"Because of the evil in the woods," Solina said.

And there it was. This was why they were here.

"Now, I've got to hear this," Curran said. "What kind of evil is it?"

"We don't know," Ned said. "That's part of the problem. It started after the last flare."

Flares were the potent magic waves that came every seven years and lasted several days. With each flare, a bit more of our world became irrevocably changed. Flares brought disasters. Gods manifested, large structures collapsed, and weird monsters went on rampages. The last flare was about five years ago.

"Three days after that flare ended, some strange-looking people walked out of the woods near Penderton," Ned said.

Solina reached into the tote bag by her feet, pulled out a rolled-up piece of paper, and opened it on the table. A sketch made in colored pencil showed a human female, but not any kind of human I had ever seen.

Her skin had an odd, almost bluish tint with a pattern of hairline cracks. One time Andrea, my best friend, dragged me to a spa where they smeared clay on my face. It cracked when it dried, and the body paint on this woman looked strikingly similar.

Her shoulders sloped down at a sharper angle than normal, her limbs and her neck were too long, and there was something strange about the proportions of her features. Almost as if her entire middle of her face was stretched along the vertical axis, flattening and elongating her nose and cheekbones. Her mouth was a narrow slash, and the corners of her lips sagged down, giving her a derisive or mournful expression. Her eyes were round, almost black, set close together, and completely blank.

The woman wore a tan-colored garment, a kind of robe or a tunic cinched at the waist by a belt. Her long brown hair was pulled back from her face and stiff. It looked like she'd taken a handful of the same bluish mud or clay that was on her face and arms, smeared it on her hair at the hairline, and let it dry. A metal collar clasped her neck, a kind of plaited band formed from strips of golden metal. Her right hand clutched something. A sack or a net?

After the Shift hit, a lot of people turned to ancient gods and long-abandoned religions. I'd seen neo-pagans wear some weird stuff, but that didn't explain the strange facial features.

"What is she holding?" I asked.

"A banner," Solina said. "That's how they communicate."

She pulled a Ziploc bag out of her tote and put it on the table. Inside was a roll of tan cloth.

"May I?" I asked.

She nodded.

I opened the bag, took the roll out, and let it fall open. Three pieces of cloth. It felt like wool. I unfolded the first one. On it, in bright red, was a single English word written in all caps. *TRIBUTE.*

Shit.

The word wasn't painted onto the banner. It had been woven into it with crimson wool.

14

"Penderton lost a town guard during that flare," Ned said. "Selma Butler. We are reasonably sure this is her handwriting. She always wrote the bar in a capital T at an angle like that."

Curran took the banner, sniffed it, and held it out to Conlan. Our son trotted over and took a long whiff.

I unfolded the second piece of cloth. A symbol for the first quarter moon, a circle split in half vertically. The left side was solid red. The right side showed moon spots with paler and darker shades of red.

"The deadline," Curran said.

Ned nodded.

There was one piece of fabric left. I opened it. A symbol for a person, one step above a stick figure and featureless, but undeniably a person, woven in red in the center of the banner.

"They wanted a human tribute," Curran said.

"Yes."

A cold, uncomfortable knot formed in my stomach. This was looking worse and worse.

"The town ignored it, of course," Ned said. "Penderton has solid defenses, and the guards are well trained. These are all tough people, lumbermen, farmers, hunters. On the deadline, at sundown, the forest people came back. The town expected them to storm the walls, but they just left. Everything seemed to have blown over. Then at noon the next day a huge brown boulder shot out of the woods, landed in the town square, and exploded into brown dust."

"Everyone who was in the open in the square died," Solina said. "Nine people. Two kids."

"In the evening the women were back," Ned continued. "Same message, but this time they wanted their tribute by the full moon. Penderton sounded the alarm, of course. It was all hands on deck. Forest service, the National Guard Magic Rapid Response unit, three teams of mercenaries, everyone came to find the cause of this disaster. They went into the forest. Four days later some of them came out. Pender Forest is a big place, over three hundred thousand acres. They'd walked around in circles. Some of them disappeared. Some were eaten, nobody knows by what."

Great.

"Why not evacuate?" Curran asked.

"People tried," Ned said. "Every single person that left the town after that first blast became sick two days later. Some came back to town and recovered. The others died. A day trip like coming here, for example, is fine. But any longer than twenty-four hours outside of town, and they start to develop symptoms."

"Nobody has any answers," Solina said.

It infected them somehow. Probably with that first boulder, although it could have been something else. And Ned and Solina weren't sick because they'd moved out of Penderton before this whole mess happened.

"What happened with the National Guard?" Curran asked.

"They stayed a month past the tribute deadline, but they couldn't stay in Penderton indefinitely," Ned said. "The day after they left, a second boulder exploded at the school. It just so happened that most of the children were in a separate building for a school assembly. Only five people died."

There was an awful flatness to his voice.

"Penderton offered tribute," I said.

"Jimmy Codair," Ned said. "Sixty-nine years old and dying of cancer. He volunteered. He walked into the woods with the women, and nobody ever saw him again. The next year, on the same day and hour, they were back."

They gave it a person.

"The town fed it," Curran said. "Of course it would be back."

"It's been five years since the flare," I said. "How...?"

"The town holds a lottery," Ned said.

I'd learned over the years that you can adjust to just about anything to survive. Penderton adjusted to the price of their survival. One person a year to let the other five thousand go on with their lives. It felt monstrous because it was.

"These people are not monsters," Ned said, as if reading my mind. "They have no other options. Whatever you think they should have done, they have done. They have appealed to everyone, from the military and mercenaries to the Order and the Covens. Everyone has tried. I've personally traveled to Washington for help. Nobody could help and in the end the town paid the price every single time."

"This is the *fifth* year," Solina said. Her voice had an edge to it.

Ned looked at her.

She inhaled deeply and looked at the sky above us.

Curran fixed Ned with his stare. "That's a terrible story."

Ned nodded. "Yes, it is. Thank you for listening to me. I've rambled on for far too long. I should probably get to the reason why I am here."

He reached into his jacket and pulled out a folded map.

"The town of Penderton is very excited about your move to our neck of the woods. But your lovely home is so far from us. We'd like to invite you to move closer."

He opened the map, presenting us with an aerial view of Wilmington and the surrounding area. The Atlantic Ocean was on the east side, a vast pale blue. The city of Wilmington sat toward the bottom of the map, a little north of where Cape Fear River and the Atlantic finally met. Above Wilmington, the map was green with dense woods, with the narrow lines of the major roads cutting through them.

Just above the northern border of Wilmington, a dotted line marked Pender County, perched like a big mushroom cap on top of the city. Almost the entire county was tinted green, indicating the massive sprawl of Pender Forest. Midway through it, not too far from I-40, a small red circle marked Penderton. And several miles northwest of Penderton, a big square of blue cut through Pender Forest, taking up about a third of the woods.

"Move closer where?" I asked.

"Here." Ned tapped the blue square with his fingertip.

Conlan soundlessly moved to look at the map over my shoulder.

"What is that?" I asked.

"Your woods."

What? "I don't follow."

"These are the woods that Penderton gifted to you. Our welcome present to our wonderful new neighbors. Eighty-two thousand acres of woodlands, two-thirds of it longleaf pine, prime timber; one third swamp with incredible biodiversity; and the thousand-acre Big Skunk Lake. Best fishing in the county."

Curran focused on the blue square of the woods as if it were a bloody steak and he'd been starving for a month.

Ned put a photograph on the table. It showed a forest of pines, straight like the masts of the tall ships, rising to dizzying heights from the sun-dappled golden wiregrass.

"Ninja forest," Conlan breathed.

"We have the prettiest woods," Ned said. "There are many suitable places to build a keep."

A keep. Like the Pack Keep. Damn it.

"I always appreciate a man who does his homework," Curran said. "You think you know who we are. But do you really?"

The flesh of his head split and twisted into a different shape. A new head formed on his shoulders, a massive, nightmarish blend of human and lion. Faint, smoky stripes marked his gray fur. His black lips trembled and opened, flashing fangs the size of my fingers. Curran's gold eyes locked on Ned and Solina with predatory intensity.

Solina jumped up and took a step back.

Ned swallowed but stayed seated.

"Think very carefully," Curran said, his voice a deep rumbling growl. "Be sure this is what you want. Because once I take this land, it will be mine."

"It's already yours," Ned said. "You have all rights, minerals, timber, water, access, everything. We have already registered the grant with the county. I have the paperwork."

"Does the town understand who they are inviting?" Curran asked. Up close, his voice shook you. It reverberated in your bones.

"They understand," Ned said.

"Even if I look like this? Even if I will bring others like me?"

"People are always more than one thing. The residents of Penderton know who you are. They know about your friends. Should they move here from down south, the town will not oppose it. Nor could it. The land is yours. Do with it what you wish."

The sky above us was completely clear, but I could've sworn I heard thunder.

"We are small town people, but we aren't bigots, Mr. Lennart," Ned said. "And we keep our word."

Accepting this forest meant our quiet lives would be over. This thing reeked of old magic power. Fighting it would be bloody, noisy, and dangerous. If we managed to deal with whatever evil had spawned in that forest and survived that fight, we'd need to defend that land. Sooner or later Curran would build another Keep, and once he did that, shapeshifters would flock to him, and we would be right back where we started.

Territory, base, money, allies, and connections...

My "low profile" was slipping through my fingers.

"Okay," Curran said. "You have me. But I don't speak for my wife. Convince her and you have a deal."

Ned stood up. "Could you open the gates for us?"

Curran glanced at Conlan. Our son jogged to the gates and swung them open. There were two large SUVs in our driveway, both with bloated hoods to accommodate the dual gasoline and enchanted water engines. Solina walked over to them and waved.

Ned invited me toward them with a sweep of his hand.

Okay. I'll bite.

I got up and crossed the yard to the gates. Curran joined me.

The doors of the SUVs opened, and people started getting out, one after another. Just normal, regular people in normal, regular clothes, some older, some younger. A young man in his upper teens, still a kid, hopped out, and helped a woman in her seventies exit. They lined up in front of us.

"The women came early this year," Solina said. "They want their tribute in two weeks. The town already held the lottery."

Ice slid down my spine.

The older teenager pulled a banner out of his pocket and held it out. On it, woven with wool the color of blood, were ten human figures.

The people looked at us.

Curran took my hand and squeezed.

I could say no. I could walk away right now, and nobody would ever call me on it.

I squeezed back.

"We'll take it," my husband said.

[2]

Curran

We waved goodbye as Ned and his people left. I turned to Conlan.

"Follow them and make sure they make it onto the main road."

"Yes, Dad."

He ran after the cars. Grendel shot out of his hiding spot in the corner of the courtyard and chased after him.

I waited until he was too far to hear us. We needed to have an adult conversation.

Kate stood next to me, flipping through a thick file Ned left behind. The record of Penderton's battle with the evil in the woods.

"Thank you," I said.

"For what?" Kate asked.

"Agreeing to help. For coming with me to the woods." I paused. Looking for the right words. "All of it, I guess."

"He put ten people in front of us and let us know they were going to die. What was I supposed to do? I would have to tell them to their faces that saving them would inconvenience me."

Oh, it would be more than an inconvenience and we both knew it. "Agreed. That was a dick move."

She stared at the forest tunnel around the road, watching the SUVs disappear into it. "Ned is a manipulative bastard."

"Yes. He's also desperate. We are who we are, baby. And I really do want those woods."

She groaned.

"I liked Ned," I said. "He outplayed us. He'll be a good man to know."

"Aha. I saw your face when you found them in our courtyard."

"I didn't know who they were or why they were in our house."

She shrugged. "Technically, they were in our courtyard."

I shook my head. "It doesn't matter. They were in our territory uninvited."

"When we were picking out this place, you told me that it was perfect because we had no neighbors and that you didn't like people."

"I like everybody," I told her.

I thought I'd get her to laugh, but she just looked at me.

"Name one person I don't like," I told her.

"My father."

"Fair enough."

"My aunt."

"We are polite and careful with each other."

"My cousin."

"I dislike him less now that he's several states away and safely domesticated by his wife and kids."

"And he stopped trying to kill me."

"That's the main part of it," I growled. "Everyone you've mentioned has tried to kill you."

At some point in our lives together, keeping her lovely family from trying to murder her became a full-time job for me. They were powerful, homicidal psychopaths, and they didn't half-ass it. When they came to kill her, they gave it their all.

Her eyes sparked. "You wanted to kill me at some point."

"No. The most I promised to do was to throw you out of a window."

She smiled, then thought about something, and her smile died. Kate leaned back and dragged her hand through her hair. I knew that expression. Something had been eating at her for a while.

"I started this by looking for Darin," she said.

"You didn't start anything. It was inevitable. And I don't regret helping Darin."

"Neither do I. I'm just acknowledging that I kicked this door open." She had that calculating look on her face she got when she was assessing someone she was about to take down. "This Penderton problem is going to be complicated. I don't like it, I don't want to get involved in it, but you're right, we need the woods and Penderton needs help."

"Good. Then we agree." I thought it would be harder to convince her. Something changed in her, and I'd missed it.

"The bad news is that we don't know what we're dealing with and it's strong," she said.

"The good news is that it has finite resources. It didn't want to tangle with the National Guard. The Magic Rapid Response Unit has 75 veteran soldiers in it. That's the max the National Guard could've sent, so we know that whatever is in the forest decided that 75 soldiers were too many. It sat back and waited for them to leave."

"And it worked."

"But we won't be leaving."

"No. We'll stay until the end," Kate said.

We didn't abandon things half done. Both of us knew that when we said yes.

Kate lifted the file in her hand. "Everything in this file Ned gave us tells me that the evil in the forest is powerful enough to snatch people from Penderton whenever they want. They don't need to formally request a tribute."

23

I thought about it. "It's about subjugation. Get the town under your thumb and keep them pinned to make sure that they won't even consider rebelling. The forest broke Penderton's will."

She nodded. "It owns the town now. It can take from Penderton, and Penderton will comply."

"We'll have to force a confrontation. How terrible."

She rolled her eyes.

Well, at least she had stopped looking so grim.

"Before we go there, I want to touch base with the Order," Kate said. "According to this file, Penderton petitioned them. They sent a five-knight team in. Only the pathfinder came out."

Pathfinders were an odd lot. To a pathfinder, there was no such thing as a maze, and if you presented them with a haystack and asked for the needle hidden in it, they would stick their hand in and pull it out on the first try. They were as close as a non-shapeshifter human could come to a trained werewolf scout.

"The Order lost four knights," Kate said. "They wouldn't have let it go, but I can't find anything else about it. They didn't follow up. I want to know what they know."

"You think Claudia will tell you? Just like that."

"She owes me a favor."

"Okay. While you're doing that, Conlan and I will go see his new favorite uncle. He can stay with them, or they can send him back here with babysitters. Either way, he won't be here alone again, and he doesn't need to go anywhere near Penderton for now."

"Agreed," she said. "He likes staying at Keelan's. Especially if Darin will come to visit."

Ever since Kate saved Darin, the merman kid made a habit of hanging out at the Wilmington Pack's HQ and safehouses. Darin had been searching for something and now he seemed to have found it. He wasn't our kind of shapeshifter, but we welcomed him all the same. He was a good, responsible kid. Everyone liked him, including Conlan.

"It's about thirty miles to Penderton from the Wilmington Pack's HQ," I said. "I want to bring at least seven or eight shapeshifters. We'll need a couple of cars."

"Are you taking ours?"

"I'll take Keelan's." The tech was holding, but sooner or later magic would come. Chanting at cars was never my favorite bit. If I could get someone else to do it, all the better. "It will take me a couple of hours to get everyone together. Do you think you'll be done by then?"

"I should be," she said.

"What do you need to bring?"

"I'll make a bag."

"Meet you on I-40 outside of town?" I asked, and leaned in to kiss her.

"Wait for me," she said and kissed me back.

"Always," I told her.

I watched her leave and wrestled that little anxiety I always felt when she left back down where it belonged.

Conlan returned a little later.

"They're on the road," he told me. "Where's Mom going?"

"Into town," I told him. "I'll meet her on the road to Penderton later."

My son's face fell a bit. "And me?"

"You and I are going to play a game on our way to see Keelan. The choice is yours: catch, or hide and hunt?"

"Is it a punishment?" Conlan asked.

"No. I'm not sure what we're walking into with Penderton, and your mother and I would feel better knowing you're safe. What do you think you've done to deserve punishment?"

"I invited Mr. Calloway and Solina into the courtyard. I fed them." He let it hang there for a moment. "Is that why you're mad at me and I can't go?"

Ah, best to nip this in the bud. "No. I'm not mad at you and, as I said, you aren't going because it's probably not safe. As far as giving cookies to Ned and Solina, that was polite. But human polite. Had they been shapeshifters..."

"Don't know them, don't feed them."

Keelan's words coming out of my kid's mouth.

"Put simply, yes. But do you understand why?"

"Because we're different."

"From who?" I asked.

"Whom," he corrected.

I let a little growl into my voice. "Conlan."

"Yes, sir. We're different from humans and other shapeshifters."

Correct again. "We are. We're stronger than both. Because of that, some people, like Keelan, will want to help us. Some people will want us to help them."

"Like Mr. Calloway." Conlan said.

"Yes, like that. And some people will want to hurt us. You need to be able to tell the difference."

"Even other shapeshifters?"

"Especially those. We both know you could handle most humans. Even adults. But you're young and there are shapeshifters that could hurt you."

"Like the pigs."

"Yes. If I wasn't there. If Keelan and his people weren't there that night, could you have fought both?"

A little bit of gold rolled over his eyes. "I would fight."

Okay. Yes. He probably would. "But would you win?"

"Maybe."

"No. You would have fought and died. I need to be sure that you know when to fight and when to run."

"Did you ever run?" he asked.

I had. I'd run for my life. And I'd hid. I had done it for so long that after a while all I could remember was running and hiding.

"Yes, and I was older than you. Faster and stronger than you are now. That is why you're going to run toward Keelan's place. I will wait, and then I will chase you. Try to get to Keelan before I catch you. This is serious, Conlan. Act like this is real."

My son smiled. "What do I get if I win?"

If it was real, everything. But he was a little boy, and this was a game to him. "If you manage to evade me and get there safe, I will take you to Penderton. If not..."

"I stay put."

"Yes. Your head start is dwindling away. Best get moving."

Kate

FALL IN WILMINGTON WAS LOVELY. IT WAS A PERFECT OCTOBER day, full of golden sunshine and happy trees. The locals told us that the foliage wouldn't turn until closer to November, and the poplars and maples shading the streets were just beginning to show hints of gold.

The sky was a crystal-clear blue, and a slight breeze stirred random hair that had escaped my braid. The temperature at our fort was always lower than inland, and I optimistically wore my favorite light hoodie, gray with a green stripe. If the weather turned any warmer, I'd have to take it off.

Around me, Wilmington buzzed as Cuddles made her way through the old streets at an unhurried pace. Since the Shift, foot traffic had increased because gas was expensive, chanting a car to life during magic took at least fifteen minutes, and horses needed to be fed, secured, and taken care of. If the destination was less than five miles away, most people opted for walking, and Castle Street channeled a steady crowd: craftsmen coming back from lunch, shoppers heading to the markets, laborers, businesspeople, a couple of mercs, all on their way to somewhere.

The hot red dot that burned in my mind got hotter. A vampire, ahead of me, not too far. I'd been watching it for about a mile, and I seemed to be getting closer.

To the left of me, on the empty lot, someone had set up a chicken market, and it had drawn a crowd. A couple of people on their bicycles stopped to crane their heads. The chicken vendor, a dark-haired older white man, waved a huge chicken around asking for bids. She was gray and fluffy and seemed content to sit in his arms like a docile cat.

"...lays five large brown eggs a week!"

That was a good-looking chicken with some serious egg-laying power. *I should probably look into that.*

The Order had chosen a historic firehouse as its lair. The old brick building rose on the corner of Castle and 5th Avenue, complete with a lovely red door and four-story tall tower housing a large metal bell. As I got past the chicken crowd, the tower came into view on my right. A green gaunt shape crouched on the tower's top floor by the bell, shaded from the sun by the tower's small roof.

There you are, precious. We finally meet.

The vampire sat perfectly still, like a mint-green gargoyle. If a navigator had come to visit the Order, they would've taken their undead inside. There were only two reasons why a vampire would end up in the Order's tower. Either the Order and the Farm were cooperating on something and the undead was keeping watch, or Barrett and Claudia were taking potshots at each other, and Barrett had one of his necromancers park an undead there to annoy the Order.

Either way, this would be entertaining.

We reached the tower. I dismounted, secured Cuddles to the rail, and walked inside.

The interior of the firehouse looked just as I had left it about three months ago: a single bright room with brick walls, sealed concrete floor, and large windows secured by thick grates. The two desks on the left were occupied, one by an athletic man in his thirties with a handsome face and a ragged scar that crossed his neck, drawing a dark slash on his light brown skin, and the other by a trim woman in her early twenties with tan skin and short blond hair, frosted with red dye.

Claudia sat at the larger desk on the right. She was in her fifties, with a round face, russet-brown skin, and a powerful build. Her short, curly hair was streaked with gray, and her eyes told you she had very little patience for your nonsense.

I gave her a big smile and a cheery wave. "Hello!"

The knight-protector gave me a flat stare.

The other two knights pretended to be absorbed in their paperwork.

"Yes?" Claudia asked me.

"I need a favor," I said.

"Don't we all."

I had sent her a report on Darin's rescue, complete with all the sins of the Order's former knight-enchanter, Aaron, spelled out in excruciating detail. And there were a lot of sins. Kidnapping, imprisonment, human trafficking, conduct unbecoming a knight, reckless disregard when practicing magic...

I tilted my head and waited.

Above us, the undead shifted a foot to the left. Claudia glanced up. If she could've fired laser beams from her eyes, a smoking undead corpse would've plummeted to the ground in a fraction of a second. So the vampire wasn't a welcome guest.

This was a flex by Barrett. He'd waited until the tech was up—otherwise the wards would've kept the undead off the building—and parked his vampire in the tower, knowing full well that the Order would never tolerate it. Claudia had to chase it off. There was no question about it. But she also would have to avoid making a spectacle or damaging the vampire. A spectacle would make the Order look weak, and any harm to the undead would escalate tensions with the Farm and, again, would cost the Order their street cred. Whichever party resorted to violence first would lose face.

"What do you want?" Claudia asked me.

"Access to Knight-Pathfinder Isaac Silverstein."

Before I left the fort, I'd called down to Atlanta's chapter of the Order and asked Nick to look up Isaac Silverstein. After he told me that he wasn't my secretary and we'd bickered for ten minutes about who was keeping score on favors, he came back with an interesting tidbit.

Silverstein was a really good pathfinder, highly decorated and experienced. He'd come to Penderton as a part of a five-man knight team specifically dispatched to handle this problem. Five knights went in, Silverstein came out alone, and after he came out, he stuck around in the area. Officially, he was on an extended mental health leave. Unofficially, he'd hung around Wilmington for the last six months, but the Order had no address for him. His mail was forwarded to the chapter.

The Knights of the Order were like soldiers in enemy territory. When possible, they preferred the company of their own and the safety of their base, so Isaac was likely inside the Wilmington Chapter right now. He'd probably lived here for the last half a year.

"That's a big ask," Claudia said.

"I realize the knight-pathfinder is working through some things," I said. "But I'm about to go into Pender Forest."

"Ask the National Guard," Claudia said. "They can brief you."

"What's the point? They didn't see anything. Knight-Pathfinder Silverstein saw something, because instead of leaving, he's here impersonating a monk. Like you said, it's a big favor, but there are five thousand people trapped in Penderton."

She sighed. "You don't need to be anywhere near that damn forest. I'm sure Penderton promised you the sky and the moon, but all you'll get is pain and death. This isn't me dissing you. This is me speaking as an expert with two decades of experience in the field: powerful people tried to resolve this and failed. This is above your paygrade. It's not worth it."

Claudia was trying to look out for me. I felt so...touched. Genuinely touched. This meant three things: Claudia was a real-deal, by-the-book knight, Nick hadn't told her who I was, and I wouldn't see Isaac Silverstein unless I convinced her that I was capable of surviving.

This would require a show of power.

If it was just about me, I might have hesitated. Showing my cards to Claudia meant she would start digging deeper. Eventually she'd figure out exactly who I was. But I wouldn't go alone into the woods. Curran would be with me, and we would be bringing Keelan and his crew. I had already made the decision to take Penderton up on their generous land offer, cracking the door open. Might as well open it all the way so I could get through.

Letting go of the need to hide was surprisingly easy.

Above us, the vampire shifted again.

"I appreciate where you're coming from," I said. "But I already gave my word to Penderton. Getting the knight-pathfinder's input would really help me."

Claudia shook her head. The world was filled with fools, and I was clearly the dumbest of them all.

I gave her a smile. "While you're thinking it over, would you like me to get rid of your unwelcome visitor? I can take it off the tower without damaging it, and if you humor me, Barrett won't ever put one up there again."

Claudia pondered me. "Let's see what you've got."

She didn't ask how I would do it. I pulled off my hoodie and held it out. "I need one of your knights to put this on with the hood up, get on my mount, and ride around the block. The undead needs to see me leaving."

I didn't want Barrett's attention focused on me. Eventually he and I would have a reckoning, but not yet. Not for a while.

Claudia nodded. The female knight walked over and took my

31

hoodie. "Which horse is yours?"

"The black and white mammoth donkey up front. Trust me, you can't miss her."

"Incoming," Claudia murmured.

"Barrett?" I asked through the undead's mouth.

"In the flesh."

Getting from the Farm across the river to the Wilmington Chapter took about half an hour. Barrett made it in twenty minutes. Either he was already in the city, or he was very motivated. He wouldn't have trusted just anyone with antagonizing the Order, so whoever piloted the vampire on his behalf had to be good. If someone had yanked an undead from one of my best navigators, I'd be motivated, too.

My new vampire crouched behind a whiteboard stand I borrowed from the Order's situation room, on the side of Claudia's desk. I'd taken a fat roll of paper from there, too. English letters were a lot easier to write through a vampire than Shinar's flowing sigils. There were few things better for training precision navigation than writing out your family's lineage in a dead language while your aunt despaired over the sad state of your calligraphy.

"He looks pissed," the other female knight murmured.

I'd locked myself in their armory, so the vampire was my eyes and ears for this little date. From my vantage point, I had an excellent view of Claudia, but the screen blocked the entrance and the windows, so I had to settle for imagining pissed-off Barrett marching across the street.

The door swung open, and firm footsteps announced Barrett approaching.

Claudia raised her head from her paperwork. "Well, this is a surprise. What can the Order do for you, Mr. Barrett?"

"You have something of mine." His voice was light. You could almost hear the smile.

"Do I?" Claudia frowned. "Oh, the vampire. Is it one of yours?"

"All of them are mine." Barrett chuckled and pushed the white-board stand aside. I twisted the undead into a picture-perfect impression of a person caught naked in the shower and tried to cover myself up with my undead hands.

The male knight made a strangled noise.

Barrett blinked.

I spun the vampire around, picked up the long roll of paper I'd been writing on, and held it out in front of Barrett. On it, in a beautiful cursive, I'd written a little song.

Old Barrett had a Farm

E i e i o

And on his Farm he had some cows

E i e i o

With a paw print here

And a paw print there

Here a paw print, there a paw print

Everywhere a paw print

Old Barrett had a Farm

E i e i o

And on his Farm he had some vampires

E i e i o...

I'd covered about five feet of paper with that nonsense. I'd mentioned the vampires, the journeymen, the cadre, and so on.

Barrett stopped smiling.

I handed the paper to him. He took it and looked at it. His face showed no emotion.

I lifted the vampire upright. It'd been undead for about fifteen years, and its hips had shifted to quadrupedal locomotion, but even the oldest vampire still possessed the ability to imitate the human posture. I put my arms down, slightly apart from my body, with the hands held up and turned around on my toes. Then I crouched slightly, bounced back up, put one hand on my hip, and held the other arm to the side, bent at the elbow, with my fingers together.

"What is this?" Barrett asked.

"I believe it's a little teapot," Claudia said, completely deadpan. "Short and stout. See, there is its handle and there is its spout."

"Cute," Barrett said.

His magic clamped on the vampire's mind, gripping me in a steel vise and trying to force me out. Wow. Barrett packed some serious power.

In its unpiloted state, a vampire's mind was an empty shell, a car without a driver rocketing forward at full speed and, like a runaway car, the undead wrecked anything it came across. Once a navigator took the driver's seat, getting them out was a lot harder than simply grabbing an unpiloted vampire. It wasn't a matter of skill but of raw power, which was why Barrett had dropped what he was doing and ran over here to see who had won the tug of war over his vampire. And the tech was up. Navigators, like shapeshifters, stored magic like a battery, which allowed them to navigate even when the magic was down, but doing this song and dance during tech was considerably harder.

The pressure intensified. He was really going for it now. This was what a walnut must feel like in a nutcracker. That wasn't all of it though. He was still holding back.

Let's see what you've got.

I shook the vampire and tilted it to the side. *When I get all steamed up, hear me shout. Tip me over and pour me out.*

A blast of power smashed into me. Like being buried under an avalanche. A massive weight crashed into my mind, squeezing, bombarding me, trying to crush me out of the driver's seat.

There it is. Welcome to the game.

Barrett's power hammered at me. It was a good, powerful punch. It even drew some blood. But I was the daughter of the Builder of Towers. My father had brought the undead into existence. I had ignored this side of my power for years, but I'd used the last decade to make up for it.

The pressure ground at my mind. Barrett stared at the vampire with a terrible intensity.

It was time for a reality check.

I raised my arms, did a pirouette to build up momentum, extended my leg to the second position, whipped it to the back of the supporting knee, bringing it to the front, and turned *en dehor.* A fouetté.

Barrett's eyes widened. He clenched his fists and pushed with everything he had.

One turn, two, three. I kept spinning. Turn, and turn, and turn, ten, fifteen, eighteen...

Uncertainty shivered in Barrett's eyes. The three knights were staring at the vampire like they had never seen one before.

Twenty-four, twenty-six...

He must have thought of himself as an unstoppable force but, in the mind of an undead, I was truly an immovable object.

Thirty...

The pressure eased just a hair. It was barely less than it had been, but it still meant surrender. Barrett was running out of his magic reserve. I won.

I finished the last fouetté, landed, and raised my right arm, inviting applause. Nobody clapped. Party poopers.

I let go. The transition back to only one pair of eyes and ears was always slightly nauseating. I stayed still in the armory, listening.

Barrett would've grabbed the undead instantly, but we both knew what had happened. He didn't win. I let him have his undead back.

"I don't know who you brought in," Barrett said, his voice low and full of contained menace. "But I'll find out."

A door swung open. I waited. A minute crawled by. Another...

"He's gone," Claudia called out.

I opened the door and trotted out. "You didn't clap. My feelings are hurt."

Claudia gave me a slow golf clap, and the other two knights followed. They were looking slightly freaked out.

Claudia squinted at me. "Who are you?"

"Someone who really wants to talk to Isaac Silverstein."

Claudia got up. "I'll ask him. No promises. Sit tight."

I sat in a client chair. Claudia opened a door leading to an interior staircase and left.

How was it that she didn't know who I was? My file in the Order's database should've been a mile long.

Unless they had sealed it. I had seen that before, during my tenure with the Order in Atlanta. The file on my father was invisible to me. I didn't have the clearance to know it existed. Andrea, my best friend and, at the time, a high-ranking knight, could only see a very brief summary that amounted to a warning sign and had to call in favors to learn more.

As a knight-protector, the head of her own chapter, Claudia should've had a high enough clearance, but then Wilmington was a lot smaller than Atlanta or Charlotte.

I wonder how tightly they have my file locked up...

I heard Claudia coming down the stairs. The door swung open, and she emerged. "He'll see you."

"Thank you."

"I hope you're ready for Barrett," Claudia said. "He won't let it go. You didn't see his face as he walked out. That man was pissed off. He's going to make it his purpose in life to find you and make you suffer every humiliation his psychotic mind can think up."

"He won't find out, unless one of you three tells him."

"He will find out," Claudia said, "because you enjoy screwing with him. Sooner or later, you'll slip up."

Slipping up wasn't in the cards. I planned to keep Barrett ignorant for as long as I could. "Thank you for the warning."

"Take care," Claudia said.

[3]

I saac Silverstein looked like a knight-pathfinder. A shade under six feet tall, somewhere between twenty-five and fifty, he had the lean build of a long-range hiker, a perfect balance between flexibility, endurance, and moderate calorie needs. His navy sweatshirt hung off his shoulders, and his dark brown lightweight pants were tapered to his legs, loose enough to allow freedom of movement but tight enough not to snag on the brush. He wore serious hiking boots that looked like they had seen a lot of miles in a rough terrain. We weren't anywhere near a hiking trail, so he must be wearing what he felt comfortable in.

Isaac's tousled hair, cut short on the sides and slightly longer on top, was a cooler shade of brown, more ash than red. His skin wasn't that pale naturally, but it didn't have even an echo of a tan, which told me he'd stayed the whole summer inside the chapter.

His hooded blue eyes still held a hint of the "woods" stare, however. Human eyes were expressive. We communicated with our glances as much as with our mouths. When shapeshifters hunted in the forest, their eyes lost emotion and communicated nothing. They simply watched, observing their prey, tracking it, cataloguing danger and weakness, and if you happened to meet their gaze, your mind might not even recognize that you were looking at a human. Isaac's eyes were a bit like that.

I paused in the doorway.

"Come in," he said.

I stepped inside.

Isaac's office was square, with a window in the wall opposite the door. On both sides of the window, mounted weapons waited —a bow with a quiver and an assortment of knives and bladed weapons that doubled as tools: axes, tomahawks, and machete-style short swords.

A desk sat on the left, filled with neat, orderly stacks of papers. Behind it, floor-to-ceiling shelves held books, rolled-up scrolls, chunks of twisted roots, jars of dried herbs, and other assorted things an outdoorsman might find in the woods and drag home.

The wall opposite the desk, on my right, was covered by a curtain.

"Claudia wants me to talk you out of it," Isaac said. He had a quiet voice, slightly raspy.

"Claudia is a good person."

"Would it work?"

"No."

Isaac leaned against his desk and pushed the wheeled client chair toward me. I saddled it backward and leaned my arms on its back.

"There were five of us," he said. "Me, a knight-enchanter, and three knight-defenders."

Standard team. Isaac would've led the way, the knight-enchanter would have set and broken wards, and the three knight-defenders would have kept all of them breathing.

"Everyone was seasoned. Everyone knew their way around the wilderness. Tim, the senior knight-defender, and I had worked together before a few times. He was a good man, reliable, compe-tent. Kept a cool head."

"SnS or SnD?"

Knight teams of this type came in three varieties, depending on their mission: search and rescue, search and scout, and search and destroy. The first one was off the table, so it would be one of the other two.

"SnS," Isaac said. "Get in, locate the threat, identify if possible, and get out to tell about it."

That meant that once things got hairy, the team would've bailed. They wouldn't have pushed their luck, and yet he was the only one left.

"We got to Penderton when the magic was up," Isaac said. "As you get closer to town, you get a bad feeling."

"Like what?"

"Like you should turn around. It starts subtly, but the farther you go, the stronger it grows. Something doesn't want you to be there."

Isaac paused. I didn't rush him.

"Did they tell you about the hill?"

"No."

The knight-pathfinder walked over to the bookcase and pulled a cord hanging on one side. A map unrolled from the top shelf, showing Wilmington and the surrounding area. It looked different. The border of Wilmington proper was larger, and a dozen or more small towns and villages dotted the area above and to the west of the city, connected by a network of roads.

"There used to be a hill south of Harrells," he said.

It took me a second to find it. A small town about twenty miles north-northwest of Burgaw, currently Penderton. A couple of miles south of Harrells, someone—probably Isaac—had put a big black dot.

I pulled Ned's file out of my bag and found the map. The hill was right in the middle of the blue square marking the land Penderton had given us. Dead center.

"How big was this hill?"

"A little under two square miles in footprint, conical, 260 feet high."

"Unusual for this area," I thought out loud. Most of the surrounding landscape was flat, with round depressions that were lakes or pastures randomly strewn here and there.

"Pre-Shift, the hill had problems," Isaac said. "People would see odd things around it. UFOs, skunk ape, Bigfoot, ghosts, the usual modern folklore nonsense. Post-Shift, the locals avoided it, because it gave them a bad feeling."

"Kind of like it didn't want you there?" I guessed.

Isaac nodded. "The hill is gone."

"What do you mean, gone?"

"When the woods started expanding, the Forest Service went up there and put a big flagpole with a flag and a feylantern on the apex of the hill to help people orient themselves. On a clear night, you could see the lantern all the way from the tower at Penderton. It disappeared during the last flare. No flag, no feylantern, no hill."

That wasn't in Ned's file.

"They tried looking for it," Isaac said. "Flew a drone up there. Something took it down, but not before it transmitted a picture of a clear sky and woods where the hill used to be."

"You bet on the hill, then?"

He nodded again. "We waited until the tech came and went in as soon as it was light enough to see. It's about twenty miles through the woods to where the hill used to be. Now, all of it was supposed to be your regular longleaf pine savanna. It's light, bright, open. The forest floor is grass, very little underbrush, with an occasional bog here and there. This was a fun, easy forest. Not even close to the Ozark broadleaf woods or spruce-fir upstate, where you have to cut your way through."

Yes, the ninja woods. Tall pines and sunshine.

"We go in, and that bad feeling starts growing stronger. After the first hour, Taylor, the knight-enchanter, said we were going in circles. She was sure she had seen the exact tree twice before, and she said she'd nicked a pine trunk, and there was the nick. The thing was, we were going the right way. She wanted to go back to town, regroup, and try again. I told her no, and Tim backed me up.

"By the end of the second hour, everyone except me was sure we were going the wrong way. We stopped at a clearing by a pond. I took one of the knight-defenders, pointed to the north, and told him to look in that direction and memorize what the woods looked like. He said he did. I had him cover his eyes, spin around three times, and tell me where north was. He had no clue. Even though he knew that the pond was on his west side, he couldn't orient himself. He said that every time he turned his head, the woods looked different. Now, tech is up this whole time. None of this shit should be happening."

"What did you do?"

"We went to ropes. I got my paracord out, tied everyone to each other, with Tim bringing up the rear and me leading the way, and told them to look at the back of the person in front of them while they were walking. We kept going. All the while I'm looking around for the shaman totems, witch markers, anything that could possibly explain what's going on, and there is nothing."

Isaac dragged his hand over his face, as if wiping memories away.

"The woods started closing in. Suddenly, there is an under-brush. I'm seeing willow, alder, and blueberry. I'm seeing quaking aspens. They don't grow south of Zone 6, so it's strange, but they are native to North Carolina. You can find them on some Smoky Mountain slopes. Then I see this."

He turned to the shelves, pulled a glass jar off, and set it in front of me. Inside was a clump of golden pine needles.

I looked at him.

"Tamarack," he said. "Also known as American larch. A conifer that loses its needles in the fall."

"Not something I'm familiar with."

"That's because it grows in Canada and northeastern US."

"Oh."

"This forest is thriving. Trees look healthy, birds are singing, squirrels are running around, deer, mice, everything is as it's supposed to be except all of it should be a lot farther north and something doesn't want us there. All of this is confirming that we're going the right way, because the farther we go, the weirder things get. We keep moving. Our path gets denser and denser. I had to get my machete out, and I'm cutting through now. In every other direction, there are clear animal trails, but directly in front of us, it's a wall of green."

The evil in the woods was trying to get them to turn back any way it could. It must've recognized them as large-caliber magic users and didn't want a confrontation. But with the tech up, there were only a handful of ways to do it. Three, to be exact, and all of them meant serious trouble for us.

"Do you think you might have gone through a portal?" I asked. "A pocket realm of some sort?"

Isaac shook his head. "No. I've gone into places like that twice. One hundred percent sure there was no portal. And the enchanter confirmed it."

It was down to two, then. I would've taken the portal over either one.

"It's early afternoon now," Isaac said. "And we're being watched. I can feel the stares. Something large is moving all around us, just out of sight. The woods end suddenly and we're in a swamp. I stop on the edge trying to figure out the path, and I see these things in the water. I don't know what the hell they are but they're furry, they're the size of black bears, and there are a lot of them. We turn to go around, and something comes out of the brush and rips Jeremiah out of our line. Sliced right through the paracord on both sides. You'd think it would hit me or Tim, but it went for the man in the middle."

"What was it?"

Isaac sighed. "A blur. Never saw it clearly. It was so fucking fast. But you want a gut-feeling call: a shapeshifter."

Crap. "What kind?"

"I don't know. I've fought shapeshifters before, and this bastard was on another level."

I didn't need to ask him if they chased the attacker. Knights of the Order didn't leave their own behind.

"It took us another two hours to find his body," Isaac said. "There was a clearing with a rock sticking out of it. He was on that rock, impaled by his own sword. The rock had carvings all over it, and his blood had run down into the grooves and painted them red."

Great.

"The knight-enchanter had never seen anything like that. She had no clue what culture it might have come from. By this point it was dark. So, we left him, alone, on that rock, and made camp away from it. Taylor put the salt circle down in case magic hit at night. We slept in shifts, two people down, two people watching. In the morning, Sander, one of the knight-defenders, is missing. None of us heard or saw whatever took him. He's just gone. It's down to Tim, Taylor, and me."

The pauses between his sentences were getting longer. He was struggling to get the words out.

"We took a vote to go in or to get out. Everyone wanted to keep going, so we did. At noon, I climb a tree to see how deep into the woods we had gone. While I am up there, something comes out of the forest. I can't see what, the brush was too thick. I hear Tim scream. I get down off the fucking tree and they are both dead. Skulls caved in, just crushed like walnuts. Blood and brain everywhere."

He fell silent. I gave him room.

"I'm pissed off, so I keep going north," he said finally. "I don't know how long I walked, but they trailed me the whole way. Finally, I see the forest thin out up ahead. I come to a clearing and see this animal chewing on some bushes. I don't know what it is but I sure as hell know it shouldn't be here, in coastal North Carolina.

"We look at each other, and this realization comes over me. This animal, it fits perfectly into this environment. It's exactly where it's supposed to be. It's me who is out of place. I'm the one who doesn't belong."

"The magic hit, and it was like someone pinned me under a microscope. I don't have words to explain. It's like whatever it was that had been keeping an eye on me suddenly stared and the weight of it almost made me black out."

He paused.

"What happened?"

"I ran. Whatever was watching me chased me, but I'm very fast when I have to be, and I was squeezing out everything I could of my pathfinding magic. It threw me out onto an abandoned, over-grown road—421 as I found out later—and I took it. Came out of the woods the next day with barely a scratch on me. Sat down. Wrote a report. Explained how I was the only one who had lived. Sent it to the Citadel in Wolf Trap."

"Why didn't they send another team in?"

Isaac crossed his arms on his chest. "The town asked me what would happen if the woods decided to retaliate. They wanted to know if the Order could protect them."

"What did you tell them?"

"The truth. We have no idea what it is, and we don't know how to defend against it. The mayor called the Citadel, spoke with the Grand Master directly, and I was told to fall back."

"And now you're here."

"The four of them are still in that forest," Isaac said. "The thing that killed them is still there, too."

All the unsaid things hung between us, making the air heavy and oppressive. That he lost his whole team. That he came out unharmed, while the rest of them had their skulls bashed in. That the town was still under siege. That he met something in those woods that disturbed the very core of his being and he needed to confront it to make the world right again.

And Grand Master Damian Angevin had allowed him to stay right where he was instead of ordering him to a new assignment. The Order had gotten a lot choosier about which fights they picked under Angevin's leadership, but once the knights went in, they saw it to the end. No matter what it cost them. Leaving this matter unfinished went against everything they stood for. Angevin was giving Isaac a chance to resolve things, but not the means to do it.

"What did the animal look like?" I asked.

Isaac pushed away from his desk and pulled the curtain on the opposite wall to the side. A big map of Pender Forest was pinned to the wall, with a twisted route leading north-northwest inked on it. Landmarks dotted the map here and there: fallen tree, pond, bog—each marked with a symbol and a piece of a string that connected the marks to pencil sketches drawn with startling accuracy on watercolor paper.

On the left, a sketch showed a triangular rock with a blond man sprawled on it, a sword protruding from his chest. His blue eyes stared up at the artist from a face twisted by fear and pain.

At the top of the map, on a thirty-inch piece of paper, a landscape unfolded, the trees framing a small slice of grassy plain. A big animal stood in the grass. It looked like an elephant, and yet it clearly wasn't. It had an elephant's trunk and elephant's ears, but the ears were too small and its trunk was too long. Very short beige fur covered it, reminiscent of a horse's pelt. Its legs seemed wider apart than an elephant's, and its profile was wrong, too. Elephants had high foreheads, and this beast's cranium sloped. But the tusks were the most obvious. They were massive and long, as long as the trunk, pointed down, and spiral-shaped.

Wow.

"How big?" I asked.

"Almost eight feet at the shoulder. Four tons in weight. Maybe more."

We stared at the drawing.

"What the hell is it?" I murmured.

"No clue."

We looked at the beast some more.

"Still plan on going in?" he asked.

"Yep. Want to come?"

"I'll think about it."

"If you decide to join us, find me in Penderton."

"I'll think about it," the knight-pathfinder repeated.

NED WAS RIGHT. THE WOODS PAST THE NORTHEAST CAPE RIVER bridge were beautiful. Massive pines crowded the old highway, drenched in sunlight, their branches thick with clusters of long pine needles that looked deceptively fluffy. The underbrush was nonexistent, mostly fledgling pines poking out of the clumps of golden wiregrass. It was a far cry from the impenetrable bramble of stunted live oak, wax myrtle, and yaupon holly that made up the maritime forest around our house.

Ahead two gray SUVs waited, parked on the side of the road. That had to be my ride.

I caught a hint of movement out of the corner of my eye. Eight shapeshifters slipped out of the woods and flanked me, with my husband popping up on my right like a jack-in-the-box. I took half a second to catalogue the familiar faces: Keelan, dark blond hair tousled, a massive claymore on his back; Da-Eun, his beta, athletic, with dark hair pinned to the back of her head; Jynx, a bouda with wild eyes and long, bright yellow nails; Andre and Hakeem, whom I first met on their cow-pawing adventure; Troy, the red-haired werejackal who was our medmage; Luiza, dark-haired and willowy; and Owen, who looked like he enjoyed bench pressing small cars as a light workout. A good team.

Curran grinned at me, his gray eyes happy. "Hey, baby. You come here often?"

I laughed.

"Your hand looks heavy. Let me hold it for you." He squeezed my hand with his warm fingers.

"Smooth," Jynx murmured.

Andre winked at her. "Hey, Jynx, your hand—"

"Touch me and I'll break you," she told him.

"Aww."

"Conlan?" I asked.

"Back at the safe house with Helen," Curran told me.

I figured he'd choose that option over having someone watch him at the fort. This way everyone could pretend that he was a guest and not someone they were babysitting.

"Luiza will take Cuddles back to the safe house," Curran said. "Helen will need backup until the patrols come in."

At any given moment, there were three shapeshifter patrols moving through Wilmington and the surrounding area, not counting the pair of shapeshifters who watched the Farm. Keelan wanted to know what was happening in the city, and he was very thorough about things.

We reached the cars. I dismounted, took the saddlebags with my gear off Cuddles, and handed the reins to Luiza together with a bag of carrots.

"If she stops in the middle of the road, don't try to force her. Show her that you have a carrot, give her a small piece, and keep the rest. She'll follow you. Also, Conlan looks like an eight-year-old, but he doesn't think like one. He's very polite, so he'll say things like 'Yes, ma'am' and 'No, ma'am,' and before you know it, he'll talk you into letting him do something everyone will regret. Treat him like a smart, conniving teenager. Above all, please keep him away from Penderton."

Luiza smiled. "I can handle him. No problem."

Famous last words.

I pulled a copy of Isaac's sketch out of my bag. I had made several at the chapter while the tech held out.

"What's this?" Curran asked, focusing on the creature.

"Something the knight-pathfinder saw in the woods. I'll tell you more on the way."

I passed the sketch to Luiza. "When you get back, show this sketch to Helen in front of Conlan and tell her that we asked you to research it. If he asks you for the sketch, tell him it's boring adult stuff."

She grinned back at me. "Got it."

"It will keep him occupied," I said. "But we do need to know what this animal is. Maybe run it by Forest Service."

"And the hunters," Curran said. "Butcher shops buy venison and other game at auction during Friday market, so a lot of hunters will be there. Ask them if they ever saw something like this."

"Yes, Alpha."

We climbed into the vehicles and started down the road. Curran drove, with me in the front passenger seat and Keelan and Da-Eun in the back.

"Did you find out anything?" Curran asked.

I brought him up to speed on my fun visit with Barrett.

Curran laughed.

"Barrett's been the king of his little island for too long," Keelan grumbled. "He needed a reality check."

"That man has the straight-A student syndrome," Da-Eun said. "He's been the most powerful Master of the Dead for so long, it's gone to his head and permanently fucked it up."

Isaac's story didn't go over as well. Neither did the copy of his sketch, which I had passed to Da-Eun and Keelan.

Da-Eun rubbed the bridge of her nose. "It's not enough that

there are mud-smeared women and human sacrifices, now we've got a weird-ass elephant."

Keelan shrugged. "It's still a herbivore, just larger. It bleeds, so it can be killed. If it gives us trouble, we'll bleed it and run it down like an oversized stag."

Werewolf thoughts, uncensored. If it bleeds, it dies. Not worried about the giant mysterious pachyderm in the slightest.

A side road came into view on our left. We took it, rolling deeper into the woods. After a couple of minutes, the trees turned into fields wrapped in barbed wire. Onion, corn, squash—most of it either waiting to be harvested or in the process of it. An occasional farmhouse and a few solid barns dotted the landscape, all reinforced new construction designed to shelter the farmers and their livestock from the weird predators breeding in the magic-soaked forest. To the right, a herd of red and white cows with foot-long horns grazed in a pasture. Three big Anatolian shepherds watched us as we drove by.

Another pasture, sheep this time. No dogs. Optimistic of them.

Something stirred on the roof of the barn and stood up. The creature was about forty inches at the shoulder, gray, with a lean lupine body and a wolf's tail. Its head resembled that of an eagle, with a dark beak the size of a dagger. Its feathery wings draped over its back.

"What is that?" Da-Eun asked.

"A wolf griffin," I told her. "A pretty good-sized one, too."

Magic hit. The SUV's gasoline engine sputtered and died, and Curran gently guided the vehicle to a stop just past the barn.

An unsettling feeling touched me. A kind of instinctual unease, as if a sniper were staring at me through the scope of their rifle.

Hmmm. I opened the car door and got out. Curran exited on the other side, and the two shapeshifters followed.

I stared at the woods, trying to sort out what my senses were telling me. Magic wasn't a specific sense like a scent or a sound. We didn't have an organ devoted to analyzing it. Instead, it was a combination of things, a pressure, a feeling, heat or ice, a faint odor, a sense of danger, sometimes overwhelming, sometimes vague.

This was... I wasn't sure what this was.

Da-Eun began to chant, priming the water engine. Behind us, the second SUV disgorged its passengers, and I heard Troy's voice launching into a monotone chant.

The wolf griffin pivoted to us. It gripped the edge of the roof with wicked, sickle-shaped talons, lowered its head, and raised its spotted wings, every feather erect, tipping them down like an owl trying to make itself larger.

"Quit it," Keelan told it.

The wolf griffin rocked side to side, fluffing its feathers to maximum capacity, and let out a low shriek.

"Stay on your roof," Keelan warned. "Don't you come down here, or I'll pluck your feathers out and make myself a nice pillow."

The wolf griffin shrieked again and gave Keelan an evil raptor eye.

The creepy feeling grazed my skin, like an itch I couldn't scratch. I turned and jogged down the road, moving in the direction we'd come from. Curran caught up with me.

We ran for about ten minutes. I stopped.

Yep, it was lighter here. Very slightly, almost imperceptibly lighter. If I wasn't concentrating on it, I might have missed it.

"What's up?" my husband asked.

"I'm trying to figure that out."

I turned and walked back in the direction of the cars. It felt like walking through a very shallow stream. The magic barely wet my toes, offering no resistance, but the farther I went, the deeper it would become, until I would be wading in it.

If I was right, this would explain some things but not the others.

I crouched and put my hand on the ground. Magic touched my

fingers, alien yet slightly familiar. There was a way to test my theory, but that would mean giving away the element of surprise.

I straightened.

"This might be harder than we expected," I told Curran.

"Do you want to turn back?"

"No. Curran, that thing Keelan does, where he sends a scout team out? He can't do it here. Nobody can go into the woods unless I'm with them. If they enter the forest without me, they won't come out."

"That bad?"

"Do you remember after Mishmar we camped at an abandoned gas station? We woke up, and the world was white with snow, and then the magic wave hit. It feels similar."

Curran's face snapped into a hard mask. "I see."

"It's not exactly the same, and it's very weak here, so I could be wrong. But if I'm right, this isn't a portal or a magic fissure like Unicorn Lane. This is deliberate and it's driven by something intelligent. It knows we're here. I don't want anyone to die because they brought teeth and claws to a magic fight."

"I'll speak to Keelan," he promised me.

NED TOLD ME THAT PENDERTON'S TOWN CENTER WAS WALLED IN. Looking at the thirty-foot wall, he might have left out some details.

Curran frowned at the big gatehouse in front of us, wide enough to accommodate the two-lane road. "What did his file say again?"

I pulled the file from the backpack resting by my feet.

"A double timber palisade filled with packed dirt," I quoted.

The gate was built with gray oversized bricks and flanked by two towers of the same gray under shingled roofs. More towers rose on both sides, about four hundred feet apart from their neighbors, connected by a wooden wall of thick pine timber. Guards were walking on it, so it had to be at least three or four feet wide.

Curran's eyebrows crept up.

"Solid," Keelan said.

"And expensive," Curran said.

"According to the file, they paid for it with a state grant, a federal grant, municipal taxes, and private donations. Ned's father built most of it. Oh, and you'll love this, those gray bricks are made out of Shift dust."

When magic gnawed on a building, it slowly ground concrete into dust, a fine gray powder that was completely inert and useless. There were small hills of that dust in the city centers, and most cities had no idea what to do with it. Ned's father would have gotten it dirt cheap. In fact, Wilmington probably paid him to remove it.

Hmm. And I bet these bricks were magic-proof, too. There was a business opportunity if I ever saw one.

"How are they made?" Curran asked.

"A proprietary process of mixing it with water, cornstarch, and sticky rice," I read.

"How strong could rice concrete be?" Keelan asked.

"They built the Great Wall with it, you ignorant savage," Da-Eun told him.

The speed limit dropped to twenty miles, and we joined the short line of pickup trucks, carts, and riders crawling through the gates.

"Ned has a house set up for us," I said. "Take the second left past the gate."

Before the Shift, Burgaw must've been a typical Southern town with plenty of space to spread out. I'd guess ranch-style houses, generous lots, and few if any front fences. Hints of the old town were still there, mainly in the layout of roads and parking lots, but the city wall only enclosed a square mile, and space inside was at a premium. The houses sat closer together, a lot of them two stories and a good number of them almost touching. The lawns had been converted to vegetable gardens and fenced in with chicken wire or short wooden fences. I saw a communal stable and a reinforced, bunker-like building with the sign South Walker Shelter. The town was compact, purposefully laid out, and ready to defend itself.

Ned's directions brought us across Penderton, all the way north. A couple of street markers were missing, so we stopped to ask a local for directions, and he helpfully told us to "go on past where Pender Prison used to be." The prison was no longer there, although some of the white one-story buildings remained. It now housed the town guard barracks, a municipal storage facility, and an emergency clinic, all sheltered behind a razor-wire fence.

"They expect the threat to come from the north," Curran said. "This is a fallback point."

"CC?" Keelan said.

"Mhm," Curran said. "The radio tower."

A command center, designed to coordinate the defense if the wall was breached. Nice.

The house Ned set out for us was just two streets over, on the imaginatively named North Wall Road. The wall was on the other side of the street. We parked the SUVs in the garage, hauled out our bags, and went into the house. It was a nice three-story place, with a porch on the ground level and wide wrap-around balconies on the top two floors. Curran and I dropped our bags in one of the third-floor bedrooms, and I walked out onto the balcony.

The wall was in front and below me, with a solid gatehouse almost directly across from the balcony, guarded by a tower on the right side. The two nearest towers rose about equal distance to the left and to the right. Past the wall, five hundred yards of clear ground offered a nice kill zone. Beyond it, the woods towered, like a second ominous wall.

Curran stepped out onto the balcony and came over to lean on the guardrail next to me. We looked at the woods.

"This is the timber gate," I said. "Before the problem started, they harvested timber in the north forest and brought it through here to the sawmills."

"Makes sense," Curran said.

We watched two guards cautiously check us out from their respective towers and turn back to the forest. That tree line five hundred yards away was where the strange women first appeared.

We still didn't know who they were or what they did with the people they had taken. Were the tribute people alive? Were they enslaved, or were they killed? Of all the magic practices, human sacrifice was the worst. It gave you a boost of magic but at a terrible cost. It tapped into the kind of powers that fed on humanity and drove us mad. They had been long banished from the world by tech, and that was for the best. Even my father steered clear of it.

The woods waited.

"Do you want to go in?" I asked.

"We have six hours of daylight left."

"Sounds like a plan."

"We're going in five," Curran called out.

A chorus of ragged "Yes, Alpha" answered him.

Five minutes later, we assembled in front of the house, a small army in sweatpants. I was the only fighter out of uniform.

"We'll enter together," Curran said quietly. "As we go in, drift into two groups. Group One: Kate, Keelan, Troy, Owen, and Hakeem. The rest with me. We'll widen the gap by five hundred yards and hold it there."

He was splitting us up to invite an attack on one group or the other. Might as well find out what sort of welcome party the forest had planned for us.

"The thing that's behind this knows we're here," Curran continued. "Whichever group is attacked will hold, while the other group will close in. The enemy uses magic. Kate is a magic expert. Obey her without question even if it goes against your training. She'll keep us alive."

Curran turned toward the woods.

"Alright," Keelan barked, "you heard the Alpha. You're going into enemy territory. This is the real thing. This is what you've trained for. Ears up, noses open, look alive."

We started to the gate.

A small group turned the corner, entering the street a block away and hurried toward us. A middle-aged man was in the lead, short, stocky, with light brown skin and short brown hair, dressed in sawdust-covered overalls with safety googles perched on his head. Beside him was a stocky red-headed woman in her twenties armed with a bow and a sword, and a well-dressed woman in her forties with dark brown skin and glossy hair pulled into a bun.

The middle-aged man waved at us. "Wait!"

Curran stopped and everyone stopped with him.

The group reached us. The middle-aged man stuck his hand out and said, slightly out of breath, "Mayor Eugene Dowell. Everyone calls me Gene."

"Curran Lennart. This is my wife, Kate, and these are my associates."

Curran and I took turns shaking his hand.

The associates, who a moment ago had put on their game faces and were ready to invade enemy territory and fuck shit up, made valiant efforts to appear non-threatening.

"This is Ruth Chatfield, city clerk and finance director."

The dark-haired woman put her hand out, and we shook it.

"And this is Heather Armstrong, our interim wall guard captain."

We shook again.

"If you need anything, please let us know," Gene said.

"Thank you," I said.

"You're not going in, are you?" The anxiety dripped from Gene's voice.

"We are," Curran confirmed.

"But the magic is up," Gene said.

"We know," I told him.

Ruth looked like she was imagining our funeral. Heather's face told me that she had seen this exact scenario before and knew none of us would come back in one piece. Or at all.

"I wish you'd reconsider," Gene said.

"Thank you for your concern," I told him. "Can you please open the gate for us?"

Gene sighed. "Heather?"

"Open the gates," Heather called out. One of the guards ran down the wall, took the stairs, and went to the gate to unbar it.

The three of them watched the gate open with resigned looks on their faces.

The gate swung open, and we went through.

Behind us, Heather sighed and said, "I'll get the first responders ready."

[4]

The oppressive feeling grew stronger. We were half a mile into the woods now. The shapeshifters had executed the drifting maneuver with flawless precision. We sort of spontaneously parted, slowly diverging from each other along parallel paths in an entirely natural, casual way. I could no longer see Curran or his group, but I knew they were there, five hundred yards to my right.

The woods around us were still pine and grass. None of the confusion Isaac told me about was happening.

"It's drawing us in," Keelan murmured on my left.

"Yep."

It wanted us far enough from town that help wouldn't arrive in time, but close enough for our bodies to be easily found.

"Any time now," I said.

The shapeshifters around me moved like shadows, fast and silent. We kept going.

"We're being stalked by some sweet shrubs," Keelan murmured. "They've been following us for the last five minutes."

Last I checked, sweet shrubs didn't move. They did, however, give off a spicy strong scent that was good enough to drown out other odors. "How many shrubs?"

"At least three."

Ahead, a couple of trees had fallen to our left, creating a clearing around a massive pine tree. Hakeem, who was slightly in front of us and to the left, stopped and picked up a stick.

"Stop," Keelan and I ordered at the same time.

Hakeem froze.

I caught up with him. "What is it?"

He pointed with his stick in the direction of the giant pine. Four stone spheres about the size of baseballs were stacked on top of each other in the clearing, about fifteen yards from the big tree. By every law of physics, they should have collapsed. They had to be held together by magic, but nothing emanated from them. From this distance, they looked like rocks. Unnaturally smooth and round rocks.

"Were you going to poke them with a stick?" Keelan growled.

Hakeem looked uncertain. "Yes?"

"When you find freaky shit in the scary woods, you don't poke it with a stick. It can explode in your face. What do you do instead?"

Hakeem clearly didn't know the answer to that question. I almost felt sorry for him. He had just turned eighteen this year, and this was likely his first real outing.

"You ask the Consort. The Consort knows everything."

"Oh," Hakeem said.

Keelan pivoted to me. "Consort, please tell us what this is."

"I have no idea."

Keelan blinked, his teaching moment temporarily derailed. He took a second to recover. "How do we proceed?"

I held my hand out, and Hakeem surrendered his branch. "I'm going to poke it with a stick."

To my left Troy snickered. Owen cracked a smile.

Keelan looked like he was about to suffer a conniption fit.

"It's a magic trap," I told him. "It's likely primed to go off when something organic makes contact with it. Wood in this case is a good substitute for a human. I'm going to enchant the stick and see if I can get a better sense of what this is."

I approached the rocks and stopped a couple of feet away. Still nothing. The question wasn't whether I could handle the trap. The question was how many of my cards would I have to show.

I whispered an incantation under my breath, focusing it on the stick. I'd learned it from my father about five years ago, and he'd learned it from some visiting mages several millennia ago, when he was trying to broaden his horizons. As a diagnostic tool, it was pretty limited. It told you if the magic was there and how much of it, it but revealed nothing about its nature. There were better spells and artifacts out there, but we were short on time and right now it was my best bet.

The magic coated the wood and saturated it, sucked into the dead branch with a snap. I raised my stick and concentrated.

Each of the rocks was a solid knot of magic. A staggering amount of it, compressed into a vessel that was way too small for that amount of power. The moment that containment broke, all of that tightly coiled magic would burst. Simple but devastating.

We had to disarm it. It was too close to town, and if we passed it, someone could trigger it behind us, hitting us in the back.

I backed away, pulled a vial out of my backpack, and looked around. A slight depression curved the forest floor about ten yards away. It would have to do.

"Fall in on me." I walked over to the depression.

The shapeshifters converged around me.

"Hit the dirt and stay down."

They dropped to the forest floor.

I uncorked the vial and brushed my thumb over the edge, testing the liquid inside. Magic nipped at me. Still potent. My father's patented secret recipe, but instead of seven herbs and spices, it used vampire blood mixed with a binding agent and primed with exactly three drops of my blood.

A blood ward was the strongest defensive spell in my arsenal. However, bleeding all over the place weakened me and was inconvenient. It also gave away the nature of my power. The undead blood charged with my magic was almost as good, and it conveniently masked the clear signature of my blood.

I circled the prone shapeshifters, dripping blood from the vial at regular intervals, and stepped into the circle I'd made. The undead blood waited, ready for my magic.

I picked up a pinecone, dripped a drop from the vial on it, corked the vial, put it away, and hefted my improvised grenade.

"Fire in the hole!"

I threw the pinecone at the rocks and dropped, activating the ward with a pulse of magic.

Magic crackled like thunder. The four spheres toppled over and spun in midair at a dizzying speed, expanding into car-sized boulders in a blink. The boulders whipped around each other in a circle like moons that lost their planet.

The magic binding them snapped like a rubber band. The boulders hurtled through the woods like runaway trains, crushing everything in their path.

One rocketed directly toward us, smashed into the ward above our heads, and bounced off, into a pine tree. The three-foot-thick trunk snapped like a toothpick. The ward shattered, its power exhausted. The backlash slapped my brain. *Oww.*

Wood cracked, trees collapsed in four directions, birds screeched in alarm, then everything went silent.

Hakeem, Troy, and Owen stared at the crossroads of destruction with wild eyes.

"And that's why we don't poke random shit we find in the woods with a stick," Keelan said.

A tree to our left, with a chunk of its trunk sheared off where one of the boulders grazed it, careened and fell. A humanoid figure dropped out of the branches, landing twenty-five feet away. A shapeshifter in warrior form. Huge, almost eight feet tall, with orangish fur splattered with dark rosettes, claws like knives, and giant fangs. A gold collar clasped his thick neck. He snarled and charged.

Keelan leaped. A human started the jump, but a werewolf landed, thrusting the claymore at the charging beast. Keelan was abnormally large for a werewolf. The enemy was bigger. Holy shit.

The collared shapeshifter batted the blade aside with his left hand and raked at Keelan with his right. Keelan danced back, slicing. The collared shapeshifter lunged at him and howled as the pain from the nearly severed wrist finally registered.

The woods came alive.

Shapeshifters closed in on us from all sides, charging through the trees, howling, snarling, a mass of fur, claws, and gleaming teeth, every single one over seven and a half feet tall.

Fear washed over me in a prickly adrenaline rush. I had forgotten what it was like to be scared of shapeshifters, and it all came back in a painful split second. It felt like the wilderness reached deep inside itself and spat these monsters out, designed only to rip and tear into flesh. Human flesh. My flesh. Every instinct shrieked at me that these things would eat me alive while I screamed.

The fear brought the world into crystal clear focus. Another massive orange shapeshifter dappled with rosettes bore down on me, her mouth gaping. Her fangs were enormous, at least nine inches long. Sarrat was already in my hand. I twisted out of the way and sank my saber between her ribs, ripping through her liver. She spun away as I withdrew and leaped on me, trying to pin me with her bulk. I stabbed up as she came down, driving my blade through her upper abdomen, past her sternum into her heart.

Her weight drove me back into a tree. She clamped her huge

beast hands on my shoulders. Her heart was impaled by Sarrat's blade. She should be dead or dying. Even a shapeshifter couldn't shrug off a ruptured heart.

Claws tore at my shoulders. My bones groaned. She was trying to rip me in half.

I shoved Sarrat deeper, twisting the blade. Her heart had to be a popped balloon at this point. Ruined beyond even the strongest shapeshifter's ability to repair.

Her jaws gaped open, way beyond the normal point. She bit at me, trying to catch my head and sink her fangs into my skull. I tucked my chin in and headbutted her lower jaw. My blood and her spit wet my face. I hit her with my head again. Teeth scraped my scalp, cutting through the skin. I pulsed magic through my wounds and let it rip.

A forest of blood spikes exploded in the shapeshifter's mouth, puncturing her tongue, her cheeks, and digging into her sinuses.

She dropped me. I stomped on her knee, kicking her leg out from under her. She went down, and I sliced her head off with a single horizontal cut.

Heal that.

The battlefield blossomed in front of me like a flower. In a fraction of a second, I saw everything.

Keelan to my right, claymore discarded, ripping at his orange opponent, both covered in blood.

Owen, a massive werebison, gripping a werewolf's head with his hand and pounding it into a tree, while another shapeshifter tore at him from the side. Owen's back was a raw, bloody mess.

Hakeem and Troy, back-to-back, fighting off three shapeshifters. Hakeem's stomach was ripped open. Troy's left arm hung limp.

Every enemy had the same gold collar.

I charged at Owen's group. The power word burst from my lips, packing a wallop of magic. *"Aarh Saar!"* All Stop.

My power splayed out in a wide semicircle.

The shapeshifters froze, petrified by my magic. Five seconds.

One. I beheaded the one attacking Owen from the side.

Two. I drove Sarrat across Keelan's opponent's spine, severing the spinal cord in two places with a crunch.

Three and four. I reached Hakeem and Troy.

Five. I decapitated a shapeshifter to my left.

Time restarted.

The two remaining collared shapeshifters in front of me spun away from Hakeem and Troy and lunged at me.

I opened my mouth for another power word.

A gray werelion tore out of the woods, his eyes filled with golden fire, and roared. The blast of sound hit me like thunder.

Curran grabbed the shapeshifter to his left and snapped his spine like a twig. Leonine jaws gaped open. Curran bit down on the shapeshifter's neck just above the collar. Blood poured. The remaining shapeshifter turned to flee. My husband tore his opponent's head off and hurled it at the escaping enemy. The bloody head smashed into the shapeshifter between his shoulder blades. He stumbled and then Curran was on him. The shapeshifter collapsed with Curran on top of him. Bones crunched. An arm flew by me.

Across the clearing Keelan pulled handfuls of entrails out of his opponent's stomach and dug up, into the collared shapeshifter's chest. The air was a mist of blood and bile.

Owen dropped the bloody stump of a body to the ground.

It was over.

WE WALKED THROUGH THE WOODS SMEARED IN BLOOD AND carrying seven bodies. The dead had reverted to their human form, but my team was too beat up, so Curran's shapeshifters got the hauling duty. Except for Owen, who carried one in spite of everyone's advice, and Keelan, who insisted on dragging the biggest shapeshifter, the one he had killed, all by himself. My husband, the overachiever, was carrying two, one on each shoulder.

I had insisted on decapitating every corpse, just in case. Originally, the shapeshifters planned on impaling the heads on sticks and transporting them that way; however, I pointed out that approaching Penderton waving around gory, blood-dripping skull sticks was not the best idea. Curran and I had both brought our backpacks with waterproof bags in each, and now Da-Eun carried two sacks filled with shapeshifter heads. At eleven pounds each head, she was hauling seventy-seven pounds and she did it with a pep in her step.

It was good to be a shapeshifter.

Clotting my blood on command was one of the first skills my aunt had taught me, so I'd sealed the cuts and wounds, but the injuries were still there. My shoulders hurt, the flesh raw where the claws had pierced the muscle. Those claws hadn't looked that clean. I'd pushed some blood out to purge the contamination, but I would need a visit to the medmage before some enterprising infection decided to make itself at home. My head hurt less than my shoulders, but I felt it.

The rest of our crew fared about as well. Keelan was hurt, but he stoically kept it to himself. Owen's back had been sliced to ribbons. His wounds knitted themselves closed, but the muscle fibers would take longer to fix themselves, so right now his back looked strangely bumpy and uneven. We had to reset Troy's broken arm on the spot, or it would heal badly and would need to be rebroken. Hakeem got the worst of it. His stomach was a mess, and Troy had chanted over him for a good twenty minutes, pushing the body into regeneration past the typical shapeshifter healing.

I glanced at Hakeem. He looked a little green, and he was walking in that slow deliberate way that meant every step was sending a fresh stab of pain through his body. A lacerated liver was a bitch.

The fight kept replaying in my mind, all thirty gory seconds of it. The shapeshifter's momentum as she drove me back, the pressure against Sarrat as it pierced her heart, the fangs scraping my skull as she gnawed on my head, the hedgehog of my blood spikes in her mouth, her head falling off her shoulders, the power word, the mad dash of the pressurized five seconds, the slicing, the stabbing, the blood...

Ahead the trees thinned, hinting at the sunlit killing ground around Penderton.

I'd do it again. In a heartbeat. It had made me feel alive. More, it had made me feel...like myself.

I was a killer. Magic provided a barrier between me and the enemy. It insulated me from the visceral immediacy of direct violence, but in the end, I lived or died by my sword. I'd been taught to kill, encouraged to do it, praised when I did it well, and in the end, I liked it. It was in my nature, like breathing.

I'd all but given it up for the past seven years. I had focused on being a mother, on building a safe life, and now... Now I had some things to think about, and I wasn't sure where I stood.

We cleared the tree line. I squinted against the sunlight.

The bell on the closest guard tower began to ring, striking a rapid, almost hysterical rhythm.

"Game faces on," Curran said.

Everyone walked a little straighter. On my left, Jynx adjusted a collared shapeshifter's body on her shoulders and raised her chin. This was our victory parade. The town didn't need to know just how badly we got our asses kicked.

It wasn't that Curran's plan was bad or his tactics had been unsound. A team of four shapeshifters—one render, two renders-in-training, and one experienced alpha—should've cut their way through seven ordinary shapeshifters like they were butter, even without my or Curran's help. It was just that the caliber of our enemy was far beyond what we expected and there was no way to know that until we fought them. Now we knew. We won but it was expensive. We'd need to adjust.

We kept walking.

The gates of Penderton swung out, and the first responders spilled into the open, two teams of three people each. Archers flooded the wall above the gate. The archers and the wall looked medieval, while the paramedics and EMTs looked decidedly modern in their reflective orange vests, and the contrast was jarring.

"Consort," Hakeem said, his voice a little hoarse.

"Yes?" This was the first time he had called me Consort.

"Thank you."

"No need. We're a pack. You are one of ours, and you would do the same for me."

He swallowed.

"Who are we?" Keelan asked.

"Wilmington Pack," a chorus answered.

"Goddamn right we are."

"Pack," Curran said.

"Pack," I answered with the rest of them.

Unity. Chosen family. There was strength in that.

We picked up the pace, falling into the familiar formation, Curran and I at the head, Keelan behind, and the rest of the shapeshifters forming a loose oval behind us. I remembered this from my time as the Consort. Ten years had passed, but some things left a lasting impression.

The first responders started toward us at a jog, and I caught the moment the leading team realized that we weren't carrying our injured. The dark-haired medic in front braked and stopped, her face uncertain. She looked almost scared.

The same uncertainty spread from person to person, as if contagious. Bewilderment and surprise mixed with jittery nervousness.

This had never happened before. Nobody had ever gone into

the woods and brought the bodies of the enemy out. The enemy was always invisible and invulnerable, watching and waiting. Now they were suddenly solid flesh. The residents of Penderton weren't sure how to process it.

We reached them.

"I need full containment for seven bodies," I told the leading medic. "Do you have loup cages?"

She blinked at me.

"Loup cages," I repeated.

The medic's brain restarted. "No loup cages, but we have cells. In the old prison."

"That will work." Magic was known to do all sorts of creative things to the dead bodies, but I'd never seen a shapeshifter survive decapitation. Even they had limits. Still, nobody ever regretted an abundance of caution when it came to magic's ability to spawn weird crap.

"Lead the way," Curran prompted.

"Follow me." The medic strode down the street and we followed her, flanked by the EMTs and paramedics.

Heather, the wall guard captain, ran up to us.

"It will retaliate," Curran told her. "Probably before the magic wave ends."

"You might want to ease up on having your people walk the wall," I added. "It will try to punish us, and the guards are an obvious target."

Heather spun on her foot without a word and ran back the way she had come.

We walked down the street. People came out of their homes and businesses. They didn't say anything. They just watched us go by with that same mix of excitement and apprehension on their faces.

The medic turned to look at us. "Can we help you in any way?"

"We'll need food," I said. "Meat. A lot of it. And we could use a coroner if you have one to help us examine the bodies. Our medmage has a broken left arm and regaining his dexterity will take some time."

"My wife needs a medmage," Curran said. "She will tell you that she is fine, and she doesn't need help. She isn't and she does."

"You made your point," I told him.

His eyes flashed gold. "I did. And I'm going to stand over you and watch you get treatment."

As a married woman, I had learned that some fights weren't worth fighting. "Your lack of trust is very disappointing."

"I trust you with my life, not with yours," my husband said.

I SAT IN A ROCKING CHAIR ON THE TOP-FLOOR BALCONY AND SIPPED my iced tea. On my left, Owen rested on a blanket in the lotus pose. His eyes were closed. He said meditation helped him with the bison rage.

It was the golden hour, that magical sixty minutes before sunset when the light turned soft and warm, and the first hints of red and yellow tinted the sky. The world was beautiful, and the tree line at the end of the kill zone turned lovely enough to frame, the tall pines spreading their fluffy branches as if trying to hold on to sunlight.

We were overdue for the forest's counterpunch. It would come. I had no doubt about it. The unseen force in the forest had ground Penderton under its heel for years, so long that it took compliance for granted. Now the town suddenly dared to fight back. It would try to stomp that resistance out, hard and fast, before hope took root.

I glanced at the closest tower. The guard hunkering down under that roof was a teenager. A boy, with short dark hair and glasses. Sixteen tops. On the surface it seemed like an easy enough way to keep teens employed: sit on the wall, watch the woods, ring the bell if you see anything. Except when the trouble started, they would be on the front line.

The door to my left swung open, and Troy padded out onto the balcony carrying a notebook and a small plastic cooler.

"Consort."

"Did you escape?"

He nodded. "Went out the back door when I heard them coming."

After the initial medical treatment was administered—Curran did stand over me while Nereda, the town's leading medic, patched me up—Penderton delivered food by the truckload. Literally. Our crew ate and went to sleep.

Changing shape took a lot of energy. Most shapeshifters could do it once every twenty-four hours with no problems, but after the second shift, they'd need mandatory rest. Under siege like this, the shapeshifters would eat and sleep every chance they got to stave off the shifting fatigue.

Troy had stayed behind in the former prison to examine the bodies. About twenty minutes ago Mayor Gene, Ned, and the entire town council knocked on our door. They wanted to view the bodies and ask questions. Keelan and Curran went with the town delegation to the prison. I conveniently excused myself due to my injuries. I didn't want to lie to the Penderton town council, and there were questions I didn't want to answer, so avoiding community outreach seemed like the best strategy. I had a feeling Troy was in the same boat.

Troy sat in the other rocking chair and put the cooler by his feet. His left arm seemed to be functional, but he was moving it carefully.

"Did you eat?" I asked.

"Not yet."

I got up, went inside, went downstairs to the kitchen, and grabbed a tray. Penderton generously provided barbecue, so I loaded a plate with brisket and smoked chicken, added a beef rib with about a pound of meat on it, a chunk of cheddar, and some fresh, crusty bread, and carried it back up to Troy.

He stared at the tray.

"Pledge of loyalty not required," I told him.

He looked even more uncomfortable. "Thank you. I didn't mean to inconvenience you, Consort."

Ah. It was the fact that an alpha got up and fetched the food that was the problem. "I won't tell anyone about it if you eat your food."

"Yes, Consort."

He set his notebook down and tore into his dinner.

I sat back in my chair.

When shapeshifters ate, they focused on the food completely. They didn't talk, they didn't socialize. They ate. Even their formal dinners, like Pack Thanksgiving, went totally silent for the first few minutes.

It took Troy about a quarter of an hour to finish devouring the barbecue. Once his plate was empty, he sat back, a small, contented smile on his face.

"I know all this stuff is weird and exciting, but you have to take care of yourself," I told him.

He nodded. "Yes, because if I die, nobody in Wilmington would have any idea how to treat a wounded shapeshifter."

"No, because if you die, you will be dead. And all of us will be very sad."

He blinked.

"Things just didn't go your way today," Owen rumbled from his blanket, his eyes still closed. "First, you got your arm broken. Then the Consort had to bring you food. Now you are getting a lecture. It's hard to be Troy today."

"Don't make me come over there," Troy growled.

Owen opened his eyes. "And do what?"

Troy showed him his teeth.

"Stay where you are, and you'll get to keep all of those." Owen closed his eyes.

Hmm. When Nereda had treated me, she found a tip of the shapeshifter claw in one of my wounds. I reopened it and dislodged the claw through forced bleeding, and it broke her brain. I told her that it was similar to a shapeshifter pushing silver out of their body, and that shocked her even more. In her ten years as a field medic, she'd never treated a shapeshifter. She'd asked a lot of follow-up questions, some of which went beyond me so Curran had to answer.

Shapeshifter regeneration was off the charts. They walked off most wounds that would put a non-shapeshifter human into a hospital for a week. They were mostly impervious to infection, they treated blood loss as a joke, and it was said that if a shapeshifter was breathing by the end of the fight, they would live.

Unfortunately, shapeshifters also often fought enemies that inflicted catastrophic damage. Their lives were much more violent, which was why the Pack Keep in Atlanta had a first-rate hospital within it.

"I take it the guidance to avoid human medmages is still in effect?" I asked.

"Yes, Consort," Troy said. "It has been a matter of concern to Pack medical staff for a while now."

The thinking behind it was simple. If human medmages knew how to heal shapeshifters, they would better understand how to hurt them as well. Except that knowing how to injure shapeshifters didn't require a medical degree. Every merc in the Guild knew that silver was toxic to them, and wolfsbane was widely available at herbal markets and pharmacies.

That policy accomplished nothing except to delay treatment until a shapeshifter could get to a Pack medic.

"Have you discussed your concerns with the Beast Lord?"

"Yes, Consort. We were told that this policy was put in place by the previous Beast Lord and the current Beast Lord sees no reason to change it."

Shots fired.

My husband had a complicated childhood. His parents had taken him and his sister to live in the woods, trying to avoid shapeshifter politics. Eventually they were attacked by loups. Only Curran survived. He was rescued by Mahon, the Alpha of Clan Heavy, the Bear of Atlanta, who pushed Curran to become the Beast Lord when he was fifteen. A lot of my husband's early policies were shaped by Mahon, who didn't trust humans. Curran altered most of them, once he had started thinking for himself, but that particular one apparently didn't get an overhaul before we retired, and Jim had chosen to leave it in place.

"Would you refuse to treat a non-shapeshifter patient, Troy?"

Green fire rolled over Troy's irises. "I took an oath to apply, for the benefit of the sick, all measures that are required. The oath didn't specify which sick."

"I assume Nereda took the same oath?"

"Yes."

"Good. From this moment, the avoidance guidelines do not apply to Wilmington. You have my permission to share whatever medical knowledge you find necessary with her and other medmages. We need to make sure that if a shapeshifter is hurt, they can access emergency medical care. And if Curran says anything to you about it, tell him that I ordered you to do it."

I couldn't imagine that Curran would have an issue with it, but if he did, pointing out that our son could require emergency medical care and that Troy might not be in range to administer it would shut that down real fast.

Troy smiled. "Yes, Consort."

"How did the examination of the bodies go? Did you learn anything?"

Troy looked at his notebook, then looked at me. "'Learn' is a strong word. I have questions. Right now, what I don't know is significantly greater than what I do."

That lined up with my own feelings. As soon as the first body reverted to humanoid form and I had a chance to look at it, I knew we were in the weeds.

The body was hairy. Excessively so. Hair on the back protruding in a ridge over the spines; hair on the chest for males that looked like something you might see on a Maine Coon cat; longer hair on the backs of the arms, ranging in color from almost black on some corpses to a muddy brown on others. The skin under all that hair was light brown and had an odd, slightly purple tint, as if their blood vessels lay very close to the surface.

Everyone was muscled like an Olympic athlete. Visible definition on the arms, back, and stomach on each one and almost no fat. Everyone was short, five and a half feet tall at most. You would anticipate some variation in height, and there were three or four inches here or there, but statistically I would have expected at least one of them to be closer to six feet.

The shapeshifter Keelan had fought was almost eight feet in a warrior form, and the rest of them weren't much smaller. The differential between their human and warrior form was huge. Although their increased body mass compensated somewhat, their transformations would have required a lot of magic.

And then there were the faces. Their teeth and ears were human enough, but all seven had massive, heavy jaws and wide mouths with very narrow lips. Their profiles were unnaturally elongated. Instead of forehead and chin being close to the same vertical line, their chins, jaws, and noses jutted forward beyond anything typical of a human.

All that alone would've marked them as drastically different from us, but there was one detail that left absolutely no doubt they were not human. They had horns. All seven of them. The horns were short and pointed straight up, as if someone had taken deer antlers and cut them off at the first branching.

Troy flipped through his notebook. "My best guess is that they are human. Just not our kind of human."

What did that mean?

"Could they be a splinter group of some sort? A shapeshifter family that went off after the Shift?" Owen asked.

Troy shook his head. "I counted three wolves, one probable hyena, something that might have been a cheetah, and two of them, like the one who'd attacked the Consort, don't track as anything I'd ever seen before. All of that in a single family?"

A good point. A splinter group wouldn't have such variety.

Troy shook his head. "Some of them might be related to each other, but overall, they are not a single family but representatives of a specific hominin group. A specific phenotype."

"Hominin? Not *Homo sapiens?*" I already knew the answer, but I asked anyway.

Hominin included modern humans, extinct human species and ancestors, and weird variations resulting from magic exposure.

"We're talking about some fundamental deviations. The hair pattern is completely different. They grow hair along their spines. I've never seen that. They have chins like us, but their facial structure is strange. And they have horns."

The horns were the sticking point. There were mythical humanoids who had horns, like satyrs, but we were a long way from Greece and the bodies didn't fit the satyr pattern. The horns were wrong, and the legs weren't goat-like.

Besides, I had never seen or heard of anyone encountering a satyr. It didn't mean they didn't exist. When we travelled to the Black Sea, I'd encountered an atsany, a tiny human only eighteen inches tall and capable of shockingly powerful magic. He was part of a whole tribe of people who had lived in the Caucasus Mountains for they alone knew how long and even built small towns. And yet if someone had asked me before that trip if tiny humans existed, I would've said the same thing I was thinking now—I had never seen or heard of anyone encountering one.

There were other humanoids out there. Some of them apparently had horns. Or antlers. Horns were herbivore weapons. These guys transformed into meat-eating predators. What the hell did we stumble into?

"This isn't a matter of some superficial differences," Troy was saying. "This isn't a different race or a close relative. This is a different species. Hakeem asked me if they are human. He meant it in cultural sense."

"What did you tell him?" I asked.

"Depends on your definition of 'human,'" Troy said.

They looked human to me.

"Do they use names?" Owen said from his corner of the balcony. "If they use names, they are people."

Troy frowned. "That's a weird criterion."

"If they name themselves, they have a language and a sense of self," Owen said. "It means they recognize that each one of them is unique and unlike the others, so they must have a separate name. That means they know that life is valuable."

Unexpected werebison wisdom.

"Where did they come from?" I muttered.

"Could there be a portal?" Owen asked.

"Yes, could it be a pocket realm?" Troy asked. "Maybe they existed in it for an extended period of time, separate from us?"

"Portals have a very specific power signature," I explained. "This entire area is flooded with the magic from the forest. Right now, we're ankle-deep in it."

Troy glanced down.

"Nothing about this magic indicates a portal. It's completely different."

It felt like something else entirely, and I wasn't ready to go there yet.

Not only were these shapeshifters different from us, but they

75

also didn't look at all like the people with the human tribute tapestries. That meant not just one group of enemies, but two. Possibly more.

"If I had to design a human adapted to shapeshifting, I would make something similar to them," Troy said. "A ton of dense body mass to work with, a skull structure that makes muzzle formation a breeze, expanded lung capacity, and a large heart. Their noses are longer, and their ears are larger and pointed. Not only are they stronger than an average shapeshifter in human form, but their olfactory and auditory senses are likely better than ours. From a shapeshifter point of view, they are better adapted."

Now there was a disturbing thought.

"I've recorded my findings." Troy patted his notebook. "As soon as the tech hits, I'm going to take some pictures and send them and some blood and tissue samples down to Atlanta."

"A second opinion?" I asked.

"The more eyes on this, the better."

Doolittle would be fascinated by this. If we weren't careful, he'd be up here within a day of those samples arriving to his lab.

"What about the collars?" I asked.

"Oh! Almost forgot." Troy jumped up and brought the plastic cooler over to me. I opened it. Inside lay a golden collar.

I held my hand above it. Inert.

I took it out, holding it carefully by the edges. The metal felt cold under my fingertips. Two rows of rectangles, one inner, one outer, similar to antique expansion bracelets. I carefully stretched the collar. The segments slid apart under the pressure of my fingers, enough to accommodate the shift from a human neck to an animal one.

"It has gold in it," Troy said. "It stings a bit."

Silver was toxic to shapeshifters, but they had trouble with all noble metals. Gold was second on the toxicity level. Wearing it would irritate the skin. Curran once described it as having a constant mild burn. The shapeshifters wearing these would feel them every second of the day. A constant reminder, but of what? Was this a badge of honor or a slave collar? If it hurt them, why hadn't they ripped them off?

There were thin glyphs etched into the inside of the collar. I turned it to get a better look.

"Company!" Troy barked.

At the tree line, a group of people walked out into the clearing.

The guard in the tower reached for the bell.

"Don't touch that!" I yelled.

The boy dropped his hand, and I tossed the collar back into the cooler and took off running.

[5]

I got down from the third-floor balcony and to the top of the wall in under six seconds. It had to be some sort of a record.

Troy and Owen still beat me to it. Unlike them, I didn't fancy dramatically jumping off the top floor balcony onto the street. I'd break my legs.

The teenage guard manning the tower handed me a pair of binoculars. I leveled them at the group waiting on the edge of the woods.

Ten people total. Eight looked like the woman in the sketch, tall and dressed in light brown tunics, cinched at the waist by belts. If you drew a horizontal line about two inches above their elbows, everything below it was relatively human skin, a kind of light ochre touched by the sun. The skin tone seemed uneven, but it could've been dirt.

Everything above the line was smeared in a thick coat of bluish clay: the top halves of their chests, their necks, their faces, and the first three inches of their hair starting at the scalp. The clay had dried, forming hairline cracks on their skin and stiffening their brown hair up and away from their faces.

The eight clay-covered people held spears, each exactly as tall as its owner and tipped by a spearhead made of some light-colored material. They looked like a group of hunters. The two people they clustered around definitely didn't.

The central pair, a man and a woman judging by the outlines of their bodies, were also tall. The woman wore a long robe dress, brown with a broad strip of white in the front and thin red symbols woven into it. The man had a matching outfit, although his robe was more square-cut. They wore identical overcoats, a kind of half-jacket, solid over their chests but which split toward the bottom into long ribbons of white fabric that fell below their knees. Each ribbon bore more red symbols and ended in an amulet of golden metal. If they spun, the ribbons would fly around them, forming perfect circles.

A two-inch-wide band of braided cloth crossed the woman's forehead. A fringe of thin fabric strips, each ending in a large gold bead, dripped from the band all the way to her nose, obscuring her eyes. The man wore a human skull over the top half of his face, studded with fangs from some sort of huge predator. All visible skin was smeared with the same bluish clay, but their hair was clean and pulled back from their faces into tight horse tails. Both held staves, and the brown stains on their shafts looked suspiciously like blood.

"What are they?" Troy murmured.

"Mages or priests," I said. "The ruling caste. No collars."

The two mages stood still. They were probably staring at us, but it was hard to tell. At five hundred yards, they were well outside of bow range.

Humans liked to see each other's eyes. Hiding them was usually done for three reasons: to protect someone's face, to obscure their identity, or to be seen as a personification of something greater than themselves. A conduit for the spirits, an embodiment of justice, a force rather than an individual.

"Nice skull." Troy's face was a harsh mask.

"I feel like he's trying to tell us something," I said. "Not sure what it is. He's so subtle about it."

Owen chuckled.

The skull mage raised his staff and tapped it on the ground. Two hunters stepped forward and unfolded another tapestry between them. Twenty red figures.

"They doubled their ask," Troy said.

"Punishment," I told them.

The skull mage pointed his staff at me and then at the tapestry.

Ah. It was my doing so I had to atone by being one of the twenty.

I crossed my arms on my chest. That should be clear enough.

The fringe mage stepped forward and spun, twirling her staff. She did it in complete silence. The creep factor was high.

The mage turned and twisted. There was a definite pattern to her dance. I couldn't feel her magic from this distance, but she was cooking something nasty.

"Troy," I said, "Go get my husband, please."

Troy turned and took off down the stairs at top speed.

The skull mage stepped aside and spun as well. His staff work was less fluid, more abrupt, as if he was trying to rip through the air. The two mages whirled, but not in unison. Their movements weren't coordinated. Whatever they were doing was similar but separate.

"You can ring the bell now," I told the guard.

The kid grabbed the rope attached to the clapper and shook it hard. The bell rang out in a hysterical frenzy.

The fringe mage thrust her staff up and plunged it into the ground. Thunder clapped. A huge creature landed in the grass in front of her, swirling with dark smoke. Massive and shaggy with brown fur, it stood eight and a half feet tall on four thick, sturdy legs. A big hump protruded between its shoulders. Its head was pure rhino, bearing a single enormous horn, five feet long and at least a foot thick. It curved like the blade of a scythe, jabbing upward.

Every bit of the rhino's bulk bore thick bone plates with foot-long spikes: its back, its sides, even its head. Gold-colored veins crisscrossed the plates, fusing them together. A broad bone carapace protected its forehead, and a segmented metal and bone collar shielded its neck.

The bone wasn't a natural part of the creature but armor added to it.

I couldn't see any belts or harness straps. The armor seemed stuck to the rhino, as if glued onto the animal's hide. Magic rolled off it, like hot air from asphalt, a shimmering, transparent corona that turned into coils of dark vapor and melted into the air.

That was a hell of a summon. And there was a second one coming as soon as the skull mage finished his dance.

The beast sighted our gate with its mean black eyes.

"Owen, how much do you think it weighs?"

"I'd say he's about five of me. Without armor."

An adult bison weighed about two thousand pounds. If that thing hit the gates at full speed, it would rip right through them and probably take a chunk of the wall with it. Shit.

The monster rhino dug into the ground with his foreleg like a bull.

It was a summon. Summons had a simple remedy. Kill the summoner and they went away.

I'd have to cover five hundred yards, and those spears looked a lot like javelins.

"We have to get to the summoners." I looked at the guard. "I need a horse. Do you have a horse?"

The kid shook his head, his eyes opened wide.

"Where is the closest stable?"

"Eight blocks to the south."

Too far.

The fringe mage pointed at the gate with her staff and let out a short, high-pitched shout. The rhino grunted and started forward, aiming for the gate, accelerating into what would become a crushing charge.

The skull mage shoved his staff into the ground. Thunder cracked again, and a pack of six gray birds burst into existence. They stood on two legs, the tallest almost seven feet. They looked like some kind of mutated ostriches, except their necks were shorter and much thicker, their wings were tiny and useless, and their heads, two feet long, were mostly eyes and a huge, nightmarish beak, flat and heavy like an axe head.

What the hell...

"Since a horse isn't handy, how about a bison?" Owen offered.

"Sold!"

Owen grabbed me by the waist and jumped off the wall. He landed with a thud, let go of me, and planted himself. He raised his arms, stretched his chest, flexed his back, took a deep breath, and blew the air out of his nose. A deep, furious red drowned his eyes.

The monster rhino picked up speed. He was almost running now. The skull mage screamed out a command, and the birds took off toward us at ridiculous speeds.

Owen's body tore in a whirlwind of flesh and bone, and a big bull bison hit the grass, his horns the size of my forearms. I jumped onto his back.

Owen bellowed. It was so deep and rumbling, it was almost a roar.

The birds overtook the rhino.

Owen charged. I grabbed his mane and held on for dear life.

The rhino barreled toward us, the birds in a tight flock in front of him. The ground shook, and I couldn't tell which stomps came from the rhino and which came from Owen. Every strike of his feet nearly sent me flying. Bisons weren't meant for riding.

We hurtled at each other.

One hundred feet to the birds.

Eighty.

Sixty. I pulled the magic to myself.

Thirty.

Ten.

"*Ahissa!*" *Flee.*

The power word punched the flock. For a moment they were still running at us, their eyes wild, and then the magic sunk in, and they scattered, fleeing for their lives. We thundered forward, straight at the rhino.

"Turn! Owen, turn!"

We didn't turn. We didn't slow down. We galloped faster.

"Turn!"

The rhino loomed in front of us, the huge horn poised to gore.

Oh my God.

I threw myself to the right, tucking my legs and arms in. The ground smashed into me. My teeth rattled. *Owww.* I rolled, and out of the corner of my eye, I saw Owen veer to the right, missing the horn by inches, and slam at full speed into the rhino's left foreleg, hitting it from the side, all of his weight and momentum hammering the leg inward.

The rhino crashed. The ground shook as if a giant had punched it.

Owen bellowed and rammed the fallen rhino, sinking his horns into the bone armor plates protecting the monster's gut.

I scrambled to my feet and sprinted to the summoners.

Curran

"AGAIN, MAYOR GENE, THEY WEREN'T PACK SHAPESHIFTERS."

We'd been over this, but the mayor simply couldn't seem to grasp that the bodies in the cells were as much a mystery to us as they were to them. I hadn't expected to give a lecture on Shapeshifters 101 but here we were.

"Meaning what?" The short, powerfully built older man leaned forward, placing his tanned forearms on the table. Visible among the scars was a blue-green blob of ink that may have been a legible tattoo at some point.

"Meaning most shapeshifters belong to one of the larger, organized packs who claim an area. For instance, shapeshifters who live in Wilmington belong to the Atlanta Pack. The Pack maintains a regional office in Wilmington, and Keelan oversees it. If new or unaffiliated shapeshifters moved into the area, they would be obligated to make their presence known to him."

"Obligated?"

"Yes. It is considered polite. It avoids unfortunate misunderstandings."

Keelan cleared his throat. "It's not really optional. They introduce themselves in twenty-four hours or we come to see them."

"You said most shapeshifters belong to a pack," one of the council members said. "So, some don't."

"Those shapeshifters who don't belong to a pack generally fall into two categories. The first would be individuals and small family units who live in unclaimed territory."

"And the second?" Mayor Gene said.

"Loups."

"The crazy ones?" one of the council members asked. Everyone at the table drew back a little.

"The correct term is magic-induced psychosis."

"These aren't loups," Keelan said, nodding at the bodies in the cells.

"How can you be so sure?" Ned asked.

"One of them was a little late to the fight," Keelan explained. "I caught a glimpse of him shifting, which means at least some of them were in a human shape right before they attacked us."

"So?" Mayor Gene said.

Keelan looked at me. I made a *go ahead* gesture.

"Loups are stuck in a sort of half form," he said. "Never fully human but unable to transform completely into their beast shape. They are trapped in a constant shift, and because of that, they burn through magic. Magic takes energy, which requires calories. They're always hungry and always in pain. No matter how much they kill, how much they eat, it's never enough. Within hours of succumbing to madness, a loup's body begins to cannibalize itself, and when that happens, they give off a stench. We all know it, we all recognize it, and it smells like nothing else."

It was Ned who spoke up. "And that particular scent was not present in the bodies you brought in?"

"No," I told him. "Before today, were any of you aware of a family or clan of people living in woods? Maybe reclusive or isolated from civilization? Do any of them look familiar?"

I pointed to the seven heads arranged on the examination table we'd rolled into the conference room. They all turned, studying them again.

"No," Ned shook his head. "Definitely not locals."

"I've lived here more than fifty years," Mayor Gene said. "Not only I've never seen them, I never saw anyone like them. The horns are hard to hide."

He had a point.

The town bell tolled. A long, continuous, frantic note.

"Well, that's not good," Keelan murmured.

No, it probably wasn't.

"Ned, would you and the mayor please get everyone to safety?"

"Of course. We'll stay here."

Mayor Gene laughed. "Yep, this old prison is the safest place in town."

Super. Keelan was already headed toward the exit. I followed.

Outside, Troy was sprinting toward us. He looked like he'd run all the way from the house.

"We've got company."

"How many?" Keelan asked.

"Ten that we could see."

"Shapeshifters?"

Troy shook his head. "Eight with spears. Plus, a couple of priest or mage types. Real creepy bastards."

That was all I needed to know. As I headed for the North Gate, I heard Keelan order Troy to round up the rest of our group.

If I knew my wife, by the time I got there she'd be over the wall and giving our visitors a warm welcome.

Buildings flew by. The North Gate loomed in front of me.

Magic slapped me. Like someone had struck a gigantic drum, except it wasn't a sound, it was a feeling that raised the hair on the backs of my arms. Kate had used a power word.

I charged up the stairs and landed on the wall, next to a terrified kid running back and forth by the guard tower.

The grassy killing ground spread in front of me with us on one side and a group of ten invaders on the other. Between us and them, Kate was riding a bison, charging at full speed toward a monstrous rhino-like creature armored with spiked bone plates and shedding coils of black vapor. A flock of big-ass birds shot away from them, fleeing in panic.

Okay. That's what we're doing today.

The bison had to be Owen, and he was barreling toward the rhino at full speed.

Kate screamed something. I focused.

"Turn! Owen, turn!"

Owen would not be turning. He was a bull werebison who had spotted a larger challenger in his territory. I knew exactly what was going through his bovine brain right now.

Hit that guy. Hit him real hard. Show him who's the strongest.

Through his brain fog and tunnel vision he had probably forgotten that Kate was still on his back. He'd ram into the rhino, right into those spikes.

Jump. Baby, jump off.

The rhino bellowed, exhaling fury.

Now! For fuck's sake, Kate!

She jumped. I held my breath.

She flew through the air, landed hard in a clump, rolled, and bounced to her feet. She seemed alright. Nothing looked broken.

I exhaled.

Owen slammed into the much larger beast. He avoided the horn and shoulder-checked the rhino's front leg.

The collision was colossal. The armored beast collapsed on his side. The impact shook the wall.

Owen galloped off, roaring like the fool he was, made a tight circle, and went in for seconds.

Kate was running toward the magic users with the staffs.

The rhino was down, kicking, and Owen was doing his best to disembowel it with its horns, except its armor and spikes were in his way.

And he got his horns stuck. Damn it.

Owen tugged his horns free, backed up, and charged again. Still on its side, the beast kicked out. His huge three-toed foot connected with Owen's chest. The bison flew back twenty feet and crashed into the grass.

Damn, that had to hurt.

The rhino struggled. The dark smoke around it thickened.

"Think it'll get up?" Keelan said.

"It shouldn't." That was a hard fall, and the armor added a lot of weight.

The smoke solidified at the rhino's side and seemed to be pushing it to its feet.

"It's getting up," Keelan reported because I was clearly blind.

"Thank you. I can see that."

The rhino would get up. And when it did, it would go after Owen or the gate. If we were really unlucky, it would go after Kate.

This wasn't a natural animal. It wasn't an animal god—I'd seen enough of them to recognize them on sight—but it wasn't a normal rhino either. That bone armor sat on it as if it were welded to its hide, and the magic boiling around it was thick enough to cut with claws.

Everyone who had been in the house was already on the wall beside me.

"Elk Hunt One," I ordered. "Keelan, Da-Eun, and I are the takers, the rest of you are drivers. Spin it around. Any direction except for the gate."

"Yes, Alpha," they answered in unison.

I leaped off the wall. By the time I hit the ground, I was in half form and roaring. The wall rained shapeshifters in warrior forms. We sprinted forward in a tight formation, howling and snarling.

The smoke picked the rhino up and set it back on its feet. It shook its head and roared. It was a sound filled with rage and hate.

"You owe me a dollar, my lord!" Keelan snarled on my right.

"I never bet you anything."

"Being stingy is unbecoming of an alpha!" Da-Eun laughed on my left.

Keelan howled, a long triumphant battle cry, calling for blood.

The rhino started forward and was picking up speed, moving from a walk into a sort of trot. The ground started to shake.

Gods, he was massive. This was going to suck.

The drivers shot in front of the rhino, snarling and snapping.

I veered right, while Keelan and Da-Eun darted left. We circled the rhino. Those plates had to be held in place by something—chains, a harness—and I would find it and break it.

There was no harness. The rhino wasn't wearing the bone plates. They hadn't been placed on him. They'd been placed *in* him, embedded in the creature's flesh and fused together by the same golden metal we saw on the collars. The hide in the narrow gaps between the plates was inflamed and bleeding. Pus wet the metal and bone. This beast had to be in tremendous pain.

The stench was the worst. It smelled like acid, burned flesh, and blood. And a hint of decay, just setting in. The rhino was dying.

I would kill it. I would make it as fast and as painless as I could. And then I would find the person who did that atrocity to it and kill them slowly.

I circled behind the beast, passing Keelan and Da-Eun running in the opposite direction. They hadn't found a weakness either.

At the front end of the rhino, the shapeshifters baited the beast, leaping in and out before it could gore them, clawing, snapping, and snarling. The huge beast tried to press forward, but the chaos was too much. It couldn't ignore the shapeshifters harassing it. Too many bodies, too much noise.

Andre lunged in and bit the rhino on the lip, the only exposed part of its head. For a moment the werewolf hung there like a terrier. That was the last straw.

The rhino rolled his head and flung Andre to the side. Andre landed on his feet. The beast screamed and pounded toward him.

Good. We'd turned him. Now we just had to bring him down.

I closed in on the rhino.

Could I pry a plate off?

The rhino kept going, totally focused on Andre. Trying to run him down.

Keelan and Da-Eun leaped onto its back, scrambling up.

Good plan. The spine was a solid target.

Keelan struck with his claymore, plunging it straight down, but didn't seem to be doing any serious damage. The bone armor was too thick.

I grabbed the edge of one of the plates along the flanks, dug my feet in, and pulled. I could yank the door off a car. I'd done it before.

The rhino didn't stop. The plate didn't come off. Instead, I was dragged off my feet and pulled along. I let it drag me for a couple of seconds, let go, landed on my feet, and ran to keep pace.

A bird swung around the rhino and tried to hammer me with its giant beak. I slapped its head and broke its neck.

"Jynx, thin the flock!"

The bouda peeled off from the pack ahead with an eerie giggle.

On the rhino's back, Da-Eun planted her feet and pulled at one of the plates along the beast's back. The weretiger strained, her muscles swelling under her striped hide. She shook with effort, cried out...

The plate didn't budge. Yeah, I already tried that.

Andre turned left, drawing a wide *U*. The rhino followed him, never noticing we were now running in the opposite direction. I caught a glimpse of Kate swinging her sword at the female mage.

The rhino thundered past me, and I got a quick peek of its head, the top half of it shielded by a thick bone plate bristling with spikes. The giant horn jutted upward, ready to impale anything in its path.

Armor or no, it still had to turn its head.

I sprinted and chanced a closer look. The rhino's short neck was protected by segmented bone plates, but they were thinner than the rest. They had to be, or they would be too rigid, limiting the creature's range of movement. The horn was its greatest weapon. It had to be able to aim it.

The neck. That was the sweet spot.

I had to find a way to pierce those plates and the monster's hide.

Kate

I ROLLED TO MY FEET. WE'D MADE IT HALFWAY ACROSS THE FIELD. The mages and hunters waited for me 250 yards away.

Crap.

The mage with the headband fringe spun her staff and clawed at the air.

I had to get there before she finished whatever she was doing. The effective spear-throwing range was about seventy to eighty yards or so, and if I ran fast enough, I should be able to dodge them.

I ran.

Behind me a deafening lion's roar filled the air.

Hi, honey.

One of the hunters jogged back and raised his spear.

No way. I was still over 150 yards out.

He took a running start, his legs pumping, left arm thrust in front of him, and hurled the spear at me. It sliced through the air, whistling like a fucking arrow. I dodged left. The spear sank into the ground four inches away from my right leg.

What the hell were those shoulders made of?

The hunters backed up in unison.

I kept moving. 120 yards. At least twenty seconds across clear ground without cover. Too far for a power word, not enough time for anything complicated. I had to run and avoid being hit.

They had seven spears left. I could dodge seven spears.

The first hunter, the one who'd thrown the spear, reached behind a tree, pulled out a bundle of spears, and thrust them into the ground for easy grabbing.

Shit.

Seven more spears screeched through the air. I zigzagged like a rabbit, guessing the direction on pure instinct. Left, right, right, left… The sixth spear plunged into the ground right in front of me. I paused for half a second, and the seventh spear sliced across my side, grazing me in a scalding burn.

They were already reaching for more spears.

I dragged my left arm across my bleeding side, yanked the canteen of vampire blood off my belt, and poured it over my left arm, right over the blood already on it. The vampire blood sparked with the magic of my blood, coating my skin and clothes. I jerked my arm in front of me and whispered the incantation. Shaping it with my will alone wouldn't be fast enough. The burn of magic expended too quickly scraped the inside of my chest with hot, serrated teeth.

The tortured whine of the new volley sliced through the air.

The blood armor sleeve snapped into place over my left arm, widening into a round shield three feet across. The first spear hit it and bounced off. The impact reverberated through my whole arm, right into my back and chest. Wow.

I sprinted, the spears hammering at my shield.

Erra would've loved this so much. I could almost hear her in my head. *You run like a toddler. Slow and clumsy.*

The spears rained around me.

A hundred yards. Seventy-five.

The hunters switched their grips and launched another salvo with a weird, underhanded motion. The spears flew almost straight. I thrust my arm with the shield in front of me and kept running.

I was almost to the fringe mage. The hunters backed away, trying to grab more distance. They were almost out of spears.

I unsheathed Sarrat, drew it against my bleeding side, soaking the blade in blood and power, and pushed my magic through it. The crimson liquid hardened into a razor edge. My pulse pounded in my ears.

The mage spun in front of me, her ribbons flying. I caught a glimpse of her eyes under the fringe, cold and dark, and then she stopped and spat fire.

A swirling cone of flames shot at me. I dropped to one knee and thrust the shield in front of me. The fire roared overhead, splitting around me. I held my breath.

She didn't build it or shape it the way firebugs did. She *spat* it out.

The air turned to scalding soup and burned my face. A little more. I just had to wait a little longer...

The fire died.

My turn.

I surged up, turning as I rose, and struck. She jabbed her staff at me, but I was faster. The staff slid by me, and I hacked at her right arm. Sarrat's blood edge cut through muscle and bone with ridiculous ease. Her right arm fell, severed just below the elbow, and the staff fell with it. She reeled back, screaming, and I beheaded her with a single vicious cut.

Her head flew off her shoulders. Her body toppled to the ground. I looked over my shoulder. Across the killing ground, the shapeshifters attacked the rhino. It chased them, bellowing its rage, and swung its giant head, trying to gore them. The birds dashed around it, taking potshots at the shapeshifters. A bouda in warrior form hounded them. As I watched, she caught up with one and slapped its head. The bird went tumbling across the grass.

The fringe mage was dead, but the rhino didn't disappear. Fuck.

I spun back and saw the skull mage charging at me. He screamed something—it sounded like words—and broke into black mist. The dark smoke streaked around me, bouncing from spot to spot in a random pattern.

What is this fresh hell?

One of the hunters jabbed at me with his spear. I batted it aside and kicked him in the groin. He went down like a log.

The smoke raked my back with ghostly black claws. Pain burned across my shoulder blades.

I turned, trying to keep it in view, but it was too fast. It zipped back and forth, like some ground-bound lightning.

The black smoke pounced around me, striking, each cut of the ghostly claws like a strike of a whip made of pure pain. Left thigh. Right shoulder. Back again. You fucker.

I shattered the shield into dust—it was getting in the way—and turned slowly. The smoke clawed my right thigh. If he got me with that across the neck, I was done.

He had to become solid to strike.

I spun left, then immediately right. The black smoke bounced where my back would've been, and suddenly we were face-to-face, me and the loose column of swirling dark mist.

I thrust my left hand into it. My fingers locked around flesh. I gripped and yanked the skull mage out of the mist by his neck. He locked his hands around my wrist, but I was pissed off and stronger. I dug my fingers into his throat and impaled him on my sword. Sarrat slid into his gut with a soft whisper, through the abdomen, through the intestines, all the way to his back. The blood edge severed his spine and broke, its power exhausted.

The skull mage went limp.

I freed my blade with a tug and thrust it into his heart. The light went out of his eyes.

I pulled Sarrat out, dropped the corpse I was holding, and turned to the hunters.

They gripped their spears, their faces shocked. The spears, the faces, the collars of unpolished gold.

I pointed at the woods. "Go."

They didn't move.

"Go!" I took a step forward, raising Sarrat.

The hunters dashed to pick up their spears and fled, melting into the trees.

Across the grass, the seven-and-a-half-foot nightmare that was my husband in warrior form ripped the rhino's horn off and jabbed it into its neck. Dark, almost purple blood gushed. The great beast collapsed, sending a cloud of shadowy magic into the air. The shapeshifters swarmed it.

Curran walked away from it, making a beeline for me. I started toward him.

Behind me, the hunters darted from the woods, grabbed the mages' bodies, and carried them off. Fine. I already told them they could go, and I didn't feel like chasing them. Right now nothing mattered except getting to Curran.

We met halfway. His gray fur was stained with blood. A deep cut across his stomach was knitting itself closed.

He hugged me to him. "You didn't wait for me."

"Things were hectic. How deep is that gash?"

"Nothing to worry about. Got caught by a spike. Looks worse than it is."

I wrapped my arm around his waist. Everything was fine. We were both okay. It was fine.

His monster hand patted my shoulders, my back, my head…

"What are you doing?" I asked him.

"Checking for broken bits." He pulled a strand of my hair. It came apart in his claws, breaking into ash. "You smell like blood and burned hair."

Damn it. "How much hair is left?"

"Enough," he said.

"That doesn't sound reassuring."

Keelan climbed up onto the dying creature and drove his claymore into its neck. The tortured beast let out a long breath and became still.

"He stopped hurting," I said.

"Yes," Curran said.

"It's not a summon," I told him. "It's an actual creature."

"I know. I smelled it dying."

"Someone did that to it to create a living battering ram. It was custom-made for us." The cruelty of it was staggering.

Curran squeezed me to him. His eyes were pure gold. "I wasn't angry until today."

"And now?"

"I'm going to find whoever put this creature through that torture, and I'm going to kill them slowly. Piece by piece."

The magic drained out of the world in an instant. Suddenly

every cut hurt a little more. A short magic wave this time. Thank you, Universe, for small favors.

Jynx had finished the last of the birds, put them together in a pile, and sat on it, grinning from ear to ear, her bouda fangs gleaming. Owen had reverted back to a human and sprawled in the grass on his back.

"Is he okay?" I asked.

"He'll live," Curran said.

My brain absently catalogued the shapeshifters on and around the dead beast. Eight. Wait a minute.

Jynx on the birds, Owen in the grass, Andre and Hakeem, Troy, Keelan with the claymore, Da-Eun in shapeshifter form, flinging blood from her claws next to another, larger weretiger...

"Um, Curran?"

"Yes?"

"Why do we have an extra weretiger?"

Curran's nightmarish face wrinkled, baring his teeth.

Da-Eun saw us looking and elbowed the other weretiger. He turned toward us. His huge striped body collapsed into human form, and Karter Byrne landed on the grass. The Alpha of Clan Cat flexed his broad, dark brown shoulders and waved at us.

"Lovely party. Couldn't help crashing. I missed the hors d'oeuvres, but I helped myself to the main course."

[6]

I sat on the balcony again, with my legs up on a wicker footstool and a glass of cold tea on my little side table, and watched Penderton's construction crews strain to remove the body of the monster rhino. I was right. That creature was more magic than beast. Once the magic sustaining its life failed, it decomposed at an alarming rate. Its corpse was falling apart into big chunks. The crew scooped them up with bulldozers and drove them off to the side, to the freshly dug burning pit, racing against the encroaching darkness.

There was a reason Curran couldn't pry its armor off. The bone armor plates were somehow fused to long metal and bone bars that passed through the rhino's body on the inside. It should've died when the first bar pierced it, but magic kept it alive. Every time I thought about it, my hand ached for my sword.

Mayor Gene and an older woman stood in front of the carnage and waved their arms at each other. According to Jynx, the woman represented the town blacksmiths, and they wanted to recover the metal from inside the rhino. They were pretty sure it was gold. Mayor Gene wanted the gold buried due to the possibility of magic contamination. If they didn't resolve it between themselves, they would come up here for my expert advice, and then the blacksmiths would hate me forever.

Curran sat in the rocking chair next to me. He was back in his human body, showered and fresh-smelling, and he was drinking beer from a big stein. He'd bought a small keg from the local brewery. It rested in the corner of the balcony now. Shapeshifter metabolism burned alcohol off in minutes, so his buzz was short-lived.

True to form, he had marched me down to the old prison, and Nereda patched me up again. The smoke claws had done a number on me. She offered me all sorts of painkillers. I settled for some aspirin. Over the years, a lot of my old scars dissolved from repeated visits to medmages and Doolittle's expert care. Today fixed that right up.

The kid on the wall wandered out of the guard tower again.

"Foster!" Curran called out.

The teenager turned around to look at us. Curran pointed back to the tower. The kid hunched his shoulders and trotted back under the safety of the roof.

Keelan sat on Curran's left, nursing his own beer and gently stretching his left leg every few minutes. Must've hurt it in the fight. We didn't lose anyone, but we had a few broken bones. Owen took the Most Hurt Trophy with a shattered femur. After he rammed the rhino, it kicked him. While he healed him, Troy had asked him if it was a good day to be Owen, to which Owen apparently said, "Hell yeah. I knocked that big bastard on his ass."

The door swung open, and Karter emerged onto the balcony. He wore a pair of pack sweats and a white T-shirt. In his thirties, Karter was six feet tall and built in that particular way of big cat shapeshifters—not bulky, but far from lean, his muscles thick, hard, and defined. The kind of muscle that could propel him up a tree or a sheer cliff, or crack an enemy's skull with one well-timed slap of his hand. His hair was short and shaped with razor precision. He had a broad nose, high cheekbones, and a solid jaw. His eyes, under thick eyebrows, were expressive, and on the two occasions I had met him, he seemed to be the kind of man who knew the world was full of fools and he found it amusing.

I didn't know him well. Karter rose to prominence after Jim became the Beast Lord.

"Beer?" Curran asked.

"Don't mind if I do." Karter walked over to the keg, picked up one of the steins waiting on the tray beside it, and poured himself a tall one.

Had Curran or I gotten up to pour him a beer, it could've been seen as an offer or demand of loyalty. This way we sidestepped it.

Karter grabbed a rocking chair, put it between Keelan and Curran, and sat. Interesting.

"Thanks for the help," Curran said.

"Seemed like a fun fight," Karter answered.

Keelan drank his beer and stretched his leg. "It was fun, wasn't it? A good, fast chase, a big prey, everyone working together... Just like old times."

Keelan, the plotter. *Look how awesome things are when Curran's in charge.*

If Karter got it, he didn't show it. They drank their beer. Two big cats, lounging about, pretending to be relaxed but very aware of where the boundary was, and a big wolf, cunning and clever, waiting to see which way the conversation would go.

"Ascanio Ferara is making a bid for the Beast Lord seat," Karter said.

I did my best not to choke.

Ascanio used to be one of my shapeshifters. I'd known him since he was fifteen, and he was the proverbial twenty pounds of bouda crazy in a five-pound bag. Add in way too much testosterone, poor impulse control, and a heartbreaker's face, and you had teenage Ascanio. Aunt B, the previous Alpha of Clan Bouda, had given him to me because although boudas cherished their children, especially males, Ascanio pushed even past their limits. She'd been afraid he'd piss off the wrong person and get hurt.

He had worked for me at Cutting Edge for several years, during which he received education, training, and a healthy dose of reality and experience. Eventually Ascanio chose to return to his clan, which was now run by Andrea, my best friend, and her husband, Raphael. I was sad to see him go, but I understood it. Ascanio wanted acceptance and respect from other boudas. He wanted to succeed on Pack terms.

Curran didn't say anything.

"Ascanio is ambitious," Karter said. "The Medranos are backing him. The kid is good at making money. It sticks to him the way it sticks to Raphael."

But being a Beast Lord was about more than money. It was not a CFO position.

"And he's good in a fight. Would've made a standout render if he'd chosen to go that route."

Being a Beast Lord wasn't about being the baddest fighter, either. I'd learned that firsthand.

"He doesn't have the power base. The boudas are rich, but there aren't enough of them. Still, they're making moves, wheeling and dealing, trying to cobble a coalition together. However, there is one thing that Ascanio needs, and nothing they can do will give it to him."

"And what is that?" Keelan asked.

"Integrity," Karter said. "The boudas always look out for number one, themselves. They're seen as cutthroat."

"They honor their alliances," I said.

"With you, Kate," Karter said. "They are a rock when it comes to supporting the Lennarts, I'll give them that. But when it comes to the rest of us, the saying is: before you enter a contract with the boudas, read every word of the fine print and then read it again. They always manage to get the lion's share of the profits. We went into business with them a couple of times. Both times Clan Cat made money, and yet both times I came away feeling ripped off."

Curran drank his beer.

"I don't hold a grudge," Karter said. "We did profit from the deals. If another one comes along, we'll probably take it again, and we will make money again, but the feeling of having to watch your back with your business partner sticks with you."

I knew that feeling. When Curran and I separated from the Pack, Jim used Raphael's expertise to make a buyout offer for Curran's shares. Jim had to do it, because as Beast Lord he couldn't afford to have an outsider own a big chunk of the Pack's businesses. Raphael had to do it because Jim ordered him to and he'd sworn loyalty to the Beast Lord, but the whole thing left me with an uneasy feeling that took years to pass.

"Clan Bouda bet on wealth to expand its influence and got all the problems that come with loaning people money," Karter continued. "And no, not all of their reputation is deserved, but it's the perception that matters. No matter how hard Ascanio tries, he can't separate himself from the clan's reputation. Jim has integrity and commands respect, but he won't be endorsing Ascanio. The kid needs someone to vouch for him if he's going to succeed in his bid for the Beast Lord's chair."

Curran glanced at him. "What is it you're asking?"

"I'd like to know if Ascanio Ferara has asked for your blessing."

"No. And if he had, I wouldn't give it to him."

Endorsing Ascanio's claim to the throne would be signing the kid's death warrant. Karter was right. Ascanio simply didn't have the kind of Pack-wide loyalty needed to hold that spot. It was that loyalty, that mixture of trust, respect, and a bit of healthy caution that kept the shapeshifters from challenging their alphas.

If he somehow took the Beast Lord title, they would challenge him again and again, until someone killed him, and the Pack would be thrown into chaos. I ran that gauntlet when Curran had fallen into a coma. I had endured it, but only because stepping down meant being separated from the man I loved while he lay unconscious in his bed, and nobody had known if he would wake up. Ascanio was a smart kid. He understood all this.

"Why is he so desperate?" I asked.

Karter decided it was a great time to drink his beer.

Here was our chance to figure out what the hell was going on with the Pack. We needed to get Karter talking.

"I know the Medranos," I said. "I know how Andrea and Raphael run their clan. They wouldn't put Ascanio in harm's way, and he wouldn't disobey them. He worships the ground Raphael walks on. Last I checked, Jim was in good health and his position was secure. Why this urgent need to replace the Beast Lord?"

"Because the Pack is heading toward a cliff," Karter said. "We can all see the sheer drop ahead. The Medranos are just trying to turn the horses."

"And what's this cliff?" I asked.

"I'm debating whether I should tell you. After all, your husband created this problem when he put that bleeding heart in charge."

Bleeding heart? I laughed.

Karter eyed me.

"Some years back," I said, "I came across a crime scene where a shapeshifter had been assaulted. Back then Jim was running security for the Pack. His crew found me in the middle of an empty plaza trying to make sense of the blood smears. Jim knew me. We'd been partnering up for gigs in the Mercenary Guild for four years at that point. He knew I worked for the Order and had a reason to be where I was. I fought for the Pack and with the Pack. I had Friend of the Pack status. I greeted his crew with my hands up in the air and he let them maul me, and when I called him on it later, he said, 'Here you have trust when you grow fur.'"

Curran turned to me, and his eyes were pure gold. Karter leaned back slightly. Keelan set his beer down very carefully and sat still.

"You never told me this," my husband said. "When did this happen?"

Crap. "It's water under the bridge."

"When?"

"During Derek's thing. My point is, Jim Shrapshire the Bleeding Heart doesn't check out."

Curran turned to Karter, his eyes still on fire. "Tell me. All of it."

"On paper, the Pack has seven thousand members," Karter said.

"How many are there really?" Curran asked.

"We don't know. Jim refuses to open the official rolls. I'd estimate upward of eleven thousand."

Curran's face was harsh. "How? There are admission protocols in place. They require an eighty percent majority vote of Pack Council to repeal."

"Oh, they're still in place," Karter said. "The background checks, the waiting lists, and the provisional period. Everything is still there. He's getting around it with the Imminent Danger exception."

I remembered that law. Curran was always very careful about whom the Pack admitted into their ranks. The Pack's organization was unique, with each clan segregated by animal form. A clan was led by two alphas, who were assisted by two betas and a number of people in administrative positions like treasurers, heads of security, and so on. The seven pairs of alphas made up the Pack Council, which met once a week, and was presided over by the Beast Lord and their Consort.

The Pack guaranteed personal freedoms and rights and protected its members from abuses of power. A higher-ranked shapeshifter couldn't challenge a lower-ranked one. When criminal conduct like theft or assault occurred, there was due process, and limits and nature of punishment were clearly spelled out by the Pack's laws. The Pack was born as a defense to chaos and constant slaughter among the emerging shapeshifter groups. It was designed to keep its members safe and enable them to live their lives without fear.

In return, the Pack demanded strict discipline. You had to be where your alpha told you to be when they told you to be there. Sometimes you had to go into battle when the Pack overall was threatened. Breaking the law wasn't tolerated.

All of this took a lot of getting used to, especially for shapeshifters who were fleeing smaller packs where abuse could be rampant. Fitting them into the Pack's hierarchy took time and patience, which was why all the safeguards Karter mentioned had been put in place. But sometimes the situation was too urgent, which is where the Imminent Danger exception kicked in. A shapeshifter could appeal directly to the Beast Lord or the Consort, and if they proved they were in immediate danger, the alpha couple themselves had the power to admit them into the Pack, sidestepping all the other regulations.

In the entire time I served as the Consort, we used this exception only twice—once for a woman who was pursued by an aggressive alpha, and the other time for a family of four who had been wrongfully accused of murder.

"You know what Jim's problem is?" Karter asked.

Give me paper and a pen, and I'll make you a list.

"He knows he's done some fucked-up shit for the Pack's sake. I had a front-row seat to a lot of it. It haunts him," Karter said. "That story you told, Kate, that's on point. Things are very clear-cut for him: Pack shapeshifters are good, everyone else is bad, and as long as he's on the right side of that line, he's golden. But all that baggage is still eating at him. Jim's goal in life is to be a savior. He wants to be the guy who finds you when things are at their worst, taps you on the shoulder, and says, 'Come with me. I will make everything alright.'"

Curran's face still had that Beast Lord expression, and his eyes were still on fire.

"That's a dangerous road to walk," Keelan said.

"He isn't walking," Karter said. "He's sprinting as hard as he can. As it stands now, doesn't matter what you've done or how long your rap sheet is. If you tell Jim that you're in danger and humans are after you, he will let you in. He admits everyone and he does it personally. You're put in a holding cell, not knowing what will happen, you sit there for a while, worrying, and then the Beast Lord walks in and personally tells you that you are in."

"Personally?" Curran asked. His voice was almost a growl.

"Every time," Karter said. "He's addicted to it: the smiles, the thank yous, the sudden jolt of happiness. It's gotten worse since his child was born. He takes his son with him now, so he can see what a great guy his father is."

This was bad.

"The newcomers see him that one time," Karter said, "and then they never see him again, because the moment they're admitted, they are assigned a clan and they become *our* problem. I had to kill a man last week who should've never been allowed in. He was a serial murderer. Not a loup. Just a psychopath who would do anything to get what he wanted and had a rap sheet to prove it."

Damn it, Jim.

"But even if they weren't violent, they are coming in numbers we can't handle. All these people need housing. They need jobs. They need food. A lot of them don't have skills, so they need to be educated and trained. I had a conversation with a female lynx yesterday who was fired from three places in a row within one week. She told me that until she was admitted to the Pack, she wasn't a working female, she was a breeding female."

Some shapeshifter packs used the fact that they turned into animals to justify a lot of fucked-up crap. I saw some of it when Curran had been Beast Lord, so I had a pretty good idea what kind of environment that woman had endured, and thinking about it made me violently angry.

"What did you tell her?" Keelan asked.

"That it's not the way we do things. That none of what happened to her is her fault—and it isn't—and that we would help her find her place, however long it takes. We had a long and gentle conversation about institutional abuse and Pack's motto of "don't work, don't eat." She is a victim, and in perfect circumstances, I would have the luxury of figuring out what her strengths are and making sure she had proper training for some sort of profession she wanted. But we are overwhelmed, so I sent her to the daycare. Child-rearing is a skill, and we've determined that she has that. That wasn't where she saw herself, but we agreed that while it wasn't perfect, it would work for now. I put her on the waiting list for assessment. There is a four-month wait. The clans can't keep going like this."

"What did Jim say when you talked to him about it?" I asked.

"He blames the problems on poor management at the clan level. He's also given the clans a lot more autonomy. He had to. No two people alone could deal with the amount of work the Pack now requires."

Karter paused, thought something over, and continued, "I tried talking to him one-on-one. He went on for a while about greater purpose and a haven for all shapeshifters, and told me that I, of all people, should understand given my history. He isn't going to stop. But he is a smart man. He knows this cart can't keep rolling forward. I think he's going to bail. He's been mentioning how he wishes he could spend more time with his family. The only reason why he hasn't stepped away is because he has no successor, and his sense of duty won't let him abandon us. Those who want the job can't do it, and those who could do it don't want to. But, sooner or later, he will quit, and when that happens, the Pack will fracture. Then it will be every clan for itself, and there are a lot of wolves out there."

"This is why Ascanio is going for it," I thought out loud. "The boudas are a small clan."

Karter nodded. "Yes. Clan Cat is a small clan, too. Wolves

outnumber us ten to one, jackals four to one, and rats seven to one. The rats are almost bankrupt. The jackals were forced to admit a woman who used to be a cult leader and her following, which seriously fucked up the stability of their clan. Clan Heavy has gotten even more reactionary and difficult to deal with. It's a mess."

And here was that thunder my aunt had warned me about.

Karter turned to Curran. "In case you're thinking I'm here for your blessing, I'm not. I don't bow, I don't cringe, and I don't kiss the ring. If I want it, I make it mine, and I don't need any person's permission. I don't want the Pack. Not like this, broken beyond repair."

Poor Curran. He had built the Pack, and now he saw it cracking.

Karter was looking at him. No matter what he said, he'd come here for help. He wasn't sure what that help would be, but I could tell that his back was against the wall.

Curran finished his beer. His eyes had stopped glowing.

"It's not Jim's fault," he said.

I almost did a double take.

"And you are right, the Pack is broken. Nobody can fix it, including me."

Karter nodded. He looked like a pessimistic man who had let a single, weak seed of hope sprout, and now it was ripped out of his soul.

"The Pack was built on a faulty premise," Curran said. "It was bound to break sooner or later."

Karter nodded again.

"Let's make something better," Curran said.

The words sunk in. Karter frowned. "Who?"

"Us," Curran said. "Let's make something better."

"Right now?"

"Why not?"

Karter blinked.

"I'll get us some paper." Keelan rose.

I OPENED MY EYES BECAUSE MY HUSBAND PULLED ME TIGHTER against himself. Soft, honey-colored light sifted through the gap below the blinds. The clock on the wall assured me that it was late afternoon.

We'd stayed up until sunrise, hashing things out. When Karter left, just as the first golden edge of the sun slipped above the forest, he'd had a big smile on his face, and he walked like a man who had a crushing weight lifted off his shoulders. We loaded him up with Troy's tissue samples for Doolittle and two golden collars for Luther Dillon at Biohazard. I needed to get a closer expert, but Karter was going back to Atlanta anyway, and Luther was the best.

I hit the sack the moment Karter had left and apparently slept nearly till the evening.

Curran kissed the back of my neck, stretching himself against me. He was so warm, and he smelled amazing. I almost purred, but then reality kicked in.

I turned around in his arms. Little golden sparks danced in his gray eyes.

"There are seven people in this house besides us. And all of them have preternaturally sharp hearing."

"We'll be quiet."

"No, we won't, and you know it. You promised me, no fish-bowl this time around."

He sighed and rolled onto his back.

Living as the Consort within the Pack's Keep was like living in a fishbowl, constantly observed by way too many people keenly interested in every detail of our private lives. They wanted to know what we ate, how much sex we had, who we met, and what we talked about. When we were working out the details of the

108

new plan, I made sure to cover that ground. We had to retain some privacy.

"Will you be okay?" he asked.

"It will be very difficult," I told him solemnly. "But I'm sure the magic will hit within the next twenty-four hours or so, and it only takes me fifteen minutes to set up a soundproof ward. We must be strong."

He laughed.

"Think pure thoughts," I told him.

"I meant will you be okay with the plan?"

"Yes. Do you think Karter can keep it a secret?"

It was a good plan. I liked it a lot. But it hinged on moving a lot of pieces into place under wraps, without most of the alphas knowing what was happening. The crack in the Pack could come without warning, and there was so much to do.

"Yes. Karter is strong enough to lead the whole Pack right now. He doesn't want to do it, and I don't blame him, but he does want to keep his people safe. He's a leader, and he accepts responsibility for everything that comes with it."

"Good."

"I'm more worried about you. Are you sure?"

That was a question with a long and loaded answer. It was best to start at an easier place and work my way toward it.

"When the shapeshifters jumped us in the forest, and that big one tried to eat my head, and then I stabbed her?"

"Mhm."

"I enjoyed it." And there it was. I said it and waited.

"I know," he said. "After you killed the skull mage, you turned to me and you were smiling. A big, bright smile. Old Kate smile."

"Old Kate?"

"Dangerous Kate. Stabby Kate. My Kate."

I raised my head and leaned it on my bent elbow. "Stabby?"

"Yes. Exciting." He grinned.

So far, so good. "More words, bigger hole, Your Furriness."

"You haven't called me that in forever."

"You haven't roared in forever."

His grin relaxed into a softer smile. "When I was on the wall, with Keelan's pack at my back, it felt right. Seeing the enemy come, and meeting them, and stopping them. I missed it. It was a battle, Kate. We haven't been in a battle together in forever."

It was time to stop dipping my toes into the water and just jump in.

Like right about now.

Now would be good.

"Some pair of homicidal maniacs we are," I murmured, buying time.

"We're not maniacs. We do what we have to do, and we do it well. Like it or not, the world needs an occasional roar. Maybe in the future it won't, but for now, it can use it... Someone is coming up the stairs."

We waited silently.

A careful knock echoed through the door.

"Consort," Jynx said. "There are two guys here to see you. They said they were 'of the Owl.'"

"Thanks."

She walked away. Saved by the visitors.

"'Of the Owl'?" Curran's eyebrows furrowed.

"My father is the gift that keeps on giving." I rolled out of bed. "Come with?"

"Of course." He chuckled low. "I'll stand next to you and look menacing."

"No need to stand. You can sit and look menacing."

"Thank you, my queen."

"Yes, be grateful that I'm a wise and benevolent ruler."

We pulled on our clothes and walked out onto the balcony.

Two men waited on the street below us, blocked by a wall of shapeshifters. The younger wore an old green T-shirt and a red ballcap. The older man had chosen a worn gray sweatshirt and a white ballcap. They both wore jeans, and their beat-up work boots looked tired. A couple of day laborers waiting to be picked up, ready to work and perfectly harmless. Wouldn't give them a second glance.

The older man looked up. His skin was like ancient parchment, a light, even umber. His face was long, made longer by a dense, short beard streaked with gray. His cheekbones stood out, the cheeks so devoid of fat that they had developed vertical creases. His eyes were dark and narrow under thick eyebrows. Everything about him, from the deep furrows in his forehead when he squinted against the evening sun to the harsh lines of his nose, was sharp, angular, and severe, and yet he was a handsome older man.

Jushur, son of Kizzura. Also known as Akku the Owl. My father's former spymaster. Those eyes had witnessed the brutal massacre of my family, the wonders of my father's rule, the zenith of Shinar, and the end of the world.

The man next to him looked less than half his age. Same profile, same pronounced cheekbones, same high forehead, and same golden undertone to the skin. Rimush possessed a kind of steady calm. Nothing seemed to faze him. He looked at me now like a man who had climbed half of a steep mountain. He knew there would be falling rocks, landslides, and hungry monsters along the way, because he had beaten some of them already, and he was determined to ascend to the apex.

Nothing good would come from this meeting.

"Let them up," I said.

- - -

MY FATHER'S FORMER SPYMASTER LOOKED AROUND THE BALCONY before sitting in his designated rocking chair. Rimush ignored his chair and positioned himself behind his father, standing quietly. Keelan took the identical position behind me and Curran.

The balcony door opened and Andre came in, carrying a coffee table filled with drinks and a platter of cookies with one hand. He set it between us, nodded to Curran and me, and went back inside.

Rimush's standing bugged me, but asking him to sit was pointless and telling him to sit would acknowledge my authority over him, which I was doing my absolute best to reject. Keelan was clearly not sitting down either.

"Do you prefer Jushur or Akku?" I took the coffee pot from the table and poured two cups. Roland had mentioned that Akku was a coffee fiend.

"Jushur," he said. "The man named Akku died when his king left the world."

How did Hugh put it that one time? The king is out, long rule the queen. Life must go on.

"Fair enough. Sugar? Cream?"

Jushur took a moment to answer. "Sugar, please."

Rimush remained silent.

I spooned some sugar into the cups and offered them to the two visitors. "Please."

Jushur gave me an odd look, took the cup, and sipped. Rimush took one step forward, picked up his cup as if it were made of gold, and took a small swallow.

"You have chosen a public place for this meeting," Jushur said.

"These are my people. I trust them with my safety."

"Some words are only meant for certain ears."

"If you wanted to discuss dangerous secrets, you wouldn't have sought me out here. You know where I live."

Jushur took a sip of his coffee.

Kate one, Jushur zero. Time to press my advantage.

"Your son pledged himself to me."

"So he told me," the spymaster said.

"I fear his loyalty is misplaced. I'm not the queen he's looking for."

Jushur met my eyes. "In this life each of us must decide three things for ourselves: who to worship, who to marry, and who to serve. Only Rimush can determine if you are suitable to lead him."

Outmaneuvered. Fine. I still had an ace up my sleeve.

"My father tells me that Rimush will need a pulse of our power to unlock his full potential."

Jushur remained silent.

"I will do this for him without a pledge or any obligation. He can serve another or no one."

Rimush bowed deeply. "You are very generous, Sharratum."

"The Consort is merciful and kind to a fault," Keelan said.

The two of them stared at each other for half a second.

"I'm sure he is," Jushur said.

Ha!

A corner of Curran's mouth curled slightly. He forced his face back into a neutral expression.

"Why would you grant my son this gift? It's a fair bargain: a lifetime of service for a lifetime of power."

"Your full power shouldn't be held hostage," I told Rimush. "It shouldn't cost you your freedom. It was wrong of my family to bind your family in this way. It's only right that I release you from it."

Jushur cleared his throat. "Your father's view is not strictly accurate."

"Which part?"

"We do not require the magic of your bloodline to reach our full potential. We can achieve it at any time."

Oh. Oh! "You lied to my father."

Jushur sipped his coffee. "Technically, we lied to your grandfather."

"Why?"

"Shalmaneser im'Shinar was a suspicious man who saw plots and betrayers everywhere. We misled him to ensure the safety of future generations. Since he believed our young ones couldn't reach their full power without his permission, he didn't see them as a threat."

Wow.

"Your father never directly confirmed it with us. He simply assumed his parent's words to be fact. He prided himself on his knowledge. Pointing out his ignorance would've caused him undue distress."

I almost laughed. Well, didn't that just take the cake?

"So you managed my father. As amusing as it is, I don't want to be managed."

"Our aim isn't to manage, but to support and assist," Rimush said.

"You lied by omission. How can I trust you?"

"And yet we admitted our lie," Jushur said. "Should that not put you at ease?"

"One can admit to a small lie to get away with a bigger one."

Jushur narrowed his eyes. "You are very unlike your father."

"Yes. All the more reason not to serve me. More coffee?"

"Yes, please."

I refilled his cup and added more sugar.

"We are all a product of our time," Jushur said.

Not all of us. Like my father, my aunt also had awakened people who'd gone into deep sleep to support her in the new age. When I spoke to them, it was very clear that they had belonged to a different time. The mannerisms, the speech patterns, even their references were all different. Jushur spoke like he was born after the Shift. He'd adapted completely.

"Your grandfather, Shalmaneser, was one of twelve candidates for the throne. He grew up in a time of bitter strife when his siblings and cousins stabbed each other in the back. Winning his trust was a feat worthy of legends. He wanted to obtain power and keep it. He was convinced he was entitled to it by the virtue of his birth and abilities and, most importantly, he didn't want any of his siblings to have it."

I'd read the chronicles Erra's staff had faithfully reproduced in the modern age. To say that my grandfather was paranoid would be a criminal understatement.

"Your father, Nimrrad im'Shinar, was a genius without equal. His star shone so brightly, it occasionally blinded him."

More than occasionally. He pretty much had permanent blinders on when it came to certain things.

"Your father sought knowledge, progress, and enlightenment. He believed in the power of his mind so much, he couldn't fathom that someone under his command might not share his vision. To him, his path was so glaringly obvious that any rational being had to follow it."

True.

"You, too, are shaped by your times. The world has fallen apart around you. It's now trying to be reborn like a phoenix from its ashes. We must endure its birthing pains even as they plunge us into danger. You want both power and knowledge, but not for their own sakes. You want them to keep your people safe and free. You fear one thing above all else."

"And what is that?"

"An unfettered version of yourself giving free rein of your power. You fear it so much, you've shackled yourself."

Okay, he had me there.

"I have served two rulers of Shinar," Jushur said. "It is my greatest reward and blessing that I will serve a third, the one truly deserving of my loyalty, before my body becomes dust and my soul passes from this world."

Full stop.

Jushur rose and took a knee. Rimush knelt behind him.

"I've dedicated many years to the survival of your family. There are others like me, brought here by your father, adrift and alone, strangers in an alien land. Your people are crying out in the wilderness, for they need a home. Will you turn a deaf ear to our desperate pleas? Will you reject us? Will you cast us out after all those generations of service?"

"Oh, for fuck's sake," Keelan muttered.

"Please, Sharratum." Jushur intoned. "Allow us to stay."

He knew exactly which buttons to push. My father did drag them here. They had followed him into comas that lasted thousands of years, not knowing if they would ever wake up. Despite all their manipulations and careful managing, they were loyal. Now my father was gone, and they needed someone to take care of them. They could take care of themselves, true, but my family owed them a debt. I could wave my hands and say it wasn't my problem. After all, I hadn't created this issue. I shouldn't be responsible for the mistakes of a megalomaniac wizard just because he happened to be my father. And yet it felt like the wrong thing to do.

They were still kneeling.

"I'll think about it," I growled.

[7]

I walked the top of the wall. The sun was setting fast, and the woods looked ominous in the encroaching twilight. After my meeting with Jushur and Rimush I wanted some solitude. I told them they could stay in the house and escaped.

I stopped between two towers and leaned on the stone.

Heather Armstrong walked up the stairs onto the wall and headed toward me. The interim chief of the town guard moved fast and looked strong, her frame broad and sturdy. Her dark red hair was put away into a braid that looked a lot like mine.

She nodded to the guard in the tower near the gate, an elderly man with a cane sitting in a chair, and strode toward me.

I really wanted some alone time to sort things out, but it was clearly not in the cards.

Heather leaned on the wall next to me. "What can we expect?"

"Trouble. As soon as the magic hits."

"I understand that. I meant what can we expect specifically?"

"I don't know. You have more experience with these woods than we do."

She sighed. "What if they launch another pod like the one that destroyed the town square?"

"We'll deal with it."

"How?"

I had a very good idea how. I just didn't like it.

"You'll see if it comes to that. But I don't think there will be another pod."

Heather frowned. "Why not?"

"Because you don't kill the cow that you're milking. You all keep giving the forest people. If it kills you all or frightens you enough to risk leaving and dying, its source of human tributes dries up."

The line of Heather's jaw hardened. "We don't have a choice about it, you know."

There was always a choice. I would've fought to the bitter end, past any reasonable point. That's why a man I respected once told me that I made a terrible leader. I had trouble with trading one life for many.

And now I had both shapeshifters and my father's former advisers to take care of. I wasn't suited for the job.

I nodded at the guard tower and the elderly man inside it. "There was a teenage kid here before."

"Foster. He finished his shift. He's due to come on in the morning."

"He keeps running out of the tower. I keep telling him to stay in, and every time I look, he's out from under that roof on the wall."

"He's a kid. Lots of energy."

"How old is he?"

"Seventeen." Heather squared her shoulders. "I know what you're asking. Why put a kid on the wall, right? Let me tell you about Foster. He isn't stupid or really smart. He's average. He doesn't like school. He could get apprenticed to some of the businesses in town and learn a trade, but he doesn't want to do that either. He's a crappy hunter, and he doesn't have the patience for fishing. He has to do something to earn a living. The wall is it. It's not big money, but it's a steady paycheck and the benefits are good."

Right.

"He's a good guard. He doesn't play around too much, and if he sees something, he'll ring that bell. We're not like you. We're not soldiers and shapeshifters. We're just townspeople who made a militia because we had to. Take Ian over there. He's in his seventies. He worked all his life. Now his knees are worn out, his hands swell up, and his back hurts. He can't do much of anything anymore, but he still wants to work. It's not just the money. It's his way of living."

Heather frowned. "If you want the truth, neither of those two were supposed to be on the wall when the forest came. I've got a better team that I rotate between the gates. But those bastards showed up a month early. If I break the schedule and rotate them out, I've got to rotate someone in. Either way, someone's son, someone's mother, someone's spouse ends up on that wall. How do I decide to trade one life for another?"

I had no answers for her.

"I'll talk to Foster," she said. "Tell him to stay in the tower. I hope you're ready for whatever comes because we aren't."

She walked away from me.

I watched her go. The house where we were staying was lit up, the windows glowing gently. The shapeshifters had slept and now they were getting ready for a late dinner.

As if on cue, the balcony door swung open. Curran stepped outside. Our stares connected. He smiled and went inside. Checking on me.

I turned back to the forest. Heather was in her twenties, but she seemed older. Putting people in harm's way tended to age you. I'd meant to ask her why she was the interim chief. Something must've happened to the original chief. Oh well. Next time.

If I had to be in charge of choosing people to guard the wall, I'd never sleep, because if a real threat came, it wouldn't matter which one of them was on the wall. None of them would be able to do much. Not with this enemy. They would die where they stood.

Curran was better than me at that. He had the steel core needed for it. He never wanted to lose anyone, and when he did, it bothered him, but he also accepted it. It punched me harder. A couple of weeks ago Conlan and I were talking about Roland, and he told me that his grandfather had failed as a king because he couldn't handle not being able to protect everyone. It was a very smart observation.

Perhaps I had inherited more from him than I realized.

Out of the corner of my eye I saw a figure in dark gray clothes drop from the second-floor window of our house. He landed without a sound, ran up the stairs, light on his feet, and slipped past Ian. The old man never sensed he was there.

The figure approached like a shadow. I let him get within fifteen feet.

"Is there something you need, Jushur?"

"Sharratum," the spymaster said. "Your senses are as sharp as ever."

He came closer and hopped onto the edge of the wall, dropping to sit, cross-legged, with the agility of a man forty years younger. I had no idea how old he really was. Fifty? Sixty? Eighty?

"I get that your heart is set on helping Rimush with my approval, but pledging yourself to me was a bit much, don't you think?"

He looked at the forest. "It was not my plan."

I looked at him. "Then why are you here?"

"We came because this is a turning point for you. As the chroniclers of your journey, we must witness it."

"A turning point?"

"Surely, you feel it. Even now, when the magic has ebbed."

Oh, I felt it. It was very weak, but it was still there, shivering between the blades of grass and coating the stones, thin like a spiderweb. And it annoyed me. So much.

"This is the moment you reclaim your heritage."

"You seem very sure of that."

Jushur shrugged. "I may be wrong. Alas, I'm not infallible. But should it happen, we must not miss it."

"Then why not just say that? Why the kneeling and the pledging?"

"I changed my mind."

"Why?"

Jushur smiled. "Your father gifted me coffee a few times, as a specific reward in appreciation of my service and loyalty. In all of the time I served him, he never personally handed me a drink in the way you offered me coffee."

I raised my eyebrow at him.

"He has never forgotten the chasm between us. He was Sharrum. He stood upon an apex of the tallest mountain and saw me as a servant below. It would never change."

"He is set in his worldview."

"You see the shapeshifters as your allies. You happen to be in charge of them, but they are not your lesser. The way you spoke to my son tells me that you view him in the same light. I decided it might be interesting to connect my life to yours. Also, your discomfort was quite amusing. We shall have to work on that. If something as trivial as a person kneeling before you can disturb you, it will be easily utilized by our enemies."

I opened my mouth. I needed to say something smart that would knock him down a peg.

"You will need allies, Sharratum, and we are very useful. We will be your eyes and ears. I have brought you something. A small token of what we're capable of."

He reached inside his clothes, took out a rolled-up piece of paper, and offered it to me. I took it and opened it. A shockingly beautiful blond woman looked at me from a photograph. She wore a grass-green gown, and despite the mane of golden blond hair cascading down her back, the Shinar blood was unmistakable. Was this some sort of cousin my aunt neglected to mention?

There was something familiar about her eyes and the expression. So famili— *Julie*. It was her. The face wasn't hers, the hair was the wrong color and texture, the eyes were green, the body seemed too muscular, but it was her. It was my kid.

"How?"

"She was dying. Erra went into a deep sleep with her for nine months to heal her. When they woke up, Julia looked like that."

And they didn't tell me. Why? There must have been a very good reason. Both Erra and Julie told me everything, from which enemies they fought to a detailed review of chicken nuggets they had for lunch.

Anxiety punched me, rolling over me in an icy rush. "Is she okay now?"

"She's healthy and strong. Her powers have grown, and she fights in the way of the old kingdom, with magic and blade."

Nothing short of a catastrophe would have stopped them from telling me about Julie nearly dying. What had happened?

Jushur frowned. "We don't know the details and, most importantly, we don't know why this happened. We will find out, Sharratum. I give you my word."

MAGIC SKIMMED MY SKIN, AS IF A COLD, CLAMMY HAND BRUSHED ME with its fingertips. My eyes snapped open. The bed next to me was empty. Where was my husband?

The magic thickened around me, like a fresh spring that broke through the ground's surface and was now quietly bubbling up, flooding the area. The sky was still dark. The clock said 5:03 a.m. Sunrise was about two and a half hours away.

Medmagic took a lot out of the body, and I had gotten two intense treatments in one day. I could barely keep my eyes open once the sun had set, and around 3:00 a.m. or so, I'd gone back to bed. When I had gone upstairs, Curran was on the second floor, eating and watching Jushur and Rimush interact with the pack. Now he was gone.

If something urgent had happened, Curran would've woken me up, so whatever took him away likely wasn't too alarming. The dense currents of magic swirling around me definitely qualified as an emergency, however. I couldn't tell if the magic wave just started or if it had happened while I slept. Either way, the source of this sudden magic influx was up to no good.

I slipped out of my bed and stepped onto the balcony.

On the wall, Ian was asleep, slumped over in his chair. To the right of him, on the wall, Andre and Hakeem were passed out, Andre draped against the stone and Hakeem curled up. The chances of them both naturally falling asleep where they stood at the same time were about a million to zero. Magic shenanigans were afoot.

Beyond them, about a hundred yards from the wall, a lone figure waited. A priest-mage, like the other two, dressed in white and red and holding a staff. A mask obscured the top half of the face, a part of some sort of strange animal skull with two scimitar fangs that were turned upside down and attached to the skull like horns. Clay-covered face and hands again. I couldn't tell by the silhouette if it was a man or a woman.

The figure pointed at me and waited.

It didn't feel like a challenge. More like a request to parley.

I'd killed two of them already. This one was by themselves. Even if they were magically skilled, I could take them down. Besides, this was my chance to find out what happened to the people they took.

I stepped back inside and pulled on my clothes. The belt with pouches filled with herbs, Sarrat in a sheath on my back, a couple of knives, hair put up, and I was good to go. I went down the hallway.

Wait. I'd have to communicate somehow.

I did a one-eighty, grabbed a notepad and a pen from the night table, and then padded down the stairs. The house was empty. Everyone had gone somewhere, and Curran must've left Hakeem and Andre to guard me while I slept.

I unbarred the gate and walked out into the open.

The priest-mage didn't move.

I got to about fifteen yards from them, pulled a knife out, and nicked the back of my arm. I'd need my own blood for this. The red fluid ran down to the tip of my index finger. I turned, letting it fall in a circle around me, and activated it with a burst of magic. A blood ward surged to life, flashing ruby red, then turned transparent. I sealed the wound and sat inside the ward cross-legged, my saber on the grass in front of me.

Let's see what you have to say.

The priest-mage spun, weaving a complex pattern with their staff. Back and forth, and turn and spin... A kind of ferocious ballet, aided by magic.

Black vapor streaked through the air, trailing the staff.

The priest-mage pirouetted one last time and planted their staff in the grass. A pulse of black shot from it and settled into a glowing circle about eight feet across. Some kind of relief, shaped with pale and dark vapor... Oh. It was an aerial view of Penderton, surrounded by woods.

They had something that could fly. There was no other way for them to get this image. Bad news.

The priest-mage stared at me, waiting.

"Can you speak?"

No response.

I pointed at the map. "Town." Penderton was a long word. *Town* was easier to say.

No response.

I pointed over my shoulder at the wall. "Town."

The priest-mage jabbed the staff at the map and then at Penderton.

I nodded. "Yes." *Yes, I got it.*

The priest-mage took a step forward and drew a horizontal line through the town, cutting it in half. The north half turned red; the southern half remained the same.

The priest-mage pointed to the red half with their staff and put their left hand on their chest, fingers splayed out.

Okay.

They pointed at the southern part and then at me.

Ah. Mine and yours. They wanted to split the town down the middle. We'd scared them. Good.

I shook my head. "No."

The priest-mage waved their staff. Spheres formed above the smoke version of Penderton and plunged down, exploding on impact into fountains of smoke. The priest-mage opened their mouth and hissed. The dark smoke swirled around their head, forming a big phantom skull, its jaws gaping in a silent scream.

Do as we say, or we will kill everyone.

I crossed my arms over my chest and shook my head. *No. Won't happen.*

The priest-mage stabbed the staff in my direction and pointed it at the ground, then clapped their chest again and raised the staff all the way up.

You are down there, and we are up there.

I rolled my eyes, pointed to myself, put my hands together, rested my cheek on them, and closed my eyes for a moment to indicate sleeping. Then I pointed at the mage-priest, pantomimed walking with my index and middle fingers, and spread my arms.

If you are so mighty, why did you come here and wake me up?

The priest-mage glared at me. Or at least it seemed like it. The skull kind of made it hard to tell.

I took my notepad and pen, drew the line of ten stick figures on it, and showed it to the priest-mage. Then I ripped the piece of paper off, slowly, deliberately tore it into pieces, and tossed them into the air.

You're not taking any more people.

The priest-mage pointed at me and drew a line across their throat. Okay, that one was clear. But more importantly, I got a good look at their hands, especially their thumb. The fingers were long, with thick nails that looked like claws.

Hmmm.

The priest-mage was waiting for my answer.

I motioned to them with my right hand. *Bring it.*

The priest-mage thrust their hand into a small bag hanging from their leather-cord belt and hurled something at me. The object expanded in midair, and a car-sized rock smashed into my ward and bounced off.

The ward flashed crimson and held.

I yawned. *Let's see what else you've got.*

The priest-mage hurled a second rock. Another bounce.

I can do this all day, buddy.

Dark smoke boiled from underneath the priest-mage's feet. They stumbled back, suddenly unsure. The smoke coiled around them like tentacles. The priest-mage spun around, frantically trying to break free. Sounds came out of their mouth, foreign, strange words that sounded like begging.

The smoke snaked to their neck. The priest-mage dropped their staff and clawed at the coils with their bare hands. Their fingers slipped through the smoke.

It jerked them up, off their feet, shackling their wrists. The smoke forced the priest-mage's right hand up, into their robes, and dragged the arm back, forcing the priest-mage to pull a large bulb out. It looked like an onion but with a thick, crusty outer skin.

The priest-mage flailed, trying to get away from it.

The smoke shoved the bulb into their mouth.

The priest-mage's skull exploded into bloody mist. The headless torso jerked about in midair, flopping like a rag doll, and deflated like an empty water bag, as if all of their organs and bones had been turned into liquid and evaporated.

The Penderton tributes from the previous years were dead. All of them.

The bag of skin that used to be a person inflated once again and exploded without making a sound. Brown powder showered on my ward. It swirled and settled on the grass in an even semicircle, held back by the magic of my blood.

"I will find you." The power in the forest probably couldn't understand me, but I needed to say it. "I will eradicate you. You're done."

The forest watched me in silence.

A CHORUS OF BIRDS SERENADED ME IN STEREO, SOME FROM THE woods and others from the town behind my back. I didn't think there would be that many in October, but here they were, singing away without a care in the world.

Logic said that they were establishing and defending their territory so when the breeding season came in the spring, they were ready for mating. They were screaming, "My spot! Mine! Stay away!" But it was still lovely.

Curran walked out of the gates and strode toward me. "There you are."

"Here I am. Might want to stay away from the dust. I think this is what they bombed the town square with."

He stopped about fifteen yards away. "Are you going to be okay?"

"Yes."

He looked at the crescent of brown powder and the spray of blood on the grass. "Blood ward?"

"Yep. They came to negotiate."

"You haven't lost your touch, clearly."

"That was all them. I didn't do a thing. I talked to them a bit and then their negotiator self-destructed. Not voluntarily."

"I've negotiated with you before. That tracks."

"Ha. Ha."

"What do I need to safely get you out of there?"

"Burn the dust. If we could get a small sample, that would be great, too."

"Sit tight. Don't go anywhere."

My husband, the funny man.

Ten minutes later the shapeshifters came out of the gates, flanking two sleepy-looking people. Troy carried very long tongs that probably came from a smithy and a plastic cup with a lid. The shapeshifters wore almost identical pinched expressions. Andre and Hakeem clearly wanted to find the nearest deep hole and crawl into it.

Troy held his breath, used the tongs to clamp the cup, scooped some of the powder off the grass, and then covered his nose, and carefully snapped on the lid. He backed away, and the two sleepy people waved their arms around and summoned two conical flame jets. Fire mages, the modern answer to magical hazmat.

It took the firebugs another ten minutes to thoroughly torch all the powder. By the end, I sat in a semicircle of blackened grass.

The shapeshifters drenched the burned area with water just to be on the safe side. I broke the ward and stepped out.

"It's good to see you safe, Consort," Keelan told me.

"It's good to be safe. I need that plastic cup."

Troy handed it over.

Jynx, who'd been rummaging through the shredded robes of the priest-mage, trotted over, and offered me a small cloth bag covered with red glyphs. I hefted it. The outline told me another one of those spheres was inside. Opening the bag was out of the question. Pulling out a rock and then being crushed under it as it expanded wasn't on the agenda today.

"Thank you."

I took the bag, and Curran and I walked back to the house.

"Where were you?" I asked.

"We did a perimeter run. I wanted to see if there were any other places they could hit us from."

"I don't think complex tactics are their strong suit."

"Agreed. The wall is the boundary. One side defends it, the other attacks. Nice and simple."

I reached for his arm and wrapped my own around it. A little reassurance.

"I left two people to watch you," he said.

"What about Rimush and Jushur?"

"Jushur is in a trance, meditating. Rimush ran with us."

Hmmm. "How did he do?"

"He kept up." He flexed a little, squeezing my hand in the crook of his arm. "I came back, my guards were asleep, and you were gone. I followed your scent trail. How'd you end up out there?"

"Pretty simple really. I felt something. Maybe the magic coming back, maybe a sort of call to the wall. The guards were out and one of the high-level magic users waited at the edge."

"So you went alone?"

"Everybody was asleep or gone."

"Fair enough." He squeezed my hand again.

"It's not Andre and Hakeem's fault. It was very strong magic."

"We'll stagger the sentries. One on the wall, another some distance away."

I told him about the priest-mage conversation, the exploding head, and the dust.

Curran smiled. "It's worried. It offered a half-assed peace treaty. It probably wouldn't have honored it. It wanted to buy time to study us and prepare."

"We're not giving them half of Penderton. Not one person more."

He stopped and looked at me.

"They're dead. All the tributes are dead. It sent one of its higher-ranking humans to negotiate. The priest-mages are not wearing collars. They are skilled and valuable, and it killed that person, just like that. Like it was nothing. It already tried with rocks and didn't get anywhere, but it threw a person away anyway on the off chance that the dust would penetrate the ward."

"Human sacrifice," Curran said. His expression was hard, his gray eyes dark.

I nodded. "I need to speak with my father."

"Go. We'll hold down the fort."

"I'll try to be quick."

Curran chuckled. "You haven't spoken to your father for three months. The only thing he loves more than talking is lecturing. He's going to keep you there as long as he can."

"It will attack as soon as it regroups. He can lecture all he wants, but I decide when I come and when I go. Thirty minutes."

He nodded. "Have a safe trip."

[8]

I opened my eyes. I stood on a square platform high above the ground, holding a plastic cooler and a small bag. A beautiful palace spread before me, a vision painted against a glowing predawn sky in cream marble and Lemurian blue granite. Terraces stretched from stately towers; balconies traced graceful rooms, held up by elegant colonnades; waterfalls spilled from the floors above into stone pools. Below, a river wound its way to sea, its waters diverted to run through breathtaking gardens, where flowers bloomed along hundreds of ponds and streams, and stone gazebos with padded loungers and carved benches offered a chance for respite.

The wind was warm and pleasant. The air smelled like flowers.

In this realm, my father was a god, and this palace, so beautiful it almost floated among the greenery, was the purest expression of his will, his vision come to life without the constraints of reality.

A soft breeze stirred my hair. I walked across the platform to a narrow bridge connecting to a terrace, which bordered my father's study, a vast chamber with tall arched windows. The doors to the study stood ajar.

"Father?"

131

Another swirl of the breeze.

"There you are, Blossom."

Roland appeared in the doorway. He wore formal garments today, a tailored blue tunic that fell to his ankles, fringed with white at the hem, and a long outer garment he called an irrok, a length of snow-white fabric, thin like gossamer. It was secured at his left shoulder and fell in structured, perfect folds across one side of his body. Sometimes, he wrapped it around his hips in spiral folds but today, the irrok hung loose.

Usually, he didn't bother with formal clothes just for my sake. I got a tunic, sometimes pants and a shirt, and one time, he had shown up in a tracksuit, which made me laugh for five minutes.

The clothes were different, but he was always the same. A man with the face of a prophet or a sage, his dark hair streaked with gray, his handsome features touched by the sun, and his eyes full of wisdom and warmth. My father, who adored me more than he loved any of my long-dead siblings, tried to kill me in the womb, murdered my mother, fought a war against me, and now pouted if I missed a scheduled visit. Complicated, our family did it right.

"It's been so long since you came to visit me."

True to form. "Disparaging my husband in front of our son might have something to do with that."

He waved his hand, dismissing the idea. "I didn't disparage him. I simply pointed out that a man who would sacrifice his position of power under pressure wasn't fit to rule."

I waved my hand in front of my nose. "It stinks."

"What?"

"Your bullshit, Father."

He chuckled.

"You keep using Conlan to deliver these little jabs at Curran. I realize you find it entertaining, but every time you jab, we unpack what you did. Like all of us, you are only human, Father, and your actions don't stand up to scrutiny. Soon Conlan will be old enough to see you for who you really are. Let's not hasten that realization. Let him have his wonderful grandfather for a little longer."

"And who am I really?"

"Someone who murdered his grandmother, tried to kill his parents, and would have killed him if given the chance."

A shadow crossed Roland's face. "Is that how you see me?"

Oy. "We are more than one thing. I still love you, Father. And Conlan will always love you. But he's his own person, and he's growing up. Teenagers see the world in black and white. Right now, you are wise, kind, and glorious. Why not stay that way? So few of us can live up to our own legend, but you are, once again, an exception to the rule."

His expression eased. "I'll consider it."

Flattery. It always worked. If I flattered Erra, my aunt would snap and tell me to stop my nonsense. But my father took it as his due. Flattery would be in short supply in a few years. Sooner or later, Conlan would ask uncomfortable questions, and Roland would have to own up. But for now, he was still a beloved grandfather, all-knowing and larger than life.

We crossed the terrace, strolling toward a grouping of couches.

"The boy is here, by the way."

That explained the formal robes.

My father waved his hand. A section of the wall slid aside silently, revealing his study. Conlan was curled up on a plush couch, hugging his backpack. His eyes were closed. A thin veil glistening with magic separated him from us. A sound ward.

"He's been here for four hours. He has something to show you and won't tell me what it is." He rolled his eyes and smiled. "He finally fell asleep a couple of hours ago."

It was still almost an hour before sunrise when I left Penderton. If Conlan had come here four hours ago, he hadn't slept last night. What was so important?

"How are his studies?" I asked.

"He's brilliant, as expected. Unfortunately, he seems to be focused on the battle arts rather than more refined, academic pursuits. He's developed an interest in defensive spells. Apparently, there was an incident. I'm not at liberty to discuss it, but you might want to ask your husband about it."

Yes, the cursed wereboar, knew all about it. "I'm very proud of him."

"You're proud because he brawled like an animal?"

"I'm proud because he put himself in harm's way to shield others."

Roland sighed. I had to shift this conversation before he went off on a tirade.

"What did you teach him?"

"The pits, the cloak of Ur, the siege shields... All those things you found boring."

I couldn't resist. "The best defense is a good offense, Father."

"That's idiocy. Who said that?"

"Your sister." And many other people.

Roland grimaced. "It sounds like her."

"I don't sit back during battles. I do my best work up front, with my swords. That's where I'm most effective."

Roland rolled his eyes.

"Is he doing well with the spells?"

"He's learning faster than anyone in my memory. However, as you recall, the incantations for the siege spells are long."

"And tedious. So tedious."

"The tedium is the point. If it were easy, Blossom, anyone could do it."

My father, the magic snob.

"You seem troubled." Roland dipped his head to meet my gaze. For all his faults, Dad was always observant.

"Did Conlan tell you about Penderton?"

"No."

"During the last flare, some sort of evil appeared in the woods

134

north of Wilmington, near a town called Penderton. It sent its human servants to demand tribute from the town."

"What form of tribute?"

"People."

Roland furrowed his eyebrows. "Dangerous and foolish. Go on."

"They come for tribute every year. They infected the town with something, and the residents die if they leave. The town offered us a lot of land if we can eliminate the threat."

"I see."

"I need your expertise, Father."

I opened the cooler, took out one of the gold collars from the morgue and the plastic cup, and put the bag with the sphere next to them.

Roland picked up the bag. It opened in his hand on its own. A stone sphere floated up, wrapped in red string. Roland flicked his fingers. The stone ball slid back, putting a few yards between us. The red string snapped. The sphere expanded into a boulder.

Roland focused on it. It shrank into a ball, expanded again, then shrank again, and expanded one more time.

"This is of them?"

"Yes. Have you ever seen anything like it?"

"No."

The boulder rotated. Thin strands of light wrapped around it —my father analyzing the enchantment.

"It feels primitive somehow," I said.

"The idea behind it is so basic. What could be more rudimentary than throwing a large rock at your enemy?"

"A very large rock."

"But only a rock still. The concept is crude, but the execution... I do not know how this is done." Excitement sparked in his eyes. "How peculiar. Simple idea, tremendous amount of magic to make it function. Grand and yet so inefficient. The work of a toddler god."

"Is it divine?"

"No. This was made by a human."

The collar was next. I watched it expand and contract in his fingers.

"Have you noticed the weight?" he asked.

I nodded. "Heavy."

"Almost pure gold and heavily enchanted. Once put on, it will not come off. The wearer?"

"Dead."

He sighed. "Of course they are. What did they look like?"

"They were shapeshifters. After they died, they turned human, but they did not look like us. They grow ridges of hair along their spines, their profiles are strange, and they have horns."

My father raised an eyebrow. "Interesting. The cup?"

I explained the meeting of minds on the killing field in front of Penderton.

He took the lid off. The brown powder snaked out, swirled around his fingers, and slipped back into the cup.

"Spores."

"What kind of spores?"

"A magical fungus, perhaps. Something that implants within the lungs when it's inhaled. How quickly did the people die once they left the area?"

"Three days."

"So it's fast-acting, and yet the population of Penderton is still alive. Something is inhibiting their growth in Penderton." He tilted his head and looked at me. "Is there something you're not telling me?"

"Do you have ink and paper?"

A piece of watercolor paper appeared on the table with an ink bottle, a brush, and a crystal cup filled with water. I took the brush, dipped it into the ink bottle, and colored a circle in a uniform, even purple.

"This is what we do."

I washed the brush, then drew another circle with water next to the first one. Then I dipped the brush into the ink again and let a single drop fall off its tip into the center. The ink spread through the water circle, a saturated purple in the center that grew paler and more diluted toward the edges. A gradient.

"This is what the forest does."

His expression shifted. The kind, wise sage was gone. An immortal wizard peered at the paper, the full power of his staggering intellect directed at the problem like a laser.

"A precursor?" he murmured. "Or a variation?"

"That's how it's suppressing the spores." The priest-mage's clawed hand still bothered me. "Father, are we the only ones capable of this?"

"By 'we,' you mean our family?"

"Humans."

"I don't know." Roland's face clouded.

What? "You know everything."

He smiled at me. "If that was so, I would go mad for there would be nothing left to discover. The family records don't specify how or when we acquired this power. However, in my lifetime, I have met three outsiders, none of them with our blood, who were capable of it."

None of this was comforting.

Roland tapped the ink circle. "This and the fact the blood ward stopped the spores makes your course clear. You already know what you must do to save them."

I looked at the beautiful vista spreading before us. He was right, but that solution was the absolute last thing I wanted to do.

"Why, Blossom? Why do you push away your birthright?"

Because accepting it would mean taking a big step toward being like you. Because when I blundered into it the first time, it came close to altering who I was, and I will never allow that again.

"It is the art of your family. It is a part of who you are and where you come from. Every one of us has a right to learn our roots, for that's how we understand ourselves."

I didn't want to get into this discussion.

"Think of your ancestors, who dedicated their lives to perfecting this magic in the hopes that future generations would use it to keep us and our people safe. Think of how they would feel if they were to witness your squandering it."

"I think it's about time we woke Conlan up," I said.

Roland sighed. The veil slid aside.

I cleared my throat. My son's eyes snapped open.

"Mom!" Conlan bolted upright.

"Your father told you to stay in the safe house. Why are you here?"

"Mom, Mom, don't get mad!"

I took a deep breath. A smile curved Roland's lips.

Conlan dug into his backpack. "It's a *Cuvieronius hyodon.*"

I looked at Roland. He shook his head slightly.

"The picture." Conlan pulled a large book out of the pack and scrambled to me. "Look!"

He opened the book and thrust it at me. On the page, Isaac's strange pachyderm posed on a rock slope next to what looked like a weird armadillo. A silhouette of a person was drawn to the side for scale. The armadillo was the size of a VW Beetle. The *Cuvieronius* was three times larger.

Conlan read nonstop, absorbing all sorts of random knowledge like a sponge, especially anything to do with animals, and prehistoric animals were his favorite. Luiza must've shown him Isaac's sketch as I asked, and he put two and two together.

"Someone saw this creature? In person, recently?" Roland asked.

"Yes," I said.

"In the area you're trying to protect?"

I nodded.

Roland raised his hand. A stone pillar thrust itself from below into our view. Rock flowed like molten wax and hardened into a colossal creature. It had four tusks, small ears, and a thick, muscular trunk, and it towered above us. I had seen an elephant before. This animal dwarfed it. Its ears were proportionally smaller, its trunk shorter, its legs longer. The resemblance to *Cuvieronius* was unmistakable. These giants were monstrous cousins to Isaac's creature, closer to it than to a modern elephant.

"The four-blade elephant," Roland said. "They had gone extinct in our part of the world long before I was born, but their statues remained. The ancients worshipped them as gods. Once, when I was young, I saw one. It was brought from the Eastern Plains as a gift to my great-aunt for her wedding."

I took the book from Conlan and flipped it over to the cover. *Extinct Giants of the Ice Age.*

Ice Age.

Wow. I landed on a couch. Sitting down seemed like a good idea.

Conlan bounced around me, talking too fast. "You know how we have all these round lakes? They're called Carolina Bays, but they're not bays at all, they are old thermokarst depressions, like the ones they have in Alaska. That's because twenty thousand years ago this area was all permafrost, and it had mega fauna, and it had *Cuvieronius*, which evolved in North America, then went to South America to escape the ice, but the ice began to melt, so they migrated back up. And there were other mega species, mastodons, giant camels, dire wolves, sabertooth cats, and lions like me and Dad..."

The shapeshifter that had attacked me flashed in my mind. Reddish spotted fur and nine-inch fangs.

Oh my God. I had killed a were-*Smilodon*.

"...and Luiza said there was a hill. And look, I found an old picture of it. I put it in the book. In the front. It's a conical hill and it looks like a pingo. They have them in Alaska. They have a core of ice, and then the ice melts, and the hill collapses. The hill collapsed, Mom! It had Ice Age animals inside!"

He stopped to take a breath.

I looked at the book in my hands. "This says *Cuvieronius* became extinct twelve thousand years ago."

"Yes!" my son confirmed.

I turned to Roland. "So whatever it is must have slept with all its people and animals for at least twelve thousand years. Is it even possible? Could something from the Ice Age pop up in our time and somehow be alive?"

"In theory, yes," Roland said. "If the enchanted sleep was deep enough. I slept for over two millennia, and when I woke, it felt like I'd gone to bed the day before. Deep sleep of this kind is complete stasis. So it is possible that a human had accomplished such an achievement, but only in theory. There have been cases of ancient animals reappearing but never a human who has slept for that long."

"That's right. You had mammoths that one time," I said. "When you attacked the Pack Keep during the first war with Atlanta."

He nodded. "A herd had walked out of the snowstorm in Alaska. I bought a few. They were hideously expensive and finicky to take care of, and they did badly in that battle. A complete waste of money."

It wasn't the mammoths who lost that battle. My father had accomplished that feat all on his own. Despite his unbearable academic brilliance, he had a questionable grasp of military tactics. His battle plan consisted of arranging his troops into a phalanx and sending them against the fortress of the Keep while he rode behind his army in a gold chariot. Because chariots made of soft and incredibly heavy metal were both durable and very mobile.

"It's a poor workman who blames his tools, Father."

He waved his hand at me dismissively. "An animal lacks the awareness necessary to comprehend the passage of time, but a human doesn't. Ten millennia is a great deal of time. In fact, before I had gone into my sleep, our greatest scholars begged me to reconsider. They were afraid that when I woke, the world would be so different, it would drive me mad."

I flipped through the book. *Smilodon.* Keelan's shapeshifter had looked like mine. If I was right, and we had fought were-*Smilodons*, his head would explode. I turned the pages. Mastodon. Nope, don't want to fight that. Giant beaver. That might explain the weird animals Isaac saw in the swamp. North American camel. Wow, bigger than the modern version.

I turned the page and stopped.

A massive lion looked back at me, its fur splattered with ghostly stripes. Huge paws, powerful frame, nearly eight hundred pounds. The African lion positioned next to it for scale looked like a skinny adolescent in comparison. *Panthera atrox.* North American lion.

Nobody knew for sure how shapeshifting had started, but the legend said that ages ago, far back in prehistory, when fierce predators ruled the planet, humans worshipped them as gods. Eventually they made a bargain, giving up a little of their humanity for the gifts of their animal deities. They then passed that gift onto others, diluting and weakening it in the process.

The descendants of those original Lyc-V carriers, those whose ancestors had made the bargain, were called the Firsts. They were exceedingly rare, and their power and control were off the scale. Other shapeshifters sensed them somehow and gathered around them, viewing them as natural leaders. Curran was a First and a *Panthera atrox.* And so was our son.

Conlan was looking at me, his eyes opened wide, trying to see if I understood what that image of the lion meant to him. I did. This was how he and Curran came to be. This was why they were different.

"I'm so proud of you," I told him. "You did very well."

Conlan grinned.

Roland's expression turned grave. "If he's correct, you are fighting something from our pre-history. I have no frame of reference. No one does. The magic you and I wield has been tamed and refined. It is a force that we have harnessed and bent to our will. What your opponent has is something completely different. It is wild and unchanged. It's chaos."

I looked into his eyes and saw genuine concern. To him, magic was a force defined by laws and rules. It was something he studied and used as a tool. It behaved in predicable ways that he fundamentally understood. He never liked witch magic or shapeshifter magic because it tapped into that primordial unpredictability that he sought to define and limit. It defied him, and so he rejected it.

This was infinitely more unpredictable than witch magic. This was wild magic, a raw power with unknown limits. It disturbed my father to his core. It disturbed me, too.

"Can you walk away from this?" he asked.

"No. I gave them my word. Curran gave them his word."

He covered his face with his hands. "Of course you did. The two of you blundered into this with no idea of what you were facing."

Conlan hopped in place like an excited kitten.

"Mom! Can I come?" His eyes were like two headlights coming at you on a dark road.

My father took his hands from his face and stared at his grandson.

"No, you may not! Have you heard nothing I have said?"

Conlan looked at me, his face desperate. "Ice Age animals!"

Power swirled around my father.

"I FORBID IT."

The palace shook from the impact.

To me, this was ancient history coming to life after lying dormant for eons and killing people. To Curran and Conlan, it was much more. My father was right about one thing: every one of us had roots.

"DAUGHTER! DO YOU NOT CARE FOR YOUR CHILD?"

The full power of his magic reverberated through me. Ouch.

"It's the origin of his bloodline."

"I AM THE ORIGIN OF HIS BLOODLINE!"

The palace trembled again.

"One of the origins. He isn't a clone of you, Father. He is a prince of Shinar, but he is also a First, and his animal counterpart hasn't walked the planet for over ten thousand years. This may be his only chance to experience the world as it had been."

Roland glared at me.

Nobody knew what we would find in the forest. Whatever it was could vanish once we took down the power ruling over it. Conlan would likely never again see it in his lifetime. Ice Age mammals didn't exactly pop out of nowhere every day like daisies.

Penderton was dangerous. But I had made up my mind. Conlan was a child, but he was a child of two trained killers. He would be fine.

"You may come."

Conlan grinned ear to ear and vanished.

My father's face was terrible.

A mountain rose in the distance, split in half with a thunderous crack, and spewed molten lava. Roland strode to the rail and gazed at it. I came to stand next to him. We watched the eruption for a while, with a stream of glowing lava flowing to the sea and very considerately avoiding the gardens. Minutes ticked by.

The eruption seemed to ebb.

"Feel better?" I asked carefully.

"Not appreciably, no. This is a terrible idea. You are putting the boy in real danger. You and that savage you call your spouse blundered into something you cannot comprehend and now you will allow my grandson to join you on this idiotic quest. Can you at least understand that?"

"What would you do in my place?"

He faced me. "I would face the threat that dared to challenge me. I would erase them from the face of the planet. They do not belong here. Their time has passed, and they have no claim to the land or the lives of the people who inhabit it. They didn't come bearing gifts. They came demanding tribute. But I am not you. I do not willfully shackle myself, denying the power my family sacrificed so much to obtain."

Again with the shackles. Him and Jushur, two peas in a pod.

"Have you ever offered a servant a drink?"

He glanced at me. "Why would I do that?"

Jushur was right. My father was the king atop his mountain. He never forgot who he was or where he came from... Oh.

"Sometimes I think we've reached an understanding," I said. "And then you manipulate me like this."

He didn't say anything.

"You focused my attention on our ancestry, trying to guilt-trip me, and then, when Conlan told us about the Ice Age, you saw an opportunity, so you dramatically forbade me from letting him join us in Penderton, knowing that if you gave me an ultimatum, I would be inclined to do the exact opposite."

"Your point?"

"You gambled with your grandson's safety for a chance to push me into doing something I don't want to do."

"No, I bet on your maternal love. Even without my nudge, you wouldn't deny him this chance to see the source of his power. It would be cruel, and you were never that, Blossom. One way or another, you would've allowed him to join you, and once he's there, you will use everything in your arsenal to protect him, including the powers of your bloodline that you are trying so hard and pointlessly to reject."

"Why are you so hung up on it?"

"Because you insist on hobbling yourself. Your fear of following in my footsteps cripples you. You don't have to be me, Blossom. You don't have to be your aunt. Our bloodline has produced many great rulers, benevolent, just, enlightened. Shinar was the beacon of progress and safety long before any of us were born. You must keep your chosen people safe. It is your duty, and your sword has limits."

The volcano smoothed itself out into verdant mountains, as if it were never there.

"We both know what you have to do to save that town. Your son's presence there is just the excuse you need to justify it to yourself. I gave you that excuse. Knowing you and the boy were safe would make me sleep better at night."

Forgetting someone there in our family of three. "You don't sleep, Father."

"Of course I do. I sleep and eat, even though I have no need of it. I live my life as normally as I can, or I would go mad in this prison of your making."

"The dragon made the prison. Your actions, your decisions put you here."

"Semantics."

"If you beat me, where would I be?"

He didn't answer. I picked up the book Conlan had left behind, turned, and walked back to the platform. It was my designated point of arrival and departure, and despite everything, I respected my father's rules.

"Blossom," he called out.

I turned to look at him.

"Wouldn't it be nice to return here after you've done it and hear me say, 'I'm so proud of you. You've done very well'?"

I kept walking.

Yes. It might be.

[9]

My eyes snapped open. I sat on the balcony, in the same spot I'd left. Rimush stood on my left, Troy waited on my right, and in front of me, Mayor Gene gripped the balcony's rail. A battle raged in front of the gates and on the wall. Big, leathery beasts swooped down on huge wings, their leonine muzzles open wide, fangs ready to rend.

Manticores. Huge and shaggy with fur. I had never seen one like that, but if Ice Age wolves and cats could be bigger, its manticores could be, too. One, two...eight. Crap.

The town guard archers were firing volley after volley from the tower. To my right, Owen spun around like a shot-putter and hurled a giant tractor tire into the air. It smashed into a manticore in midflight. Its wings folded and it plunged to the ground. Three shapeshifters closed in on it and ripped it apart. A second shapeshifter group to the left dug into another manticore, deboning it like chicken.

Where was Curran?

I scanned the field. Where... There, on the wall, in warrior form. A manticore swung away from town, a limp body in its claws. Oh no. Foster. The realization stabbed me. The boy was dead. His head hung from his neck, twisted almost completely around. When manticores hunted, they killed like leopards, falling on their prey from above. The neck and the upper spine were their favorite targets.

Curran compressed himself, powerful muscles bunching across his frame, and leaped. His claws caught the manticore's flank. It dropped Foster's body and clawed at Curran, trying to dislodge him. He heaved himself onto the beast, gripped its left wing, and wrenched it off. Blood gushed. The manticore screeched like a dying bird, falling in a corkscrew spiral.

"Sharratum," Rimush greeted me.

Mayor Gene whirled around. "You're back."

"How long?" I pointed at the carnage.

"Six minutes," Rimush said, "and twenty seconds."

"Do we fight?" Troy demanded. A bright white glow coated his irises. Curran must have left him here to watch over me until I came back.

The magic that saturated Penderton was moving, flowing back into the forest. It hadn't retreated completely, but it had thinned, the bulk of it returning to its source. That thickness of magic was the only force suppressing the spores and now it was barely there.

I glanced at Rimush. "Do you feel it?"

"Yes."

"This is a diversion."

I jumped to my feet. Suddenly things became very simple. There was no room for doubt, and no time to waste. There was only a town filled with people who were counting on us to keep them safe.

I turned to Mayor Gene. "What's the highest building in town?"

"Two choices: courthouse or water tower."

The water tower wouldn't have enough room for what I needed to do and there was a good chance it would blow up.

"How far is the courthouse?"

Gene pointed. I looked in the direction he indicated. A three-story brick building rose above the other houses, its white bell tower stretching to the sky.

"Half a mile, in the center of town."

We could end up needing Gene to get into the courthouse without wasting time on guards and locked doors.

I turned to Troy. "Pick up the mayor and follow us."

"I can walk," Mayor Gene protested.

"Not fast enough."

"Excuse me." Troy scooped the older man into a bridal carry.

I took off down the stairs. Rimush followed. We burst onto the street and raced to the courthouse.

Streets flew by. A few more minutes and we emerged into the town square. The courthouse rose in front of us, a lone guard, a teenage girl clutching a sword, protecting the door.

"Let us through, Jenny!" Mayor Gene growled.

She jumped aside. I shoved the door. Locked.

"Troy!"

The werejackal set Gene down and kicked the door. It burst open. We ran inside, into a large chamber.

"Stairs?"

"In the back!" Gene hurried forward, to a double staircase at the back of the chamber.

Troy picked Gene up again and we took the stairs two at a time. Second floor. Third.

The stairs ended in a landing that opened to a long hallway.

"Left, around the corner!" Gene yelled.

I sprinted to the left, slid a little across the polished floor, and rounded the corner. Another short hallway ended in a door marked *TOWER ACCESS. AUTHORIZED PERSONNEL ONLY.* I hit it. Locked.

I kicked the door. It held.

I didn't have time for this shit. I kicked it again.

It splintered around the lock and swung open, revealing a

spiral staircase. I pounded up the metal stairs and burst into the tower. A waist-high wall encircled a square space under a domed roof. The bell was right above me.

I leaped over the wall and landed on the roof. The town spread out below me. Good enough.

I unsheathed Sarrat and took a deep breath.

Magic stirred inside me, a heavy dense mass that had slumbered deep in my soul.

Wind fanned my hair. The sun shone bright. Everything became crystal clear, as if someone had turned a dial, bringing the world into sharper focus.

I had done this a hundred times in practice, but I'd truly meant it only once. Every cell in my body remembered how that first time felt. The power of it. The burden. The weight of life and the heady flow of magic it generated.

A distant sound split the air, like an enormous slingshot snapping. A huge, dark object shot up above the forest, an ominous darkness growing larger as it sped toward us.

"Good Lord," Gene breathed.

"What the fuck?" Troy snarled.

It had to be now.

I raised my sword point down, locking both hands on the hilt, and the ocean of magic inside me rose with it, building into a massive wave. A tsunami cresting.

The object had reached its apex. It was a bulb the size of a house. The forest had decided to devastate Penderton.

My body shook with the strain. There would be no do-overs.

On the street someone screamed.

The bulb was flying straight at us. Its bulk blocked out the sun.

I plunged Sarrat into the roof.

The wave inside me broke. Its power jerked me off my feet. I rose into the air. The geyser of magic burst out of me, pulling my arms out wide and arching my back. Words appeared on my arms, a poem written in the language of power and etched into my skin in the womb.

I opened my mouth and spoke with all the power of my blood. "HESAAD." *Mine.*

A pulse of red shot out of me, rolling over the town. My magic drenched the land. I felt it touch the wall and roll past it, over the farms and settlements, into the woods. I let it go for another couple hundred yards and held it back. That would be enough.

In a split second, my magic had soaked into Penderton, and the land responded, its power flooding back into me like a clear mountain stream. I wrapped myself in it, soaking in its energy and strength, and focused on the bulb falling onto the courthouse.

The bulb ignited. It was a flameless burning. It glowed like a piece of charcoal, turned to ash, and melted into nothing.

I closed my eyes and reached with my power, looking for the minuscule sparks of spores embedded in my land. A moment and I found them. All of them. They lay before me like a dusting of glitter across black velvet.

I snuffed them out.

THE MAGIC DROPPED ME LIKE A BAD HABIT. I LANDED ON MY BUTT and slid down the slope. The edge of the roof rushed at me. I dug my feet into the shingles and ground to a stop just before taking a dive onto the pavement below.

Phew.

If I claimed the land and then faceplanted to my death on the street, I'd never live it down.

Troy hopped over the rail, ran across the roof as if his feet were glued to it, and braked next to me. "I've got you."

Rimush landed on my other side and locked his hand around my wrist. "Apologies, Sharratum. I must not let any harm come to you."

"I'm good," I growled.

I climbed back up the slope, with the two of them hovering behind me, ready to grab me if I slipped. Roofs were not my favorite. Being hovered over wasn't either.

We made it back to the tower. Mayor Gene gaped at me.

I gave him a little wave and climbed over the rail to the safety of the tower.

"Was that—"

"No time," I told him and took off down the stairs.

The explanations would wait. Curran was fighting prehistoric manticores, and I had a score to settle for Foster's death.

I ran to the ground floor, across the chamber, and burst into the autumn sunshine, my two self-appointed bodyguards at my heels.

A big, gray shape sprinted toward the courthouse, coming recklessly fast down the street. I couldn't remember the last time I'd seen him run so fast. I had done the thing I told him over and over I'd never do, and now he raced here, worried about me.

"Wait here," I barked and dashed toward him.

We met halfway across the square. Curran grabbed me by my shoulders, peering into my face. His eyes were on fire.

"Are you okay?"

"Yes."

"What happened?"

He was actually out of breath.

"The forest had claimed Penderton. Probably years ago, during that first flare. While you were fighting, they pulled their magic back from the town and threw a massive spore bomb at us. Without their magic suppressing the spores, it would have killed hundreds. I had to claim the town."

I hugged him, and he gripped me to him, his chest rising and falling fast. I heard his heart hammer.

"Are you okay? Do you feel okay?" he asked.

"Yes."

I felt better than okay. The magic of Penderton splashed around me, strong and exhilarating. The urge to claim and hold land was bred into my family. We called it the Shar, and it was a possessive, overwhelming beast. But like many things, controlling it got easier with practice, and I had practiced for years, claiming and releasing a small patch of land every week. I felt it nip at me now, but its bites were shallow.

This wasn't my land. I'd picked it up into my palm like an injured bird I had to shield until I could take it to safety, and once the danger passed, I would whisper my goodbyes and release it. The thought of it brought me no anxiety.

"It's only temporary," I told him. "I'm okay. Really."

"Good." He took a deep breath and exhaled.

"Sorry," I told him. "There was no other way."

I'd had no idea what I was doing when I had claimed Atlanta years ago. I didn't know about the Shar back then, and I had no defenses against it. It had almost twisted me into a tyrant. Curran had witnessed me descend into the dark hole, and he was the one who helped me climb out.

"It's not a problem. I mean it." And of course, that sounded like denial. "And if it becomes a problem, I'll tell you. I give you my word."

"I believe you," he said.

"I promise—"

"You don't need to convince me, baby. I trust you. You've known this place was claimed from the moment we've arrived. You told me that on the road."

"Yes."

"Your aunt always said that the Shar is the strongest when there is competition. It would've pushed you to make the land yours, but you didn't claim the town until you had no choice. If you had an issue with control, you would've grabbed Penderton as soon as we got here."

He was right.

"I'm not worried about it," he said.

"I love you," I told him. I meant to tell him how much it meant to me, but *I love you* was what came out.

"I love you, too. I think I need a damn heart transplant."

"Why?"

"I saw you almost fall off the fucking roof," he growled.

Oh.

"I thought I'd have to catch you." He looked past me at Troy and Rimush in the doorway of the courthouse. "What the fuck were you two doing?"

He hadn't lost it because of the claiming. He lost it because of my graceful slide down the roof. I was so stupid.

"How did neither of you manage to grab her?"

Troy winced. Rimush blinked.

"What were you going to do?" I asked. "Were you really going to try to catch me?"

"Yes."

"From the third floor? Your arms would break off."

"They'd grow back," he growled.

Technically, he was right, but it would take years. I needed to redirect this before he started roaring at my two nannies. "Shouldn't we go back to the fight?"

"It's over," he said. "We won. Why the hell didn't you stay in the tower, Kate?"

"Because the last time I claimed something, the roof above me exploded. You were there, remember? I didn't want to blow up their courthouse tower. It's pretty..." Also, that bell could've fallen on our heads.

He swore, turned around, his fingers locked around my wrist, and started back the way he came, pulling me with him.

"You're the best husband ever," I told him.

"No more fucking roofs, Kate. I mean it."

Troy and Rimush followed us. Out of the corner of my eye, I saw Gene, who had finally made it down the stairs, appear in the doorway of the courthouse. He watched us with an odd expression on his face. I'd freaked out Mayor Gene. I'm sure he wasn't the only one. There would be fallout.

That was fine. Better freaked out and alive than calm and dead.

"I met Conlan at Dad's," I said. "He identified Isaac's weird elephant critter. It's a *Cuvieronius hyodon*, a species of gomphotheres, which are loosely related to modern elephants."

"Mhm," he said.

"They've been extinct for twelve thousand years."

Curran stopped and looked at me.

"According to my father, it is possible for a living creature to survive in a magically induced coma from the Ice Age until now, although he doesn't recommend it. This explains the unusually furry manticores and the abnormally large lupine shapeshifters. They are not *Canis lupus*. They are *Aenocyon dirus*. Dire wolf shapeshifters."

He was still looking at me and not saying anything.

"Also, I think I might have killed a were-sabertooth tiger. I did wonder why her fangs were so long."

"Doesn't matter," he said. "Ice Age or not, we're going in there and clearing that place out. That's all there is to it."

"I told Conlan he could come."

"Good," Curran said. "He's earned it."

Curran

THE CLEANUP OF THE MANTICORE BODIES TOOK A GOOD TWO HOURS. There was some discussion about burning them, but we'd been traumatized by the awful sooty smoke that had risen from the rhino when it was burned. The stench had been indescribable. I could still smell traces of it.

A decision was made to dump the bodies into a conveniently

available trench that had been dug out by the town previously because it needed dirt for some municipal reasons. Kate had assured me that unlike the rhino, the manticores were magically inert. That the chances of them springing out of the ground as something dangerous were relatively low. I trusted her on it.

We dragged the manticore bodies to the trench, and then Kate caused a tiny earthquake, collapsing the pit walls to bury the corpses. I knew she was already pretty tired from the claiming, and spending any more magic would probably knock her off her feet. There would be no going into the woods today. She'd need a day to recover, and I wanted my people to rest a little. They'd earned it.

We needed to discuss Conlan's theory, so I decided we'd have lunch on the edge of the woods, where we wouldn't be overheard. Keelan's shapeshifters brought out food, drinks, and blankets to sit on. The day was warm. The sun shone bright from the blue sky, and a light breeze kept things refreshing. It felt almost cheerful: a cozy little picnic, just us and some friends, eating by the scary woods, across from a mass grave and a burning pit filled with corrupted, toxic ashes. I'd need to do something about that before I left Penderton to its own devices.

Kate explained the Ice Age theory and passed the paleontology book around. They took it better than expected.

"Explains the rocks and the spears," Da-Eun said. "I've been wondering why they didn't deploy archers. They probably don't have the technology."

"They might not have needed to develop it," Troy said. "Their throwing skills are above and beyond."

"What about the spearheads?" Hakeem asked. "Bronze?"

"Bone," Kate told him.

We'd managed to retrieve only one spear, the first one the hunters had thrown at her. They had picked up the rest. I hadn't looked at it until today.

"So I've killed a *Smilodon*," Keelan said.

155

Kate took a sip of her iced tea. "Probably."

He'd be insufferable now. We'd never hear the end of this.

Andre turned the book around, showing off an illustration of a huge bear. "Bulldog bear. Fastest bear that ever lived. Five feet at the shoulder on all fours, twelve feet when standing on hind legs. Runs at forty miles per hour and weighs one thousand five hundred pounds."

Jynx whistled. "Fun."

Andre grinned, nodded, and passed the book to Owen. The werebison flipped through it.

"I don't see my rhino."

His rhino.

"Look under *Elasmotherium*," Kate told him.

"Look under *things that kicked my ass*," Troy muttered.

Owen ignored him and flipped the pages. "It says that they were native to Eurasia. Also, mine was a lot larger."

"We only have a fossil record and it's not exactly complete," Troy said. "We can't say that there wasn't a rhino of this size in North America. We can only say that we haven't found any bones that would indicate the presence of such species."

"So the shapeshifters are one species of human," Hakeem said. "The hunters are another?"

"Possibly," Troy said.

"And they fell asleep during the Ice Age and just now woke up? Why now? Why not when the Shift happened?"

"We don't know," Troy told him. "Maybe we will find out when we get to their home base."

I'd been thinking about that home base. I had no idea what it would look like. We didn't know how many fighters we would find there. We didn't know who was in charge and how powerful that person would be. I didn't like not knowing things.

"The two *Smilodons* came for us first," Keelan said. "The rest followed their lead."

"Hierarchy," I said. Most shapeshifters were born and died in one.

He nodded.

"If there is hierarchy, there is an alpha," Andre said.

"Kill the alpha and you take the pack," Da-Eun cracked her knuckles.

"Or break it," Troy said.

"Either way works," Keelan growled. He was giving the wolf more leash today.

They'd settled too comfortably into *our pack vs their pack*. There was more to this problem than simply biting everyone's heads off. It was time to point them in the right direction.

"Both the shapeshifters and the hunters are wearing collars," I said. "The priest-mages are not."

Everyone fell silent.

"We don't know what the collars mean," Kate said. "We do know that they can't be taken off until the wearer dies."

Da-Eun's lip wrinkled in a precursor of a snarl. The humor vanished from Andre's face. Jynx bared her teeth.

"Is that why you didn't kill the hunters, Consort?" Keelan asked.

He knew perfectly well it was. He was throwing her a softball question to keep the rest of the pack in the loop.

"Yes," Kate said. "If Conlan is right, these people have been plucked out of their time and thrust into ours. They may not even understand what's going on."

"When a unit from the Pack loses an alpha, what happens?" I asked.

"Betas step up and become alphas," Da-Eun said.

"When Kate killed the two priest-mages, nobody stepped up," I said. "Given a choice to fight or flee, they fled. It didn't even occur to them that one of them should take charge."

"So what does that mean?" Jynx asked.

"Do everything you must to defend yourself and our Pack," I

said. "If they give you no choice, respond with force. But if you see an opportunity to show mercy to someone with a collar, take it. Don't hesitate."

I let it sink in. Our kind had been used as little more than guard dogs before. Every Pack shapeshifter knew about it. We wouldn't allow ourselves to be used again.

"When the third mage-priest came to deliver their 'proposal' to split Penderton in half, I tried to communicate."

Kate took another sip of her tea. She looked ready to fall over. Taking the territory away from the power in the forest must've been harder than she let on.

"The priest-mage didn't speak until the very end. When it became clear that I wasn't intimidated and my ward protected me from their rocks, someone, some great power, conjured up that dark smoke and attacked the priest-mage with it. That's when they spoke."

"What did they say?" Hakeem asked.

"I couldn't understand the words, but I recognized the tone. They were begging for their life. The priest-mages are valuable. In a fight, they are powerful opponents, skilled in magic and probably trained over a long period of time. And yet, the person in charge killed that priest-mage like they were nothing, on an off chance that I might get infected with the spores. Those are the actions of someone who habitually murders their own people. Someone who'd tortured that rhino. Someone without empathy or compassion."

"That's our target," I said.

The pack fell silent.

"Hypothetically," Keelan asked. "How powerful could that person be?"

"You've seen what I can do," Kate told him.

Another silence.

"We don't know what we will find in the woods," I said. "I

won't lie to you. It will be an ugly fight. Eat and rest. Make the best of it because we will be fighting for our lives tomorrow."

Kate laid down on her blanket, on her back, and closed her eyes. Good. She probably needed a nap. I laid next to her. Naps were always nice.

"Company," Keelan called.

Damn it. I sat back up.

Penderton's town council, with Mayor Gene and Ned in the lead, came out of the city gates and was making a beeline for us. Gene looked upset. Ned looked like he was spoiling for a fight. The rest of the council seemed alternatively anxious, freaked out, and alarmed. Well, at least nobody was carrying any torches or pitchforks.

I was too tired for this crap. Oy. I stood up. Kate started to get up. I laid a hand on her arm. I had this. She nodded and laid back down, half raised on her elbows.

The shapeshifters rose and moved. The pack reoriented itself. I was now in the front, with Keelan directly behind me, and the rest of our people arranged in a ragged crescent on both sides of him.

The town council arrived. For a few moments nobody said anything.

"Hello, everyone," Ned said.

"Howdy," I said.

Kate raised an eyebrow. She must've recognized my tone.

"I'm told that what you did, on the roof, was a claiming," Mayor Gene finally said to Kate. "Have I got that right?"

"You understand correctly," I answered. "My wife is tired. Address all your questions to me."

Kate laid back down and closed her eyes. *Rest. I've got this.*

"What does the claiming mean, exactly?" he asked.

"It means she saturated an area in and around Penderton with her magic."

"Why?" Ruth asked.

"Because it helps her protect it."

Simple explanations were best. No need to disclose that she could drain all of them of their magic, murdering everything within Penderton in a matter of minutes.

An uncomfortable silence fell.

"You invited us here to deal with the threat in the forest," I said. "We're dealing with it."

"Two people died today," another man said.

"Regrettable, but two is much fewer than you would've lost if we weren't here," I said. It sounded harsh, but it was the truth and they needed to hear it.

Another tense silence.

"You said 'claim,'" a man in fatigue overalls asked. "So, what, she owns the town?"

"No. I'm only protecting it," Kate said, still lying back with her eyes closed.

"And we're supposed to just trust you?" an older woman asked.

"Yes," I told her.

"Why?" the woman pressed.

"What choice do you have? Really?" I asked her.

They stared at me.

It was Ned who finally spoke up. "All of you are questioning these folks, but what I haven't heard yet was a 'thank you.' I know you were raised better than that."

"Meaning, what?" Mayor Gene demanded.

Ned stepped closer to Gene. "Meaning, stop acting like an ass, Eugene. You're here demanding answers from Mrs. Lennart when what you should be doing is expressing gratitude for not being dead."

Mayor Gene took a step toward Ned. They were almost chest to chest now. "You don't even live here, Ned. Stay out of this."

Ned drew himself up straighter. "No, I don't believe I will. You and I discussed this prior to me inviting the Lennarts and their people here. I told you what might happen. You agreed that it was a small price to pay. Now you're just playing it up for the crowd."

Mayor Gene crossed his arms over his chest. "That's right. You told me, Edward. I don't recall you asking me for permission to do it."

"Ask you?" Ned's voice was very quiet. "Since when do I need to ask you for a damn thing, Eugene?"

Gene's face turned red. "Since I'm the goddamned mayor of this town! What gives you the right to have a say?"

"Because I'm the largest employer Penderton has. I'm responsible for the welfare of the people I employ, and that's damn near two-thirds of Penderton. You carry the keys, but I feed the town. You know it, I know it, and everyone here knows it. And I will do whatever I have to do to protect my employees and my family. Sanders is right here." Ned pointed to a man with thick, dark eyebrows. "Ask the builder union president if he'd rather be dead or let her claim the town for a week."

"I don't need to ask Sanders a damn thing!"

Sanders raised his fuzzy eyebrows. "I didn't just hear you say that."

"I may not live here," Ned declared, "but my mother and my sister still do, Eugene. And the acreage that's brought these people here is my acreage. I owned it and I gave it to them. What have you done to save this town and the people in it?"

As amusing as it was, this was getting out of hand.

I raised my voice. "We have no plans to take control of the town, demand anything from you, or interfere in your governance."

A small group emerged from the gates and headed for us at a quick trot. Conlan, Darin next to him, followed by Helen, Luiza, and two other shapeshifters. Always happy to see my son, but the timing wasn't great.

The town council turned to look at the new visitors.

Conlan reached us and went down on one knee, looking down at the ground. The rest of the group did the same.

A formal Pack greeting. What was he playing at? I glanced at Kate. She propped herself up on one elbow, her eyes wide. She seemed as surprised as I was.

"Greeting, Beast Lord and Consort," my son announced. "We've arrived as ordered."

The town council people gaped at us.

"Rise," I told him.

The small group rose at the same time, as if they'd choreographed it, with Conlan looking straight ahead. Out of the corner of my eye I caught Keelan close his eyes for a second and nod in approval. Mystery solved.

The group scattered, everyone taking a spot, with Conlan moving to stand next to Keelan and Darin behind him.

This conversation was growing tiresome. "As my wife said," I told them, keeping my voice calm but putting a bit of finality into it, "we don't have any reason to keep Penderton."

"So you say," a man in overalls called out.

"We do," I told him. "When one of us gives their word, we mean it."

Kate nodded. "Once we neutralize the threat, we'll take ownership of the land you've given us."

Technically, it was land Ned had given us but I didn't want to restart that fight.

"That land is in the forest, miles from here," I said. "Keeping Penderton would make the town our territory. We would have to defend your town from threats, and as welcoming as you all are, we're not running down here through the woods every time you have an issue."

The man in overalls opened his mouth, but Mayor Gene waved his hand at him.

"I'm just trying to wrap my head around this claiming thing," he said. "What does this mean in practical terms? For us?"

"Basically, nothing. Your area has been claimed for years already by the forest," I said. "Your daily lives will remain the same."

"I don't remember anything like that happening," Ruth said. "There was a red flash when you did it. Everyone saw it. I don't remember the flash."

"You may not have noticed it if it was done during the flare," Kate said.

"How do we know you didn't just make this up?" another woman asked.

"People, please," Ned said.

Kate sat up fully and addressed the woman. "When the forest bombarded the town that first time, it infected you with spores. That was the brown powder you saw. The spores stayed dormant in your lungs because the magic of the forest suppressed it. When some of you tried to leave the area, the spores sprouted and made you sick. That's how you know this area was claimed."

They took a moment to digest it.

"What happens to the spores now?" Mayor Gene asked.

"Nothing. I killed them all when I claimed the town," Kate told them.

The small crowd stirred.

"You can leave at will now," I clarified. "You won't die outside of Penderton's boundaries, at least not from the spores. Although, I would recommend staying here until we've dealt with whatever is in that forest. You are safest here, where her magic can shield you."

Nothing.

They still weren't getting it. Okay. I laid it out: "Your choices were a giant spore bomb exploding in the center of town or being magically protected for a few days. Consider us the lesser of two evils."

"When are you going into the forest?" the man in the overalls demanded.

"Tomorrow morning if the magic holds," I said.

"Don't take too long," the man said.

Really? I hadn't realized we were on the clock.

Mayor Gene turned and looked at overalls guy.

I let a little gold roll over my irises. The tiniest hint of an alpha stare.

The man took a step back. *That's better.*

Ned heaved a sigh. "Brighton, what are you even doing here? Did your folks let you out of the basement? Bless their hearts, they must think it's Thanksgiving."

"We'll take volunteers," I said. "Does anyone want to go into the woods with us to save your town from the evil?"

Nobody moved.

"Mr. Brighton, is it? Would you like to join us? Make sure we stick to your schedule?" I turned the stare up a bit and held his gaze.

Mr. Brighton swallowed and looked down. "No."

"Glad we have that settled," I said. "If there's nothing else, we have sandwiches to eat and injuries to heal. I'm sure you all have things to do as well. Please don't let us keep you."

Mayor Gene looked at Ned. Ned didn't say anything.

"Thank you," Heather said.

People looked at her.

The interim head of the town guard squared her shoulders. "Thank you for saving the town and looking out for my guys. And for killing the spores. We appreciate it."

I turned off the alpha stare and smiled to put her at ease. "You're welcome," I said.

[10]

Kate

The cold evening breeze swirled around me. I leaned on the rail of our third-floor balcony and watched the last glowing coals of sunset burn down to a cool indigo. The days were growing shorter and shorter. Winter would come soon.

Voices and laughter floated up from the floors below. The shapeshifters were having one last feast before the battle tomorrow. Conlan was in the middle of it, soaking up all the jokes and the friendly snarling.

The forest hadn't attacked again. Where their magic had been shallow and faint, mine was a deep, potent lake. It must've been quite a shock. If they tried something during the night, I'd know instantly.

The door swung open. Curran walked out onto the balcony and leaned on the rail next to me.

"Hey, baby."

"Hey."

We looked at the woods. Tomorrow would suck.

I sent a pulse of magic through the glyphs drawn in the

corners of the balcony floor and our room. A soundproof ward surged up.

"Look at that. I'm trapped," Curran said. Gold sparked in his gray eyes and vanished.

I dragged my mind out of the bedroom and back to the balcony. I'd been putting off this conversation for a long time. We had to have it.

"We need to talk, and I don't want anyone to overhear," I said.

"Never a good opening."

"I claimed a town after I swore up and down that I would never do it again. And when we root out whatever is in the woods and find a good site for our new Keep, I will claim that as well."

He nodded.

"You swore to never lead another pack. When Mahon came to you three years ago asking you to restart the Pack out of Jim's territory, you told him that Hell would freeze over first."

"True. I said that."

"I have my reasons. You have yours. Let's share."

"On three?" he asked.

"One, two..."

"Conlan," we said at the same time.

Right. "I'll go first. You left the Pack because of me. Both because you knew I didn't like it and because my father forced us against a wall. It worked for a while in Atlanta, because we lived in a village inside the city where everyone was friend or family. I thought people would get over my claiming the city and Roland invading, but they didn't. Staying in Atlanta became more and more difficult. Again, that's on me. My presence created that problem."

"That's not the way I look at it but keep going."

"We decided to live in Wilmington, and we ended up in the exact situation that led to the deaths of your parents and sister. We are isolated and vulnerable. If Keelan and the Wilmington pack weren't there, that fight with the Red Horn would've been a lot harder. As you said, Ned was able to walk right up to our door, and Conlan opened it for him. If Ned had been an enemy with power, our son could be dead right now. You built the Pack so when you had a family, it would be protected. I took that away from you and put you back into a place you worked so hard to avoid. I'm sorry. This isn't what I wanted. Making you deal with the possibility that history might repeat itself isn't what I wanted. I never meant to hurt you."

An uncompromising harshness claimed Curran's face. His eyes turned hard. An air of authority and a controlled, tightly coiled menace emanated from him, his presence expanding to take over the entire balcony.

The Beast Lord.

He never stopped being one. He just let him sink below the surface of an easy-going husband and father the way I had hidden my psycho killer inside my soul for the last seven years. Now the Beast Lord was out and in control, not because he was trying to intimidate anyone, but because I had brought up the moment his childhood had died.

"What I'm trying to say is that I was wrong," I said. "I've tried for normal, but normal isn't in the cards. Whether we live a quiet life or a loud one, someone will come for us either for help or for a fight. You and I and everything we can do isn't enough to keep our son safe. We need others."

"We had two obvious choices," Curran said. "To raise our son in a pack, where he would be a prince and treated like one, or to raise him on our own, forging him into an exceptional fighter much faster than would be good for him. I understand why you reject both. The first way is what your father had done to his children. They all died. The second was what Voron did to you and it was cruel."

When put that way, it did seem obvious.

"We tried a third way," Curran said.

"And we did our best. But it's not enough. I realized that when he killed that wereboar."

"How did you find out?"

"Every time he saw the skull, he smiled at it. That's why I asked you to take it down."

"I didn't tell you because you had enough on your plate that night," the Beast Lord said. "I meant to talk about it later."

"I know. I understand why you didn't."

Because talking about it would be shining a light on how close we came to ending up in the exact same situation as his parents.

"Conlan has too much of me and you in him to live a calm life where he doesn't take risks or face threats."

"Have you come to a decision?"

"Yes. Tomorrow I will accept Rimush and Jushur's pledges and I will use them to the best of their ability. I'm going to accelerate Conlan's training. When we develop a stable base, I will bring in vampires and train him to work with them. I've decided to embrace who I am. The violence, the blood magic, all of it. For Conlan's sake but also for my own."

He didn't say anything.

"I want to bring Conlan with us tomorrow. We will be fighting for what might become our permanent home. I want him to be a part of it."

No response.

"If you have any objections to any of this, tell me now. Please."

The Beast Lord squared his broad shoulders, his face grim.

"I didn't leave the Pack because of you. I left because I wanted to. The Pack as it exists now was never my vision. I was a damaged fifteen-year-old kid who shouldn't have been in charge of anything, let alone other people. When I went to fight Andorf, you know what was going through my head? A part of me wanted a challenge, but a bigger part thought, 'Oh, shit. If I don't do this, Mahon might kick me out and I'll be on my own again, alone and starving.'"

Oh no. "He wouldn't have."

"Now that I'm an adult, I know that. Back then, I didn't."

If Mahon ever realized that, it would crush him. He thought of Curran as his son. He was so proud of him, Beast Lord or not.

"I was given a framework and I implemented it. It put me at the top of the pyramid. Women fell over themselves to date me. When I entered a room, people looked at their feet to acknowledge my power. If I wanted something, it was brought to me. But none of that really mattered. It was safe."

But it wasn't. Not really.

"I never got off on adoration or bowing. To me, every shapeshifter who bowed his head was one more person I could've brought with me to fight the loups who killed my family. I had a mental count in my head: how many people would be enough? At first, Mahon and his bears were enough, but soon I needed more. I needed the clans. Then I needed a specialized fighting force, so I made the renders. It still wasn't enough, so I established a security department that would give me advance warnings when a threat was coming, and I put the smartest, the most paranoid, the most meticulous man I knew in charge of it. I hoarded fighters the way some people hoard gold. And I did it without realizing it. I didn't gain this clarity until I left."

I shook my head. "How could you? If you had taken a second to try and get some clarity, Barabas would have put another piece of paper in front of you to sign. I remember days when we didn't have time to breathe. There was always another administrative issue, or conflict to adjudicate, or threat to the Pack we needed to kill. No matter what happened, it came back to us. We had to take care of it, and you had done it by yourself for years."

"It was a contract," Curran said. "The Pack would give their lives to protect me, but I had to protect them in turn. It hit me somewhere in my early twenties—I was responsible for every shapeshifter under my command. Every single one."

"That's too much to carry for one person." I thought so at the time, and I still stood by that.

"It is. And the worst part of it, I knew the Pack was broken. I started seeing cracks even before we met. We were turning more and more xenophobic. Rules and laws adopted on trial basis became set in stone. The rigid structure that was meant to provide stability made it difficult to expand and evolve. We fell into a pattern: the clan alphas bickered in constant competition, and I played the dealmaker and roared when they got out of hand. Every attempt at reform was met with resistance. When they attacked you while I was injured, it was the last straw. They broke the contract. I decided I was no longer bound by it."

"But you stayed."

"I did." He looked at the woods. "By that point I had been the Beast Lord longer than I hadn't. I didn't know how to exit. I didn't know what I would do if we left the Pack."

"You don't like uncertainty."

"I don't. What clued you in?"

"The morning after we spent our first night together, you asked me how long I would need to pack, because all my commitments and responsibilities were now over, and I was coming to the Keep with you. And when I said no, you told me we were done."

"You weren't safe. Your aunt proved my point for me that same day."

"'I want you with me,'" I quoted in my Beast Lord voice. "'It's not a request.'"

"I was dumber and more arrogant back then." He reached for me and pulled me close to him, my back to his chest, and wrapped his arms around me. "I'm older and wiser now. I've learned how people interact outside of the Pack. How relationships work. I still want you with me."

And he would have all of me. He was my world.

He hugged me tighter. "I love you the way you are. If you choose to change, I will love you still."

The cold, hard knot inside my chest melted.

"You didn't make me leave the Pack," he said. "You didn't make me move to Wilmington. I was the one who suggested it in the first place."

"If you want to build a new Pack, I will help you," I promised.

He squeezed me tighter to him. "I thought that to fix the Pack, I'd have to turn it over to someone else. I couldn't do it because there was too much history. People expected me to act a certain way because I had done it for so long, and they wouldn't have accepted a radical change. I thought Jim would make the reforms, and he has. Just not the kinds of reforms I would've expected. But it's his Pack now and I'm good with that."

I tried to turn to look at him, but he was holding me too tight, and pushing against those arms was like trying to move a building.

"I will start over. But I want more than just another Pack."

"What do you want?" I asked.

He kissed my temple. "A new kind of place. Where we can be ourselves. Where our kid won't be raised as a prince. He will never be a boy king, because a boy king has no need to grow up. We will give him a kind of place where he earns everything he achieves, and he won't have to give up his human friends to do it."

He kissed me again. "Stay with me, Kate."

"I love you. Where would I go?"

His hold relaxed. I turned in his arms.

"When I finished that rhino and saw you," he said, "you were walking to me. There were two dead bodies behind you. You were splattered with blood. Your sword was in your hand. You were smiling, Kate."

"You told me."

"I would fight the whole world for that smile."

My heart made a funny little jump in my chest.

"You can't say things like that."

"Yes, I can."

Oh my God. He was looking at me like I was the center of his universe.

"Because you're the Beast Lord?"

"Because I'm your husband."

He pulled me closer, and his mouth closed on mine. It was the kind of kiss that seared itself in your memory. It was possessive and hungry, infused with love and lust, a pledge and a declaration in one. It would chase you through the years, and decades later it would remind you, *Do you remember how he kissed you? Do you remember what it felt like?*

My head was spinning. Every sense had jumped into overdrive. I tasted him, I smelled him, I felt the warmth of his skin and the hard muscles of his body tensing under my fingers.

The kiss ended, and I would have staggered if he weren't holding me.

He picked me up and carried me into the bedroom, slapping the balcony door shut behind him.

I wound my arms around him and kissed him again, tracing his mouth with mine. His lips pressed against mine, deceptively light.

"Lock the other door," I whispered into his ear.

"Locked it when I came up." His voice was a deep rumble.

He sat on the bed, with me in his lap.

Curran's eyes were a molten gold. We'd been together for over a decade and yet they glowed with an intense searing need.

I slid my hand along his chest, under his T-shirt, feeling the strength in the hard muscle. Strong and warm... He cupped my cheek with his hand, lifting my head at just the right angle and kissed me again, slowly, deeply.

His hands slid under my clothes, stroking my back, pulling me closer to him, and I arched against his touch. Making love with him was more than sex. It was a connection, and I

172

craved him like a woman dying of thirst craved a drop of water.

He pulled my clothes off and let them fall on the floor. The cold air kissed my skin. I shivered.

"Cold?"

He said it like it was a challenge.

"Yes."

He stripped. "Let me help."

Yes. I need help. So badly.

He pushed me onto the bed, trapping me under him. The heat of his big, powerful body warmed me, his chest almost searing my nipples. His hands slid along my body, cupping my breasts, stroking, teasing, touching. His thumb brushed against my nipple, and the glide of it sent little shocks through my body. His thick, hard length pressed against me.

He nipped my neck, just below the ear. "Still cold?"

I wasn't. I was burning up, and he was the only cure. "Yes..."

He smiled. His body slid down. His hands pushed my legs apart. His head dipped.

Oh my God.

The wet heat of his tongue shrank the world to the insistent pressure between my legs. It built with each stroke, until it was so powerful, it was almost too much.

His fingers dipped into me, into the slick heat. He licked me again, and the pressure inside me broke into ecstasy. I floated in it, reveling in the pleasure and somehow shocked it felt that good.

"Need a minute?" he asked, smug satisfaction in his voice.

I pushed him to the side and onto his back. He let me, and I took him into my mouth, sliding my tongue over his blunt head.

He groaned, and the sound of him was so male and irresistibly erotic. I wanted to hear it again.

I sucked.

His hand slid into my hair.

Growl again for me.

I moved, licking, sucking, turning, teasing, pumping...

He snarled, grabbed me, and slammed me onto the bed, caging me with his body. His eyes were two burning coals. He pushed my legs apart and thrust into me.

Yes. That's what I want. That, right there.

He built to a furious rhythm, and I matched him, cherishing every thrust. Another climax washed over me, dissolving into a sea of bliss. I screamed my way through it.

His body tensed, his muscles shaking. He came with a growl. I opened my eyes. He kissed me.

I loved him so much. My Curran. In the whole world, there was only one of him. I would do anything for him.

Later, as I lay wrapped in his arms, all my worries seemed far away. I felt strong and happy. I didn't care what tomorrow would bring. Tonight it was just me and him, and nothing else mattered.

[11]

I found Conlan on the wall. He perched on the parapet as far to the west as he could get and still keep the house in view, a small, compact shape, easy to miss in the pre-dawn light. He was looking at the woods, where a green flag marked the direction of our march.

Inside the wall, on the street in front of the house, the shapeshifters were going through the last equipment checks before we set out. Each one carried a small packet of panacea, the complex herbal remedy that helped prevent loupism; knives or other weapons they'd been trained with; a canteen of safe drinking water; and packs of high-calorie trail mix, nuts, jerky, cheese, and chocolate.

Heather's archers were going through a similar check. Pender-ton's town guard had shown up this morning and informed us that they would be assisting. We got eight archers, and Curran had had to modify our strategy slightly to account for the surprise auxiliary. We were fielding fourteen shapeshifters, including Darin, my husband, and my son, and three not-shapeshifters—me, Rimush, and Jushur. Someone would need to protect the archers, and that someone couldn't be me because I was taking point.

According to the old Google Maps, the site of the former hill lay about 19.7 miles away from Burgaw. The top walking speed of a human hiker was about three miles per hour. Expecting people to walk twenty miles straight into a battle was unrealistic. Everyone would be exhausted. Also, we would likely get hit along the way. If this was a hike through dense woods, we'd have to budget two to three days for it, but our situation was different.

We wouldn't be cutting through the forest as the crow flies. We would be taking the old NC-53, heading west, and then we would turn onto US-421 North. Both roads were too overgrown and too damaged by the forest to be accessible by vehicle, but they still provided a relatively clear route for human hikers. There were other options, like Piney Woods Road or State Road 1332, but both of those were narrower and therefore in worse shape. Our route added another mile to our trek; however, walking would be a lot easier. Shapeshifters would have no problem, and Heather assured me that all of her people could handle the hike.

We weren't the first group to try entering the woods via the old roads. Isaac had taken 421 too, at some point. But all those groups had had to wade through the territory claimed by the forest, and the farther in they went, the deeper the magic ran. Sooner or later, the power behind it managed to push them off the roads into the wilderness.

We wouldn't have that problem.

The plan was simple. Go in until noon, less if we had to fight our way through. Stop. Make camp. Rest. Keep going. If the night caught us before we got there, we would camp again. Shapeshifters had an advantage in the dark, but I needed daylight. Also, I would be tired as hell by the end of this march, and a lot of that final fight was riding on me.

I put my hand on Conlan's shoulder. Every muscle on his back was tight. He was like a kitten watching a butterfly dancing in the wind.

He glanced at me. "The archers will slow us down. And we have to protect them. We should leave them here."

"Fighting a war involves more than just calculating the odds. I've claimed Penderton, but I told them that I would never interfere in their governance. The decision to send the archers came from the town council. They are volunteers, and they come as allies rather than subordinates."

"It's not safe for them."

"Wars are not safe for anyone. They're brave. We must respect that. How would you feel if we left you behind?"

He looked back at the forest. "You're my parents. I can't just wait here... I want to help."

"So do they."

"But they will make things harder for us."

A little of my father coming through. I needed to deal with that here and now.

"For five years the forest has terrorized them. It killed people in the town square. It demanded human sacrifice. Yesterday, it killed two of their own right in front of them. A boy about Darin's age who was guarding the tower in front of our house. A manticore grabbed him off the wall and broke his neck. How do you think they feel?"

He seemed to consider it. "They are angry."

"People are ruled by their emotions, Conlan, and anger is one of the most powerful emotions we can experience. It can fester if you don't vent it. Always take that into account."

"Are you angry?" he asked.

"Very."

"Because of the boy who died?"

"Yes. And because of other things the power in the forest has done. It has no regard for the value of life, human or animal. Your father and I will end this today."

"Is Dad angry too?"

"Yes."

"He never gets angry."

Oh, you have no idea.

Conlan looked back at the woods. Logic told me that he was only eight, but it didn't seem that way. I was his mother. I gave birth to him, I have raised him, and yet there was something about my son that remained beyond my understanding. Sometimes I wanted to open up his head and see what was going on in there. But then all parents probably felt that way at times.

"Do you feel the magic of the claiming?"

He nodded. "It feels welcoming. It feels like I'm home. Like safety."

"Good."

Erra had told me that it was supposed to feel like that. The Shar was an ugly beast, but it affected the members of my family in different ways, and children experienced it the least. For them, being in their parent's territory brought feelings of safety and content. They knew they were protected.

It would be another decade or so before Conlan might want his own territory. Or he might never claim one. Erra hadn't until she'd settled at her current base in California, and even then, she'd only claimed the immediate area around it.

When Erra and Julie had left Atlanta, my aunt had gone as far west as she could while staying on the same continent. She was giving me a lot of room. My father and she thought not in years but in centuries. They expected me to claim territory and grow it. Fortunately for everyone, I was a champion when it came to failing parental expectations.

"Come with me," I told Conlan.

He followed me along the top of the wall toward the gates. Two men waited by the stairs leading up to the wall, Jushur and Rimush, wearing identical green and gray garments, a kind of tactical uniform on the crossroads of modern military and ancient assassin. They each carried two curved swords, one on each hip, and bows on their backs.

178

They looked up at me. I nodded, and the father and son came up the stairs.

I pointed to a spot slightly behind me and to my left. "Stand here."

Conlan moved to it.

I raised my hands, dropped the magical cloak that obscured my power, and let the flow of magic fill me. It surged through me, through every cell, through bone, muscle, and skin, like a light beam entering a prism, and then it poured out of me in a golden light. I had become a glowing beacon.

On the street everything stopped. People stared at me, some in awe, others in alarm. Luther, my friend at Biohazard, had put it best. Magic was wild and unpredictable, and humans, who always had trouble with chaos, searched for ways to understand and codify it. They tricked themselves into thinking that some things were impossible because it made them feel safe. Without my cloak, I was that impossible thing. The very idea that a person with that much magic could exist shattered the established illusion of safety. Some found it exhilarating, others feared it, and some sought its protection through service. I was a great and scary beast, and it was warm and safe under my wings.

Jushur took a knee.

"Jushur, son of Kizzura, the first of the Eyes and Ears, the Fourth Blade of Shinar, declare your intent."

Jushur spoke, pronouncing each word with deliberate exactness, as if carving it into stone.

"I swear upon my honor and my soul to pledge my life to you, my queen. I swear to protect and honor you in victory and in defeat, in times of famine and in times of plenty, and even if the entire world turns its hand against you, I will serve as your shield. I shall place your life above my own and speak nothing but the truth to you. My blade, my mind, and my soul are yours."

He'd modified the oath. The bit about not lying was ad-libbed.

"Do you swear that you are free to make this oath? That no other has a claim on your loyalty?"

"I do."

"I accept your oath. I shall protect and honor you in victory and in defeat, in times of famine and in times of plenty. I will never forsake you for my own gain. I will care for you until the moment you pass from this world. I will defend you as I defend my own life, and your deeds in the service of our common cause shall be recorded and made known so our descendants may honor and celebrate your life. I shall treat you not as my servant but as my valued friend, who stands at my side. My oath to you shall be true until the end of my days."

Jushur's eyebrows rose. I also went with a nonstandard oath because if I accepted someone's allegiance, I'd do it on my own terms. There would be no queen and servants. There would be a brotherhood of equals, or as close to equals as they would allow themselves to be.

"Do you accept my pledge, Jushur, son of Kizzura?"

"I do," Jushur answered. "With all my heart."

I reached out. The golden flood of magic bathed Jushur. The oath was symbolically sealed.

He continued to kneel.

"You don't need my permission to rise," I murmured.

"This might take some getting used to," he murmured back. He got up and stepped back.

"Rimush, son of Jushur, the ninth of the Eyes and Ears, the Seventh Blade of Shinar, declare your intent."

Rimush swore the same oath. I accepted it and pulled my magical protection back on. The show was over.

"Your father would not approve," Jushur told me.

"He never does." I turned to Conlan. "Jushur and Rimush are our people. If something happens to your father and me during this battle, it's your responsibility to safely get them out of danger. Jushur is an older man, and he might need your help."

Jushur and Rimush bowed their heads.

Conlan blinked and bowed back.

"Do you understand?" I asked.

"Yes, ma'am."

"Good."

Uncertainty flared in Conlan's eyes. Up until now he hadn't considered the possibility that his father and I might not make it. It was a lot for an eight-year-old.

"Where would I go?"

"You would go to your sister and your grandmother. Jushur knows the way."

"What about Darin?" he asked.

Darin had volunteered to join our party, and Curran had let him. His merman side gave Darin faster reflexes and enhanced regeneration, and like his father and uncle, he was really good with a bow. But more importantly, Darin wanted desperately to fit in, and he had decided he belonged with us and the Wilmington Pack. Curran and I were fighting for the lives of Penderton and our future home; Keelan, Da-Eun, and the other shapeshifters were fighting for the future of the new Pack; and Darin was fighting for himself.

"If there is a chance to save Darin, I'll make sure he is safe," Rimush said.

On the street, in front of the gates, the shapeshifters and archers formed up behind Curran. He looked up at me. Our gazes met. It was time.

"Your father is waiting." I nodded in Curran's direction.

Conlan took off down the stairs.

Jushur and I'd had a conversation this morning. He and Rimush carried Roland's water necklaces. When broken, the necklaces would teleport them and whomever they were touching to the original source of the water. Teleportation was risky and dangerous. It was the last of last resorts, but if Curran and I both died, they would get Conlan out of there. They would grab Darin too, if they could get to him, and take the boys to California. Erra and Julie would take it from there.

Of course, for that to happen, the forest would have to kill me and Curran first. Conlan had guessed correctly. We were both angry.

"Sharratum," Jushur said softly.

Getting him to call me Kate in private was harder than convincing my father that democracy was a valid form of government.

"It's not too late to change the plan," the older man said. "Nobody, in my memory, has ever attempted what you are trying to do. The magic drain may be beyond what even your body can endure."

"There are some things that I won't tolerate," I told him. "I won't lose another civilian to the forest. They are done killing these people. It ends today."

He bowed his head.

I followed Conlan down the stairs and took my place next to Curran at the head of our little formation. We'd arranged our forces into a column. Curran and I were in the lead. Owen was directly behind us, carrying the big tent we borrowed from Penderton and two gallons of undead blood, which I would need for my blood armor. Behind Owen were Conlan, Darin, and Jushur, followed by Heather and her archers, two per row.

The shapeshifters formed a loose protective envelope around the column, starting with Keelan behind Curran to his left, and Rimush, who technically wasn't a shapeshifter, behind me and on my right. The rest of the Wilmington Pack formed up behind those two, on the flanks, keeping the archers and the kids between them. Da-Eun, Jynx, and Andre brought up the rear. With those three, nothing would surprise us from behind.

Ned came up to us, with Mayor Gene trailing him. They'd been chatting off to the side, and judging by their body language, neither man felt uneasy. They must've patched things up.

"This is it then," Ned said.

"Yes," Curran said.

"I won't say goodbye," Ned said. "I will say, see you soon."

"See you soon, Ned," I told him.

"Good luck!" Mayor Gene told us. He looked past the shapeshifters to the archers. "Penderton is proud of you! All of us are proud of you! Don't take stupid chances. Come back in one piece."

The gates swung open, and we started across the killing field toward the green flag. All the things that had to be said had been said.

We crossed the grass to the flag. The sun hadn't broken above the horizon yet, although the sunrise wasn't far off, and in the early light, the flag looked more gray than green. Gray was the Pack color. I decided to take it as a good omen.

The beginning of NC-53 stretched in front of us, the asphalt crumbled at the edges and crowded by trees, but still solid.

I stepped forward and gathered my magic. It strummed inside me, like a heartbeat reverberating through my entire body. I plunged Sarrat into the ground.

A beam of magic shot out of me, straight as an arrow, dashing along NC-53, claiming a strip of land fifty feet wide. I pushed it for three miles, to where NC-53 made a slight turn and cut it short. I'd carved a path through the forest's territory. A safe zone. I would need to do this again when we reached its end.

I slid my sword into the sheath on my back. Curran reached out, took my hand, and squeezed. I squeezed back.

He raised his voice. "Walk behind me and Kate and stay in formation. No straggling, no running off. You are in a fifty-foot-wide safe zone. Do not leave it."

A chorus of "Yes, Alpha" answered him.

Curran grinned, his eyes sparking with feral gold light. "Time to hunt!"

Keelan stopped. Curran stopped too, half a second later. The entire column halted in the middle of the battered, crumbling road and stared at the woods beyond the pavement.

I listened.

Around us the forest was full of life. Leaves and pine needles shivered in the breeze, stretching over the road to grab every bit of light. Squirrels chased each other through the branches. A feral cat trailed them, sneaking by the tree roots. A faint whiff of old skunk musk lingered, emanating from somewhere to our left. Birds sang and chirped in the canopy.

No visible threat. No strange noises.

I glanced at Keelan. *What?*

He inhaled, sucking the air into his nostrils, then turned and leaned, looking down the length of the column.

"Come out slowly," Curran said.

A shape emerged from the brush on our left, just behind the rear guard, their fatigues perfectly blending with the forest.

Da-Eun swore.

The person stepped into the light filtering through the gap in the branches and onto the old road.

Isaac. I should have known.

"The Order's pathfinder," I murmured.

We'd been walking for over two hours. About thirty minutes ago, we'd passed the remains of an old gas station swallowed up by magically boosted trees and made the turn onto US-421 North. I'd performed the claiming for the third time, taking over a chunk of that road. By now we were probably ten miles in.

Isaac had managed to sneak up on a pack of shapeshifters, and he had even evaded Keelan's nose, which put most werewolves to shame. Had he followed us all the way from Penderton? No, probably not. If I were him, I would've waited for us at that gas station and then tagged along behind the column, keeping downwind.

"Don't you think you'd do more good in the front?" Curran asked.

Isaac shrugged. "Not my party. I'm just tagging along. If you want me on point, though, I can do that."

Curran waved him forward. The pathfinder nodded and moved through the column, completely silent. He took point and we kept moving.

That third claiming took a bit out of me. My body ached, fatigue adding a phantom weight to my legs.

The forest should have attacked us by this point, but so far Isaac was the only human we'd seen. Although, there was a hawk hanging above us. Hawks were territorial, and their range was about two square miles. This one had been with us since we left Penderton. I had noticed it when we set out and then again after the second claiming, and Curran and I had been watching it since.

He saw me looking.

"They're letting us in," I said. "We are vulnerable on the road, but they haven't made a move."

He nodded. "You took away their trump card by creating a safe zone for us. The priest-mages are powerful, but they take a while to cast their spells. Their spear-throwers would be at a disadvantage in the forest. Even if they managed to ambush us, which isn't likely, they might get one volley off before we went in and took them apart. If they want to attack us on the way, they'd have to use their shapeshifters, and they must not have enough of them to overwhelm us with numbers. They attacked four shapeshifters and a human with a pack of seven and they lost. They would want a significant numerical advantage."

"You think they have a spot picked out ahead? Somewhere with open ground?"

"I think they will let us walk all the way to their base. They can deploy the hunters and priest-mages in addition to the shapeshifters they have left. They're counting on having more people than us and the home field advantage. All the better if we're worn out by the time we reach them."

"So it's a last stand?"

"Looks that way. They are marshaling all their forces in one spot rather than risking losing them piecemeal by attacking us along the way." Curran grinned. "Also, I think your claiming really freaked them out."

He had a point. Whoever was in charge of the forest must have been accustomed to their claiming being the final word. Their ultimate move. Chances were that nobody had ever challenged them after that. Claiming gave you control and advance warning. It made you feel safe. It allowed you to kill your own people with fucked-up smoke.

When I took Penderton away from them, it must have been a shock. And my claiming was much stronger and more uniform. It would be like having the best knife in the world and realizing your opponent held a sword.

And now they were sitting in their base and feeling me carve my way straight through their territory. One narrow strip of forest at a time. And they could do nothing about it. They had to watch and wait, helpless.

"I think we should freak them out a bit more," I said.

Curran smiled and it wasn't pretty. "Darin, drop that hawk."

The merman raised his bow and fired in one smooth motion, taking no time to aim. The hawk fell from the sky and landed on the road, an arrow in its chest. Coils of black smoke curled up from it, and the hawk melted into nothing.

Keelan chuckled.

We kept moving.

I WAS RESTING. NOT REALLY SLEEPING. JUST LINGERING ON THE edge of consciousness, with my eyes closed and my body still. My legs hummed, my back hurt, and my chest felt tight. Four claimings in a row was my limit. I would need to practice more. It wasn't the distance—I could've claimed a ten-mile chunk with no problems. It was the sequence of it. Every claiming took a big bite out of my magic reserve.

Unfortunately, the roads weren't straight. There were places where they veered a little from the safe zone, which slowed us down. Given a straight shot to the hill, I would've tried to claim it all in one go.

Around me, our small party had gone to ground. There was a trick I'd learned early in childhood when my adopted father would drive me into the wilderness, drop me off with a knife and a small canteen of clean water, and expect me to make my way back on my own. The best and fastest way to recover was to lay completely flat. Heather's archers were forest people. They'd stripped off their gear, lain down on the road, and gone to sleep.

The shapeshifters had sprawled out as well, but unlike me and the archers, they were still fresh as daisies and most of them were munching on their supplies and talking.

"Should he be climbing that?" Curran asked next to me.

I opened my eyes halfway. Our son was scrambling up a big pine like an overgrown squirrel.

"It's in my territory. I claimed a circle three hundred yards in diameter." I yawned. "He can feel the magic. He knows where the boundaries are."

"You should sleep," Curran told me. "I'll keep watch."

"One hour," I told him.

"One hour," he agreed.

Curran's warm hand touched my arm. "Time to get up, baby."

"It hasn't been an hour."

"No, it's been two."

My eyes snapped open. I sat up and groaned. There was no fucking way.

I looked up at the sky. Definitely past noon. Damn it.

Curran studied me, his gray eyes concerned. "Do you need more time?"

Yes. About twelve more hours. A solid meal and a soft bed would be lovely as well. But we had another four miles to go, and the sun was rolling across the sky.

"I'm good."

"We can wait another hour."

"No need."

He nodded and put a small rectangle wrapped in foil on my lap. "And before you ask, I gave one to Conlan already."

I raised my eyebrows.

Curran walked away and crouched by the shapeshifters sitting in a loose circle in the middle of the road.

I unwrapped the foil. Chocolate.

Best husband ever.

"We're almost there," Curran said. "There will be a fight. There will be other shapeshifters. For those of you who missed the first fight, they are different. You won't be facing gray wolves. You will be fighting dire wolves, prehistoric cats, and possibly giant bears. In their warrior form, they're larger, stronger, and faster than most of us."

I took a bite. Almonds. Oh my God.

"One on one, in a contest of brute strength, we lose." Curran's voice was reassuring and steady. "But they fight on instinct, like animals. They're brawlers. We are trained killers. They will mark each of us for individual duels. We will not oblige them. Stay calm. Think. Remember your training. Look out for each other."

"I know you're trained," Keelan said. "Because I trained you. Don't embarrass me by getting killed by amateurs."

A light laughter rippled through the circle.

Keelan flashed his teeth in a happy grin. "You are a unit.

They've never encountered shapeshifters like us. Organized warfare. It worked for the Romans, it will work for us."

"Pick a battle buddy," Curran said. "Stay close to them. Watch out for them, watch out for the others. Take them two on one when you can. If you see someone in trouble, jump in. Remember, the people we're fighting may not have a choice in this fight. Kill if you have to, disable if you can."

Isaac walked over and crouched near me. "I want to show you something."

I popped the last of my chocolate into my mouth and got up.

He led me off the road into the brush. Ten yards into it I stopped.

The forest here was different. Gone were the mast-straight pines flooded with sunshine. These were much darker woods. Denser, with huge aspens and massive birches vying for space with balsam firs and cedars. Hemlocks spread their green branches. Honeysuckle, yew, and gooseberry bushes crowded into the rare patches of light. The air smelled different, clean, without a trace of salt or ocean, and spiced with a hint of Christmas conifers.

Wow.

"This way," Isaac said.

I followed him deeper in. We rounded a huge balsam fir. Ahead the forest parted, as if someone had cut a perfect circle out of the green growth. In the middle of it, a jagged stone thrust up and out of the forest floor, like the rib of a mountain. On top of the stone lay a body in tactical camo.

Isaac took another step forward, and I put my arm out in front of him. We had reached the end of the safe zone.

The body lay bathed in sunlight, perfectly preserved. I could see every detail: the blond hair, the face of a man in his thirties with two-day stubble on his chin, the eyes opened wide, gazing at the sky. He didn't look dead. He looked like a man who had decided to take a break after a long trek through the woods, except for the sword thrust into his chest, the Order's mark on its pommel.

No animals had touched him. No insects swarmed above him. The forest had formed a perfect ring to avoid him. Just the rock, the man, and the red symbols scratched into the stone and traced with blood.

"Jeremiah?" I asked.

"You remembered."

"Of course I did. Knight-Defender Jeremiah Gardner. The first man taken out of your team."

"When this is over..."

"I'll find a way to get him off that rock, Isaac."

The knight-pathfinder nodded and looked back at the body. "Not too much longer," he promised. "I'll come back for you."

[12]

The magic of the forest slithered in twisting currents, boiling at the borders of my safe zone. Thick like syrup, deep enough to drown in. We were at the center of the forest's power. It gnawed on the edges of my narrow claiming, trying to sink its teeth in and failing. The trees had grown thick and tall, their branches reaching for each other over the road, blocking out the sun above our heads. We were moving through a green tunnel.

Conlan slipped through the column, edging dangerously close to the boundary, lingered there for a few moments, and wove his way to my side.

"Mom." His voice was barely above a whisper.

"Yes?"

He shifted into the language of Shinar seamlessly. *"You're stronger than it, right?"*

"We will soon find out."

He looked at me wide-eyed. That wasn't the answer he was looking for.

"Raw power is important, but there are times when training matters more. And you, although you are only eight, are better trained than whoever claimed this land."

He looked at the woods.

"Remember what your father said about the other shapeshifters?"

He nodded.

"It's just like that. Look at it, Conlan. Yes, that's a lot of magic, but feel how haphazard and uneven it is. Now feel the power of my claim. When we painted our house, we didn't hurl paint cans at the walls. We dipped a roller and covered it evenly."

He looked at the woods again, and then at the road in front of us. His shoulders straightened. He raised his head.

"This is why we train," I told him in English. "With magic, especially, it's about control. A blood spike the size of a needle, thrown at the right moment, can kill the enemy before they ever get a chance to hurl a giant boulder at us."

He smiled and fell back into his place by Jushur.

This was a hell of a lot of magic though. At first, carving off a chunk of forest territory was relatively easy. This last time it was like trying to push a giant rock across a field through the mud. When I was done, my whole body was drenched in sweat.

Whatever awaited us at the end of this road, it wouldn't just roll over. It hadn't run away, though a part of me had hoped. No, it was biding its time, marshaling its power, condensing its magic as it drew it in to defend itself.

My sword hand itched. I was tired of walking and waiting.

Not long now. I could see the light directly ahead of us, where the forest ended, and the road would run into the clear ground. We were drawing closer with every step.

Isaac suddenly stopped, poised on his toes. I looked past him at the nearly blinding glow of daylight.

A giant deer stood in the light, just beyond my safe zone. Bigger than a moose, seven feet tall at the shoulder, it stared at us without fear. Enormous antlers crowned its head, two massive blades of bone with points the size of swords, protruding almost five feet out. Clumps of grass dripped from the horns, as if the creature had dug them into the turf.

It was majestic and beautiful, as if the forest had sent a herald to greet us.

"An Irish elk," Keelan whispered.

More like the stag-moose, *Cervalces scotti*, which was native to North America according to Conlan's book, but I didn't want to ruin Keelan's moment.

"Damn, that's a lot of meat," Jynx breathed behind us.

And the bouda had done it for me.

Keelan glared at her. "Shut it."

The stag looked at us for another long moment, then strode off to the side, into the light.

"Alright, people," Keelan called out. "It's time to do what we walked all this way for."

"Fight, survive, go home," Curran growled.

"Yes, Alpha."

A change came over the shapeshifters, as if everyone had gotten shots of espresso directly into their veins. Arms stretched. Eyes shone. Gear was shifted, ready to be shed in an instant. Keelan pulled his claymore out and swung it like it was a toothpick.

"Ready," Heather called out behind me.

I glanced over my shoulder. The archers stopped and strung their bows.

I looked at Owen. "I'm going to need that blood."

The werebison shrugged off the tent roll and pulled the big Camelback off his shoulders. "Where do you want it?"

I detached my blood canteen from my belt, took off Sarrat's sheath, and pulled my sweatshirt off. "Dump it right here."

He frowned. "Just dump it out on the ground?"

"Yep."

He unzipped the backpack, unscrewed the cap, and turned it upside down. The undead blood splashed out onto the pavement. I dumped the contents of my canteen into it.

Normal human blood would have coagulated without refrigeration after a full day of riding in my canteen. The magic in my blood had kept it fresh longer and, as it collided with the puddle of vampire blood, my power shot through it like fire along a detonation cord. The two liquids fused into one pliable, obedient mass. It streamed to me, guided by my will, climbing up my feet, over my legs, over my waist and chest and arms to coat my entire body up to my chin. It felt warm against my skin, the arcane power within it shimmering and ready.

One final push, and it snapped into shape. Blood armor sheathed me, flexible, thin like a second skin, and yet impenetrable to claws and normal swords.

Everyone had stopped what they were doing and was staring at me.

"Okay, I'm dressed," I announced. "Let's get this party started!"

Curran grinned.

"You heard the Consort," Keelan growled. "Fall in. We don't have all day."

Everyone decided to simultaneously look somewhere else. I swiped Sarrat off the ground, poured my leftover blood onto the blade, and hardened it to a razor-sharp edge. It wouldn't last long once I started using it, but while it lasted, my sword would cut through bone like butter.

I walked over to Conlan and hugged him.

"Mom," he said quietly. "I'm not a baby."

"You will always be my baby. Deal with it. When the fight starts, stay with the archers. They're vulnerable to melee and they'll need your protection."

"Yes, ma'am."

"Listen to your mother," Curran said.

"Yes, Alpha."

We started toward the light again.

"Can you do that?" Darin murmured to Conlan.

"Not yet," my son said.

The gap in the trees grew closer and closer. A hundred yards, fifty, twenty-five.

The safe zone ended.

Curran looked at me. I shook my head. There would be no more claiming. The forest's magic was too deep, and I was too tired. We'd have to solve this problem the old-fashioned way. A claiming broke when its creator died.

Curran squared his shoulders. He seemed larger somehow, looming, his face predatory and fierce, almost cruel. He was a lion who had sighted a territory he wanted, and he was ready to take it.

We hugged the greenery and carefully moved to the edge of the forest.

A grassy plain stretched in front of us, still green and vibrant despite it being fall. In the middle of the plain, a low hill curved, and on top of that hill a fortress rose, ancient and massive, dominating everything around it. We were looking at the outer wall, and it was all round towers, almost a hundred feet high, packed nearly side by side, with very little actual wall in between.

Built with clay bricks and partially sheathed in slabs of granite, the towers went on and on, in two straight lines that met at a right angle almost directly in front of us. The two sides we could see were each over a mile long. If this fort was square, the entire town of Penderton would fit inside that wall.

It didn't look like any architectural style I knew. I had never seen anything like it.

Curran closed his mouth with a click.

"Where did they get the granite? The nearest quarry is hundreds of miles inland."

"I don't care. I want it," Curran growled.

"It's a fine castle, my lord," Keelan called out. "Let's liberate it and all the people in collars with it."

We had a lot of open ground to cover between the woods and the walls. The archers especially would be vulnerable. Their effec-

195

tive range was about two hundred yards. If the evil in the fortress opened this fight with shapeshifters, there would be no point in shooting them. The arrows wouldn't do enough damage, and the shapeshifter charge was too fast. The archers would be better used against the hunters. For that, we'd need to walk them closer to the walls.

Something moved at the top of the corner tower. People came into view. Two dozen hunters armed with javelins, six priest-mages, and in the middle, a tall woman in white.

Rimush passed me a pair of binoculars.

She looked like one of the hunters. The same slender build with an odd shoulder line and limbs that looked too long. But unlike the hunters, she hadn't smeared any clay on her hair. Her long locks streamed in the wind, and they weren't black, brown, or blond. Her hair was a light, ethereal blue. The exact same shade that tinted all that clay on her followers' hair and faces. She had marked them as hers.

Her face was unnaturally white, probably tinted with powder or some kind of paint that was a lot smoother than the blue clay. Bloodred pigment stained her eyelids and the space under her eyes. Her whole face looked like a skull with two bloody holes where the orbits should be. The priest-mages hovered around her, anxious.

Hello, evil in the forest. I've come to borrow a cup of sugar and to chat about Penderton. Is it a bad time?

The woman said something, baring her teeth. They were sharp and triangular like those of a shark. The skin on her exposed arms was an odd, faded ochre and patterned lightly as if someone had painted a ghostly brindle over it with bluish-green pigment. Teeth, hair, skin...

Turn your head, turn your head...

She snapped at one of the priest-mages, presenting me with a view of her ear. Pointed. Got you.

"Fae," I said.

"What?" Curran said.

"She isn't human. She's fae."

"Fae?" Keelan asked. "Here?"

"Fae legends aren't confined to Ireland. They pop up in folklore all through Europe and Asia in various forms. The leading theory is that modern humans and fae had a common ancestor but diverged in prehistory. We had interbred at some point after that divergence, which is why human parents sometimes give birth to a fae child. Magic activates the dormant genes. Our Pale Skull Queen is a prehistoric fae."

And Dad would just love that little tidbit. When he was building the Order of Sahanu, his assassins, he'd specifically looked for fae children because of their significant magic reserve. *Father, did you know fae are capable of claiming?* His head would explode.

I lowered the binoculars and turned to look at our crew.

"That explains a lot of things," Curran said. "Like the absence of iron. Okay, the Pale Queen on that tower is our primary target. Their society is rigidly structured. She's on top, then the priest-mages, then the hunters and shapeshifters on the bottom."

"If you don't have magic, you're not shit," Keelan said.

"Yes," Curran confirmed. "She's going to assess us by what she knows. She's seen Kate do magic and claim the land, so she will view her as a queen and us as her disposable underlings."

"We're going to use it to our advantage," I said. "Once the fight starts, she will key in on me because she thinks I'm the biggest threat."

"She'll sit in her tower and field her shapeshifters," Curran said. "Judging by her previous actions, she thinks of her subordinates as subhuman. She'll hurl them at us because she doesn't care if they survive. When that happens, we're going to pull the fight to the left to give Kate room to work. We need to get to those walls with minimal casualties."

I nodded. "I'll be throwing magic around so don't be in front of me. Heather, your people, Conlan, Darin, and Jushur will need to hang back and to the right. Don't be directly behind me but stay close enough until you get in range that I can close the distance and protect you if there are surprises. Be careful. This is her territory, and we don't know what she's capable of. She could collapse the ground under you or blow up her walls to crush you."

"Questions?" Curran asked.

There were no questions.

"I need a volunteer for my left," I said.

Owen stepped forward, brandishing a huge hammer. Where the hell had he pulled that out from?

"Stay. Close. To. Her," Curran ordered, enunciating each word. "Don't get distracted."

Owen nodded. "Yes, Alpha."

"Okay, let's get her attention." I stepped into the light and raised the binoculars to my face.

One of the priest-mages pointed at me. The Pale Queen stared. Dark smoke boiled around her, sliding along her arms and shoulders.

I raised my hand and waved.

The Pale Queen bared her teeth and stabbed a finger in my direction. A harsh cry echoed through the fortress. Internal shutters slid aside, and suddenly windows peppered the corner tower. Shapeshifters rained down onto the grass.

"Here we go!" Curran snarled.

I thrust the binoculars back at Rimush, scanning the bodies running toward us. Ten, twenty, thirty. Over sixty shaggy shapes, every one of them bigger than the average shapeshifter. Shit.

Curran burst into warrior form and roared.

The blast of sound tore through the plain. The attackers in the rear slowed, as if unsure, but the front line kept charging.

Curran broke into a run.

"For the Pack!" Keelan screamed.

Our shapeshifters dashed past me.

I dropped my cloak and started forward, slowly, deliberately. Rimush was on my right and Owen was on my left.

The magic in front of me thickened, the dark smoke swirling and pooling, reaching out to me like the tentacles of some nightmarish creature.

I channeled my magic into Sarrat and spoke the incantation. *"Terrat sahatur."*

Power slammed into my sword. Suddenly it was impossibly heavy. Gripping it in both hands, I strained and slashed. A wave of golden light tore from Sarrat and shot above the grass, shredding the dark smoke like tissue paper.

One of my aunt's favorite spells. Nice and short. Easy to remember.

My arms felt like I had tried to lift a car.

I kept walking. On top of the tower, the Pale Queen gripped the parapet. I wasn't close enough to see her face, but her body language was clear enough. It was the Ice Age version of *WTF*.

Ahead of me, the ragged line of our shapeshifters broke into pairs and collided with the enemy. Blood flew. Howls and snarls rent the air.

The Pale Queen waved her arms. Her magic shifted in response and I focused on it, trying to gauge the direction of the flow.

The first shapeshifter to slip through our line sprinted toward me. Huge, gray-furred, he charged me at full speed, counting on his bulk and power to knock me down.

Owen let him get within ten feet of us, stepped into his path, and swung his war hammer. Bone crunched, and the enemy shapeshifter flew to the left and landed hard on his back. Owen jabbed the hammer at him. "Stay down!"

We kept moving. The currents of magic built around the tower, roiling above it like storm clouds.

That's a lot of magic you pulled from the land. What are you doing with it?

199

The second shapeshifter lunged at me. Rimush disemboweled her with a single swing, stabbed her right lung, and slashed across her spine as she collapsed.

On the tower, small magic explosions popped like firecrackers. Boulders shot up into the air, spinning and expanding. The priest-mages had launched their first salvo.

Were they aiming for me or the archers? I glanced over my shoulder. Conlan and Heather's people were twenty-five yards away. Too vulnerable.

"To me!"

The archers sprinted toward me, Conlan in the lead and Darin right behind him.

Where the hell was Isaac? He wasn't in the shapeshifter charge. He wasn't with the archers either.

Magic crested at the tower. I looked back.

The Pale Queen thrust her arms up, toward the mass of magic gathered above her head and brought them down in a sharp motion. The storm cloud of her power plunged down and sank into the soil.

Got it.

"Gis Addir, ar arryt..."

Understanding flared in Rimush's eyes.

The ground quaked.

"...leru skar..."

The archers reached us.

"Bunch up!" Rimush ordered. "Lock your arms together!"

"...us gytam..."

The first boulder hurtled at us like a pebble launched from a giant's slingshot. It whistled over our heads and crashed into the dirt with a boom. The ground shook.

Ahead, the hill swelled and rolled forward, as if a giant ball sped at us just underneath the turf.

Rimush grabbed Owen and locked his hand around my left arm.

"... sar udurum!"

The grassy field under my feet burst open. My magic snapped in place, and we landed on a glowing bridge fifty yards long. A thirty-foot-deep pit gaped under us, magic swirling at its bottom. The bridge barely spanned it. If I had miscalculated by a few feet, we'd be buried alive right now. Someone behind me screamed.

"You're fine. Don't panic!" Heather called out. Her voice shook.

The bridge was only seven feet wide. I hadn't made any rails. There wasn't time for anything fancy or complicated. I had made a giant magical board that rested on the edges of the pit, and we were right in the middle of it.

"Two by two," I ordered. "Don't run."

We started across the bridge toward the fortress and the fight raging by its walls. The magic gave a little under my feet but held.

The second boulder smashed to our left and rolled into the pit. If one of these hit dead center, we'd have a problem.

"Conlan! The Shield of Mush Azebtu!" I glanced over my shoulder.

He looked at me, his eyes wide and freaked out.

"Show me what Grandfather taught you!"

Conlan thrust his hands in front of him as if trying to block an invisible attacker with his palms. The language of Shinar spilled out of him, words moving and twisting his magic.

A shaggy brown shapeshifter broke away from the fight and sprinted toward us. I was in front, with Rimush and Owen behind me.

"Don't do it!" I warned.

The shapeshifter leaped onto the bridge, her shoulders hunched, her ursine muzzle gaping open, her eyes locked on me.

I ran at her, light on my feet.

We met in a split second, her claws against my sword. Her talons found empty air. Sarrat found her throat. Her body fell to the left, and her head flew to the right, into the pit.

A few more feet and I landed on solid ground. Rimush and

Owen were a step behind me. Conlan and Darin were next, my son still chanting.

A boulder smashed into the ground directly in front of us and rolled down, bouncing, crushing two enemy shapeshifters in its path.

Conlan's chant faltered. The magic was there, prepped and ready. I could feel it. It just needed that final push, and he must have forgotten that crucial last word.

A second boulder dropped behind the first. There was no place to go. The archers were still on the bridge, and the rocks would smash directly into them.

"The words are yours," Jushur intoned, his voice calm and reassuring. "They will obey."

Rimush sprinted into the path of the first boulder. His twin swords leaped into his hands almost on their own. He jumped. Magic rippled from his weapons, stretching into glowing blades of light. They scissored the giant rock, cleaving it in two. The two halves fell apart, spinning away from each other, driven by the sudden release of magic. The surface of the cut was smooth as glass.

The impact tossed Rimush into the air. He flipped head over feet and landed gracefully on his toes. The second boulder rolled by him, straight at us.

"Eibur uru atamet!" Conlan screamed.

Golden light shot out of his hands, forming two big translucent shields, each fifty feet across and twenty-five feet wide. They hung twenty feet in front of us, in midair, mirroring the angle of his hands.

Conlan lowered his palms, thrusting the slanted shields in the path of the boulder.

The stone missile smashed into his magic and bounced off, over our heads, into the hole.

He had done it!

"Good job!"

He grinned back at me.

The others gaped at my son. Too bad Curran had missed it.

A third boulder flew overhead and crashed into the far end of the bridge. Shit.

The translucent plank cracked.

Hold. Hold, damn you.

The end of the bridge fractured and shattered, the cracks running toward us.

"Run!" I screamed.

The archers scrambled to safety, the cracks on their heels as the bridge melted into nothing. Rimush and Owen grabbed them and shoved them out of the way, flinging them to the sides and the safety of solid ground.

The cracks accelerated.

Heather was the last one on the bridge. I caught a glimpse of her face, her eyes opened wide, her mouth ready to scream. The bridge fractured under her feet. She leaped, a desperate jump that would fall short, and then Rimush caught her, hanging off the edge, one hand holding Heather's shoulder and the other gripped by Owen. The werebison grunted and heaved them both out of the pit.

Conlan exhaled, his shields dipping a little, following his hands.

"You did so well. Can you walk with the shields?"

He nodded. "I'm good."

"You're doing great. Everyone, stay behind me, four people per line." I started toward the fortress. Rimush and Owen flanked me again.

The boulders crashed around us, some aimed to land on us and others dropped in the middle of the battlefield to roll into us. No other direction. We were the only target.

I could see the Pale Queen now without binoculars. She'd slumped against the parapet, watching me advance, hatred plain on her face. That pit had cost a lot of magic. She was trying to recover.

"In range!" Heather announced.

We halted. The archers aimed as one. The arrowheads glowed green. Explosion bolts. Nice. Penderton had dug deep into its budget.

"Turn the shields!" I ordered.

Conlan raised his hands and turned his palms toward each other. The shields in the air above us turned sideways.

"Fire!" Heather barked.

The arrows whistled through the air and bit into the hunters atop the tower. Magic splashed with bright green sparks.

A man screamed, and a body toppled and plummeted to the ground. A priest-mage. Good hit.

Darin smiled.

"Stay here and fire just like that."

I resumed my trek forward. I was close enough, but I wanted to put a little distance between me and the archers.

The ranks of enemy shapeshifters ahead and to my left had thinned. Bodies littered the ground, most still alive and groaning, others still and silent.

Owen made a strange noise, half bellow, half roar.

"What?"

"They're elderly," he snarled. "And children! Look at them."

What?

Oh. He was right. At least a third of the enemy shapeshifters had gray fur, and not the darker healthy gray of adult wolves or jackals. No, it was the silver gray that came with age. Their bodies were thin, without the heavy bulk of shapeshifters in their prime. Of those who weren't gray, some were clearly too young. Their bodies were clumsy, their attacks unsure. She must have emptied her citadel and sent anyone with a heartbeat against us.

This had to end now. I was close to my limit, but I still had some magic left.

I sent my power into Sarrat, spoke the incantation, and let it rip. A slash of light tore from my blade and carved its way up the hill, plowing through the dirt. The bitch on top of the tower jerked her arms up, screaming. A wall of smoke blanketed the wall. My sword strike bit into it and sliced through, gouging the tower.

She threw herself against the rampart, her face shocked. I pointed my sword at her. She blocked that one, but she wouldn't block the next one, and we both knew it. She was almost out of juice.

The Pale Queen screeched. It sounded like a command.

Nothing happened.

I shrugged my shoulders. I would have to make this next one count. She was close to her limit, but so was I.

A shutter slid open in the tower, and a dim figure, half hidden in shadow, appeared in the new opening.

The Pale Queen thrust her hand at me and yelled, her words as jagged as shards of glass.

The figure stepped into the light and dropped to the ground behind the line of shapeshifter defenders.

A roar rocked the battlefield, a wall of sound that burst through the air like a shockwave.

I knew that roar. Oh no.

Bodies flew out of the way. Something was coming, bulldozing its way through the lines of fortress defenders, knocking them aside like they were bowling pins.

The front line of enemy shapeshifters parted as they scrambled out of the way, tripping over themselves. A lion burst into the open. Enormous, gray, striped with black, a mane crowning his huge head.

I knew Curran's maximum size. I knew exactly how far he could push his body. This lion outweighed him by at least two hundred pounds.

The lion's golden eyes sighted me. The alpha stare burned me, heavy, commanding, difficult to hold. Not just any lion. A First.

Oh my God.

The lion charged.

Owen jumped in front of me, bellowing a challenge. I lunged around him, and saw the lion coming as if in slow motion, the massive paws striking the ground, the eyes glowing with deep, furious amber. He was unstoppable. It was as if the Ice Age itself, brutal and savage, was bearing down on me.

The burning eyes locked me in place. I knew I had to move, but I couldn't do it. I couldn't...

Curran smashed into him from the side, knocking him off course. The impact staggered the hulking beast. He whirled around, shocked, and roared in outrage.

Curran roared back.

The two male lions, one a beast, the other in warrior form, glared at each other and collided. The enemy First reared up on his hind legs and slapped at Curran's neck and head, his knife-long claws slicing through the air. I'd seen Curran kill a feral bull with a single slap. A hit like that would crush a shapeshifter's skull like a walnut. Instant kill.

Curran leaned back, let one giant paw slide by him, stepped in, and drove a straight right hand into his opponent's face. The enemy lion's head snapped back.

I was halfway to them.

Curran turned to me. "No!"

I stopped. It nearly killed me, but I stopped.

The enemy First snarled and charged again, lifting up, swinging his left forepaw, trying to knock Curran to the ground. If he managed to pin him down with all that weight, it would be over.

Curran danced out of the way. The claws rent the air in front of him. The momentum of the strike pulled the lion to the right, exposing his flank. Curran turned his body and drove a short, vicious hook into the lion's ribs. Bone crunched. Before the other lion could react, Curran thrust his hand into the same spot and dug a bloody chunk of flesh and bone out. Blood poured from the wound, the yellow shards of ribs stark against it.

The other lion whirled, lunging.

Four clumps of dark smoke appeared in a ring around the lions and coalesced into priest-mages.

Oh no, you don't. If I don't get to help, you don't either.

The Ice Age First roared in outrage. The Pale Queen screamed at him from the tower. The priest-mages dashed around the two shapeshifters, fading in and out of existence.

Jushur and Rimush shot from behind me, like two dancers perfectly in sync.

Curran hammered another punch into his adversary's ribs. The other lion snapped, so fast I almost didn't see it. His jaws locked around Curran's left arm. He reared, throwing his colossal front legs over Curran and dropped his entire bulk on top of him.

Curran went down.

The two Blades of Shinar sped through the smoke, their twin swords slicing in precise, brutal movements. Four bodies fell onto the grass.

The Ice Age First bit down, snarling, his hind legs digging into the dirt on both sides of Curran, giving him leverage. I couldn't even see Curran under the lion's mass. I grit my teeth.

Come on, honey. *Come on.*

The Ice Age lion raised his head, and his mouth was bloody. I caught a glimpse of Curran under him, his shoulder drenched in crimson. The lion bit down again.

"Dad!" Conlan screamed. He tried to run past me, and I caught him and gripped him against me.

All fighting had stopped except for the two Firsts. Both sides watched in silence.

The lion raised his head again. His forepaws pinned Curran's shoulders, the huge claws gouging into his flesh. The Ice Age First roared, announcing his imminent victory.

Curran was a grappler.

His arms slid between the lion's front legs and knocked them up and out. The lion's paws landed on the ground above Curran's shoulders. Curran slipped his right arm under the lion's left front leg and caught it in the crook of his elbow. He thrust his left arm up against the lion's throat, barring him from biting, and twisted his body to the right, wrapping his legs around the lion's flanks.

An armlock. He'd done it to me more times than I could remember. But human bones were a lot weaker than a lion's.

The Ice Age First still hadn't realized what was happening.

Curran crunched, bringing his body up. The muscles on his arms and back bulged, shifting as he built more bulk in a split second.

The lion's left foreleg snapped like a twig. He howled in surprise and pain. His hind legs clawed the ground as he tried to free himself.

Curran wrenched the broken limb off and hurled it aside. Long claws sprouted from his toes, and he kicked the lion's gut, tearing through flesh and organs.

The lion flailed, frantic, and rolled to the side in a last-ditch effort to get away. Curran rolled with him, and as he ended up on top, he thrust his monstrous hand into the lion's chest.

I had beheaded people. I had stabbed creatures in the heart. But I would never forget Curran ripping another First's heart out of his chest. It sat in his huge, clawed hand, a bloody clump, and contracted one last time, sending a mist of blood into the air.

The First's body collapsed into a humanoid shape. He was large, almost six feet tall, and sheathed with bluish hair. Two large antlers crowned his head.

Curran stood up. He raised the heart up, showing it to everyone, walked over to me, and dropped it at my feet.

Umm. What was I supposed to do with it?

His eyes were pure gold, still mad with bloodlust.

I stabbed the heart with Sarrat. It seemed like the thing to do.

Curran turned away from me and roared.

Every shapeshifter knelt as one. Heather's archers, the Blades, Darin, Conlan, and I were the only ones standing on the entire field. On the tower, the Pale Queen stood frozen.

Curran had taken the Pack. It was his. The fight was over. We had won.

The magic permeating the field vanished, sucked toward the tower in an instant.

Magic crackled like lightning above the Pale Queen. The few remaining hunters who had survived Heather's arrows ran from her. Some of them leaped off the tower and slid down its side, crashing into the grass.

The dark smoke boiled and expanded in slow motion, rolling over the tower, out and down. It caught the shapeshifters kneeling by the wall. Their gold collars flashed. Their heads exploded.

She was out of magic. Her best fighter and her priest-mages were dead. She was sacrificing her own people for a last boost of power. There were at least forty of them still alive on the field, most too injured to fight or run. She would kill them all, the elderly, the children, everyone with a collar. All of them would die.

"No, Sharratum, no!" Jushur screamed.

The magic shot out of me almost on its own. The very last of my reserves. All I could give. It rolled from me, pitifully weak. The world went gray. I fell but didn't land.

There was a noise. It came from far away, as if I were deep underwater and someone was screaming for me on the shore. I floated in the desaturated mist, disconnected and scared. So scared.

I wanted to hug Conlan again. I wanted to kiss Curran and see him grin at me.

I still had too many things to do. I wouldn't let it end here. No, not happening. I needed to get back to my family.

A faint tint of green began to spread along the edges of the colorless mist. The land. It was exhausted, its magic depleted and drained by the Pale Queen, and still, it was reaching out to me as it reached out to everyone.

I stretched my hand. A thin green shoot wove its way through the mist toward me.

Just a little more. A little bit.

The green touched my fingertips.

Reality rushed at me in a swirl of color and warmth, the sounds too loud, and I heard Conlan screaming into my ear, "Mom! Don't die, don't die!"

I made my lips move. "It's fine," I lied. "You're fine. Everyone is fine."

Conlan sobbed.

"Where is your father?"

"I'm here," Curran said. "I've got you."

Oh. He was holding me. That's why it felt so nice.

"Love you," I told him.

"Don't do that again," he snarled.

"Is everyone dead?"

He shifted me in his arms so I could see the fortress.

I had claimed a chunk of land, about a hundred yards wide and maybe three hundred yards long. All of our people were safe. A handful of Ice Age shapeshifters stood and sprawled inside my claim, bewildered but alive. Their collars lay at their feet. A couple of hunters, somehow on their feet, staggered toward me. Everyone else, all of her people, the hunters and the shapeshifters, were dead. The grass outside my territory was littered with headless corpses.

In front of us on top of the tower, an enormous phantom gripped the tower with five-foot-long bony fingers armed with huge claws. Her face belonged to the Pale Queen, but her mouth was full of fangs. A crown of bony horns and antlers rode on her head. Dark smoke swirled around her like a robe.

I had seen the smaller version of it before. That was the phantom the priest-mage had threatened me with in front of Penderton.

That was it? You killed all of your people for this? To turn yourself real big?

"Will she be okay?" Curran asked.

"Yes," Jushur said. "She survived through no fault of her own. She will need food and rest."

I need that bitch to die. Did she transform or was she projecting this phantom?

"I will get you that rest, baby. Wait for me."

Okay, I'll just wait right here.

A shape dashed across the rampart toward the giant phantom, a sword in his hand.

"Isaac," I said.

"Where?" Curran squinted and saw him. "What the hell."

The ranger leaped and scrambled up the phantom's arm.

"She's solid," Jushur said.

Isaac reached the phantom's shoulder, climbed up, and jumped. His body flew through the air, his back arched, both hands on his sword, and he plunged the blade into the phantom's cheek. His dead weight hit it, and the sword ripped through the magic flesh, carving a gash in her face all the way to her lower jaw. Smoke and blood poured out of the wound.

The Pale Queen screamed and batted him aside like a fly. Isaac hurtled through the air out of view.

"She's solid and she bleeds." Curran lowered me to the ground. "Wait with Kate. Guard her."

"Always," Jushur told him.

"Conlan, protect your mother."

"Yes, Alpha," Conlan managed.

"I'll be right back, baby."

"Come back alive," I told him.

"I promise."

My husband roared. The shapeshifters pivoted toward him. He pointed at the monstrosity on the tower.

"Kill her!"

The Ice Age shapeshifters stared. Their eyes lit up.

Curran sprinted to the tower.

"For the Pack!" Keelan howled.

The Wilmington Pack charged the tower, and the Ice Age shapeshifters who could still move followed, joining in with deep guttural howls. Those too injured to run stared at the tower, their eyes on fire.

Rimush looked at me.

"Go," I told him. "They will need help."

He ran after the shapeshifters.

The creature reached down with her colossal hands, trying to crush the attackers, but they were too fast. A couple of breaths and they were scaling the walls, propelled by superhuman strength.

"I'm an old man," Jushur told me. "Please don't do this to me again, Sharratum. I don't know how much of that kind of anxiety my weary heart can take."

I smiled at him.

On the tower, the shapeshifters swarmed the phantom and ripped into her.

A lone shapeshifter, left behind a few yards away from us, shifted into a human shape. She was young, maybe fifteen or sixteen, and thin. Her ribs stood out under her pale skin. Her long brown hair was matted with blood. Her little horns protruded from her forehead.

She twisted her body into a sitting position, dragging an injured leg, and cried out a little.

Shapeshifters had enhanced regeneration, but it needed calories to work. All of the calories the Pale Queen had to spare for the shapeshifters must've gone to the fighters, those in their prime, not to the young and the elderly.

Conlan pulled something out of his clothes, walked over, and crouched in front of the girl.

She eyed him as if expecting a punch.

My son unwrapped the thing he was holding, broke off a small piece of the chocolate bar, put it in his mouth, and chewed.

She watched him.

He held the rest of the bar out to her. "Chocolate. It's good."

The girl reached out, hesitant.

Conlan held perfectly still.

I thought she would snatch the chocolate out of his hand, but she took it very slowly, watching him the whole time, brought it to her mouth, and bit into it.

Her eyes went wide.

Conlan smiled.

I sighed and watched as my husband and our people tore the Pale Queen to pieces.

EPILOGUE

Four days later

"He's taking this herding thing a bit too far," Troy said.

I glanced up from the piece of paper in my hand. We sat on the porch of what we were calling the front office. The building had three levels, and we were on the second floor, accessible from the ground by a wide stone staircase. The new front gate was directly in front of us. Technically it wasn't a gate yet. Right now, it was a gap in the wall, located where the Pale Queen's favorite tower used to be.

I had done more damage than I thought with that sword strike, and once Curran and the Pack had taken the Pale Queen down, the tower cracked and was judged unsound. My husband and the rest of the shapeshifters demolished it.

He was standing by the gap now, with Paul, our general contractor, who was saying things. I couldn't hear them from my spot—they were a full hundred yards away—but I knew that expression. *Yes, it can be done. It will be expensive.*

Expensive now was relative.

Between my husband and us, Owen was walking along,

carrying a large stick. He had a big straw hat on his head. Behind him, three juvenile giant rhinos ambled along. One of them nudged Owen with its horn. The werebison turned around and tapped the rhino with his stick. The rhino ran in a circle, making short hops like an overly excited baby goat. Owen rolled his eyes.

I'd offered to get him a cowboy hat instead of the straw one, but apparently, he had an intense dislike of all things cowboy.

"Where are you taking them?" I called out.

"Southern pasture, away from the mastodons," Owen yelled back.

I waved.

My guess had been right. The fortress was square, although calling it a fortress was grossly inaccurate. The outer wall, composed of a multitude of towers, enclosed an area of almost one and a half square miles. The towers doubled as storage facilities, and we had managed to look at the first eighteen so far, although the shapeshifters had done a quick run and checked all of them to make sure nothing alive was trapped inside. We had found some crazy stuff.

In the center of the inner space rose a crude palace. A multitude of structures surrounded it: barracks, living quarters, more storage facilities, some weird platform that was likely used for rituals, and barns. Lots of barns housing a variety of Ice Age animals. We found a small family of mastodons, all of them freaked out beyond all reason, some kind of weird huge camels, more stag-moose, and the juvenile giant rhinos. Owen immediately declared that as the only herd wereanimal present, he wanted to be in charge of all the herds, and Curran and I couldn't sign off on that fast enough. The baby rhinos were his favorite.

"As long as he isn't herding us," I told Troy.

The werejackal shook his head.

"How are the Agers?" I asked.

"Better. Food, clean water, and showers can do miraculous things."

My desperate claiming had managed to save the lives of nine horned shapeshifters and two hunters. A drop in the bucket. They hadn't been treated well by the Pale Queen. In fact, the animals had been probably treated better, and they were all still traumatized. The shapeshifter living quarters didn't even deserve that name. If I could've set that place on fire, I would have.

We installed the shapeshifters into barracks, where Troy administered first aid. The hunters must've been higher in the hierarchy, because their barracks were a little better, but not by much. Although we had found a room filled with dried meat, we dumped it all because we had no idea what it was and we'd brought food in from Penderton. Watching people try fresh bread for the first time was an unforgettable experience.

"Here she goes again," Troy murmured.

One of the hunters, a tall woman with light brown hair, climbed up the stairs. Her legs had been damaged in her desperate attempt to escape the Pale Queen. Troy had healed her, but walking was clearly difficult. Even so, as soon as she could walk, she climbed the stairs and parked herself on the side guarding them. If I got up and went somewhere, she would try to hobble behind me. She took the morning shift, and the other hunter, a man about her age, would take the evening.

After watching her stand there for thirty minutes the morning after we took the complex, I asked Keelan to find a chair. He couldn't find one, so he brought a big log he cut from a tree.

She and the other hunter had washed off the blue clay. Their ears, teeth, and the ghostly bark-like swirls of green and brown pigment on their skin told me they were fae or at least had some of the blood in them. Despite the growing magic, fae were still rare. The few I'd met held humanity in low regard, and several of them had no problem eating human flesh. But then most of the people I came across in my previous line of work weren't exactly upstanding citizens. I would have to make some calls and figure out if there was a fae expert we could invite to visit us once things settled down.

We still had no idea what the horned people were.

The hunter reached the top of the stairs. I got up and nodded to her. She nodded back and sat on the log, holding her spear.

"Why is she doing this?" Troy said.

"They are trying to show that they are useful," I told him. "If she could talk, she would be saying, 'Please don't kill me. I can work. I will guard you. I will be loyal.'"

The language barrier was a problem, but we would get past it eventually. Conlan has made a lot of headway with the two younger shapeshifter teenagers. They were up to five words. *Water, food, yes, no,* and *chocolate.* Eventually we would explain to everyone from the Ice Age that they were free to do as they wanted.

I looked back at the paper.

Isaac had survived. Not only had he walked away from that fight, he had gone all the way back to Penderton, and when the tech hit that evening, he called back to the Order HQ. Now I was in possession of a letter from Grand Master Damian Angevin, sealed with his sigil and signed by his hand. I'd asked Isaac if he had any shades so the golden light of the Grand Master's magnificence wouldn't blind me when I opened it. He hadn't even cracked a smile.

The Order was officially requesting permission to establish a one-knight chapter at our temple complex to "facilitate the retrieval of our brothers and sisters so their bodies can be returned to their families." Unofficially, Angevin wanted to keep an eye on us, and I had no doubt that once the bodies were retrieved, he would find some pretext to keep Isaac or someone else stationed here.

I had dealt with him before. He had a thing for Erra, but besides that, my aunt and the Grand Master were a part of a much larger strategy involving the higher levels of federal government. So far, the feds had wisely left Curran and me alone.

Having a knight of the Order on hand brought both advantages and disadvantages. He would, of course, report everything to Angevin, probably directly, considering that the Grand Master knew exactly who Curran and I were. Our family was likely at the top of Angevin's Watch Me list. But having access to the authority wielded by the Order could prove beneficial down the line.

Curran and Paul were walking toward me.

"Hey, baby!" my husband called.

"Hey, handsome! You come here often?"

"Just to see you. Hey, did those files you got from Ned mention any kind of caves or anything in this area?"

"No. Why?"

"Where does the sewage go?"

Good question. The fortress had almost no furniture, and what little there was was made of stone mostly, but it did have toilets. Sort of. If you could call a hole in the floor a toilet. I had thrown a match in there, which in retrospect wasn't the brightest thing to do, but it hadn't illuminated anything and went out before it hit the bottom.

"No idea."

"First priority," Paul said. "That and running water. The wells are good and all, but there need to be sinks and showers. This will take a lot of manpower."

"We'll hire Penderton people," Curran said.

"It will be expensive."

Curran grinned. "We're bucks up."

Paul shook his head. "Whatever you say."

They walked away.

We had just finished renovations on the other house. None of the buildings around me were fit for human habitation without serious construction. I would be stuck in renovation hell forever.

What to do about the Order? I looked at the paper some more. It didn't say anything new.

If we did allow the Order to establish their one-man chapter here, it would have to come with a lot of conditions attached. For one, I would want its existence to be sealed. I should be able to count the number of Order people who knew about it on one hand, and Nick Feldman couldn't be one of those people. Curran's Pack rescue strategy relied on surprising the alphas. Nick was in love with Desandra. He would do anything to keep her and her two sons safe. If he found out what we were planning, he would immediately tell her. We had to keep him in the dark.

Come to think of it, we'd need to stick to our schedule as well. Before we had left for Wilmington, Mahon and Martha made us promise to return for holidays and during summer, so they could spend time with us and especially with Conlan. We'd need to keep that up no matter how busy things got here. As far as Atlanta knew, we were chilling on the beach. The last thing we needed was for them to come looking for us before we were ready. And Mahon would, too. We didn't need that old cranky bear stomping through our woods.

I was reasonably sure Penderton would keep our secret. I had released my claim on the town, so I held up my promise. That and getting rid of the Pale Queen made us trustworthy, and Penderton wanted to maintain a good relationship with us. First, we proved we were handy at dispatching threats, and if Penderton came to us for help, we would take care of it to be neighborly. And second, renovating this place would require a lot of manpower and skilled tradesmen. Curran already talked to Ned about supplies, and judging by the way Ned's eyes lit up, we would be keeping Penderton's builder guilds happily employed probably for years to come.

I would have to discuss all of this with Curran tonight over dinner.

A commotion broke out at the gap. Jynx appeared in it and

took a deep breath. "Consort! There is a man here to see you! He says he is a wizard!"

I needed to invest in a bullhorn or something. "Is his name Luther?"

"Might be. He looks like a Luther! Let me check!" Jynx disappeared from view and came back. "Yes!"

"Let him in!"

She stepped aside and a man strode through the gap, looking like an academic who had gotten lost in the woods and was now seriously put out. His dark hair was damp with sweat. His naturally pale skin still showed a little of his summer tan. He wore hiking pants and a sweatshirt that said A WIZARD IS NEVER LATE. Tolkien. Of course.

Luther adjusted his glasses and noticed me. "You!"

"Troy, this is Assistant Director Luther Dillon. We are in the presence of Biohazard royalty. We are not worthy."

Troy executed an elaborate bow.

"Laugh it up, you philistine. I hiked twenty miles to get here!"

"What brings you to our neck of the woods, Assistant Director?"

"You sent me a kilogram of enchanted gold and a blood sample with DNA from an extinct American cheetah! Of course, I..."

He trailed off. I couldn't blame him. Seeing a ten-foot-tall furry mastodon coming around the corner with an eight-year-old boy riding on her back would give anyone pause.

"Conlan, where are you taking Mona?" I called out.

"Southern pasture."

"You can't. Owen went there with the baby rhinos."

"I will take her to the west then."

"Where is Darin?" I asked.

"He went to the lake again. He found some sort of magic freshwater clams in it. He's very excited about it." Conlan shrugged.

"Okay," I told him.

Mona trotted her way past Luther and exited through the gap, carrying Conlan with her.

"What the hell is going on?" Luther demanded. "What is...all of this?"

I got up. "Come. I'll show you."

WE WALKED THROUGH THE ANTECHAMBER OF THE PALACE, TAKING IT slow so my hunter guard could keep up. The palace felt eerie, its ceiling too high, its contours too severe. Shadows pooled in the corners.

Luther hadn't said a word in the entire fifteen minutes it took us to walk over here. I had done the impossible. I had rendered Luther Dillon speechless. It only took a magical scheme roughly twelve thousand years in the making to accomplish this feat.

We entered the main hall. I whispered an incantation, and feylanterns ignited on the walls, bathing the room in bright light. I'd had them brought specifically from Wilmington just so I could see everything in this hall clearly.

The hunter halted in the doorway. She didn't want to enter.

Murals filled the walls, painted in red, brown, black, and white on massive stone panels. I stopped before the first one.

"Some time ago, probably between 15,000 and 10,000 B.C., when the world was covered in ice, and North Carolina was sheathed in boreal tundra, a fae woman was exiled from her tribe."

In the mural, a lone figure with long blue hair walked away from a group of people. Some of them had blue hair, some, like the hunters I'd saved, were brown-haired. Dark dots peppered the space between the crowd and the blue-haired figure, rocks thrown at her. Behind the group, rectangular shapes portrayed houses, with the largest house towering above them. A palace. One of the smaller houses was on fire.

I moved to the second mural. "She was driven away into the

woods, but she was powerful, and she survived. Her magic grew, and she found acolytes who followed her."

In the mural a fae woman stood in the center of the forest, lit up by inner fire. Figures knelt around her, their arms raised in supplication.

"When she was strong enough, she came back."

The third mural was smeared with blood. It had dried to a dull brown, and someone had added red pigment on top of it. Just a sea of blood with people in random poses drowning in it and the blue-haired woman's inner fire. In the distance, all the houses burned.

"She killed most of her old tribe, enslaved those who had survived, and ruled over them from this palace. She became the Pale Queen."

The fourth mural showed a lone figure with blue hair in the center of the palace, her inner fire surging to encompass everything. Many figures with gold collars knelt before her, her acolytes bowing on both sides.

"She fought a war with a neighboring shapeshifter people and enslaved them, too."

Another panel filled with blood, portraying horned people and animals dying. The next one showed her back in the palace, with lions, wolves, and horned people kneeling before her in collars.

I crossed the chamber to the other side. Luther followed me.

"Then the world began to warm. The climate was changing."

This panel had the sun, bright and scorching, wreathed in fire.

"She decided to put her kingdom into slumber."

On the next panel, a massive hill formed over the palace and the houses, all people lying flat, including the blue-haired woman in the palace.

"A fae queen asleep in the Underhill," Luther murmured. "How fitting..."

The next panel was blank. I stopped before it. "And then the fae woman woke up and found herself in the new world, which

222

she decided to rule. She sent her emissaries to the closest town and demanded human sacrifice to bend them to her rule. At first the town paid, but eventually they asked us for help. We came, killed her, took over her house, and freed the people she didn't manage to sacrifice. The end."

Luther stared at the walls, taking it in.

"I will tell you the whole thing in more detail over some tea, if you want."

"I want," he said. "What do you think woke her up?"

"I don't know. Although I'm maintaining a cordial relationship with the Order, and I've asked a knight-pathfinder I know to check their records. During the last flare, this entire area froze over. Nobody knows why, but apparently, they'd had a record drop in temperatures with three feet of snow and ice on the ground. It took weeks for it to thaw. Perhaps she had structured her sleeping spell in such a way that it awakened her when the world turned cold again."

"But how? By what mechanism? Look at these buildings. They are primitive to the point of crudeness. How could she put all of these people and animals to sleep for fifteen thousand years?"

"I don't know," I told him. "We will probably never find out."

"Did you have to kill her?"

"We really, really did."

He sighed. "There was so much we could've learned from her."

I nodded at the guard in the doorway. "Do you see her? She refuses to enter this room. Even if she had been forbidden, the person who issued that order is dead, but she still wants nothing to do with this place. Bad things happened here. Some magic isn't worth learning."

Luther surveyed the walls again.

"As soon as we get the urgent basics taken care of, I'm going to tear this palace down," I told him. "If you want the panels for posterity, I will send them to you."

Luther looked around. "You want to tear this down? This giant building?"

I nodded. "I'll level it, purify it by claiming all this land so none of her magic remains, and then we're going to build a nice modern Keep in its place."

Luther looked at me. "Is that 'Keep' with a capital letter?"

"Probably."

"So this is the new Pack HQ?"

"Yes and no. Penderton has given us eighty-two thousand acres and you're standing in the exact center of that plot. I will claim all of it and keep it safe. If years from now things don't go well in Atlanta and any shapeshifters decide to move down here, we will have housing ready for them. But this will never be a Pack-exclusive place, Luther. We're done with that. Shapeshifters don't need to live apart from other people. In fact, the more we all interact, the better."

Luther would keep our secret. I had no doubt about it.

He dragged his hand through his hair. "I will take the panels. Of course, I want the panels. This is a wealth of magical knowledge. And I understand the sentiment and the plans, but the cost of all of this will be prohibitive. Just transporting the panels alone out through the woods. I may have to get a grant from the Mage Academy..."

I motioned him to follow me and walked to the back of the chamber, past the big stone chair that must've served as the Pale Queen's throne.

We walked through a wide doorway into a hallway, and then through another doorway. I whispered a word, and the feylantern flared to life.

A long chamber spread before us. Chunks of gold and heaps of uncut precious stones littered the floor, piled against the walls on both sides. Here and there strange crystals glowed, fluorescing gently with magic. Odd bones, skulls and femurs, lay between the gold nuggets. Some I recognized. Some were too weird to identify. Everything in the chamber was either a precious metal, gem, or magically potent item. The chamber kept going, its end lost in the darkness. I had only installed enough feylanterns to light up the first twenty-five yards.

Luther stared, stunned.

"We don't know how long the Pale Queen was alive," I said. "Long enough that she noticed the world was warming up. That didn't happen overnight. It must've taken centuries. Some people think fae could live for several hundred years if their magic is strong enough, and she had a lot of magic at her disposal."

Luther was still staring. I let him come to terms with it all.

"Gold?" he said finally.

"It takes enchantment well and it's malleable with minimal tools. You don't even have to dig for it that often. Sometimes you can find it on the ground. All those boring looking rocks lying about are uncut gems, and every gem here carries potential for off-the-charts enchantment. She wanted them because they are magically potent. Emeralds, garnets, sapphires, aquamarines... I'm guessing she went on field trips to the mountains, and she must've had some way to sense them because there are way too many here. We took a small one to Wilmington to be appraised. Just one of those good size ones will pay for an apartment building."

Luther made a small, strangled noise.

"This wasn't her treasure room," I told him. "It was her craft closet. The source of the collars and some other things we found. We will pay for the transport of the panels. No need to worry."

Luther closed his eyes for a second, then opened them. "You mentioned other things?"

I smiled. "So many other things. Come with me. I'll show you."

ACKNOWLEDGMENTS

This was supposed to be a novella. We were supposed to finish it in a couple of months. But the story ended up growing and growing, and eventually we gave up on trying to figure out how long we wanted it to be and let it be as long as took. It was so fun to write, and we hope you'll enjoy reading it.

Many people helped us along the way. We would like to thank Nancy Yost, Natanya Wheeler, Sarah Younger, and Cheryl Pientka of NYLA for their help and expertise in bringing this manuscript to publication. We are grateful to Rossana Sasso for the editorial input, to Stefanie Chin for a thorough copyedit, and to Gina Nicholls for proofreading.

We are deeply indebted to our beta team: Michelle Badillo, Harriet Chow, Gloria, Dr. Chrissy Hall, Katherine Heasley, Jessi Halligan, Elżbieta Jaskulska, Veronika "Lyra" Kovaničová, Maura O'Toole, Jeanne L.D. Osnas, Sarah Platt, and Chiara Prato. Thank you for making our book better by sharing your insight and knowledge. We had the benefit of their expert advice on anthropology, archeology, zoology, botany, all things Irish, and even ballet. All errors of fact and science are ours alone.

This novel took some liberties with earth and biological sciences in the name of artistic license.

ALSO BY ILONA ANDREWS

Kate Daniels: Wilmington Years

MAGIC TIDES

MAGIC CLAIMS

Kate Daniels World

BLOOD HEIR

Kate Daniels Series

MAGIC BITES

MAGIC BLEEDS

MAGIC BURNS

MAGIC STRIKES

MAGIC MOURNS

MAGIC BLEEDS

MAGIC DREAMS

MAGIC SLAYS

GUNMETAL MAGIC

MAGIC GIFTS

MAGIC RISES

MAGIC BREAKS

MAGIC STEALS

MAGIC SHIFTS

MAGIC STARS

MAGIC BINDS

MAGIC TRIUMPHS

The Iron Covenant

IRON AND MAGIC

UNTITLED IRON AND MAGIC #2

Hidden Legacy Series

BURN FOR ME

WHITE HOT

WILDFIRE

DIAMOND FIRE

SAPPHIRE FLAMES

EMERALD BLAZE

RUBY FEVER

Innkeeper Chronicles Series

CLEAN SWEEP

SWEEP IN PEACE

ONE FELL SWEEP

SWEEP OF THE BLADE

SWEEP WITH ME

SWEEP OF THE HEART

Kinsmen

SILENT BLADE

SILVER SHARK

THE KINSMEN UNIVERSE (anthology with both SILENT BLADE and SILVER SHARK)

FATED BLADES

ABOUT THE AUTHOR

Ilona Andrews is the pseudonym for a husband-and-wife writing team, Gordon and Ilona. They currently reside in Texas with their two children and numerous dogs and cats. The couple are the #1 *New York Times* and *USA Today* bestselling authors of the Kate Daniels and Kate Daniels World novels as well as The Edge and Hidden Legacy series. They also write the Innkeeper Chronicles series, which they post as a free weekly serial.

For a complete list of their books, fun extras, and Innkeeper installments, please visit their website.

CPSIA information can be obtained
at www.ICGtesting.com
Printed in the USA
BVHW011853310523
665181BV00005B/29